Praise for the stories in *Wild Wishes*

A Happy Effin Valentine by Stephanie Burke

"An author who couldn't do tame if you threatened to pull her toenails out, Stephanie Burke brings another tale that takes you from zero to sixty in five seconds flat."

– Rachelle, *Fallen Angel Reviews*

"*A Happy Effin Valentine* by Stephanie Burke has to be one of the funniest books I have read in a long time. Full of mishaps and just plain bad luck, it is a keeper."

-- Talia Ricci, *Joyfully Reviewed*

Into Temptation by Lena Matthews

"Readers will find themselves entranced by the sensual love scenes and powerful passion this couple creates. Lena Mathews has created a tale of desire and love on the most romantic day of the year."

-- Angel, *Romance Junkies*

"Lena Matthews pens a wickedly amusing and adventurous romp for her pair of star-crossed lovers."

-- Sarah W., *The Romance Studio*

Tag's Folly by Eve Vaughn

"This is a marvellous, heart-warming story with a believable cast of characters. Ms. Vaughn is an excellent storyteller, and her characters demand to be heard."

-- Autiotalo, *Enchanted Ramblings*

"*Tag's Folly* is the perfect read when you're short on time, but need a big dose of romance. This erotic story really hits the spot."

-- Vicki Turner, *Romance Reviews Today*

LooseId®

ISBN 10: 1-59632-026-5
ISBN 13: 978-1-59632-026-0
WILD WISHES
Copyright © 2007 by Loose Id LLC

Cover Art by April Martinez

Publisher acknowledges the authors and copyright holders of the individual works, as follows:

A HAPPY EFFIN VALENTINE
Copyright © February 2006 by Stephanie Burke
INTO TEMPTATION
Copyright © February 2006 by Lena Matthews
TAG'S FOLLY
Copyright © February 2006 by Eve Vaughn

Printed in the U.S.A. by
Lightning Source, Inc.
1246 Heil Quaker Blvd
La Vergne TN 37086
www.lightningsource.com

Contents

A HAPPY EFFIN VALENTINE

Stephanie Burke

Chapter One

Effin was not having a good day.

In fact, not since Vesuvius had erupted and tons of hot volcanic ash had descended upon the denizens of Pompeii had anyone had a bad day like this.

Come to think of it, bad was too minor a word. Her day had been vile, loathsome, horrid, terrifying, disgusting, and monstrously illogical.

And it all started on February thirteenth -- *Friday, February thirteenth,* when Effin Damnwell Hurtzs opened her mouth.

Her mother had always warned her to think before she spoke, a trait that she lacked and a tendency she shared with her mother. "That little pink thing in your mouth is going to get you into a world of trouble, Effin." Her mother sighed, shaking her head as if she knew that trouble for her eldest daughter was inevitable.

Hell, she was born during a leap year! Double hell; if Effin'd had any luck at all, Trouble would have been her middle name.

She came upon her unusual moniker by accident. When her mother, doped up with painkillers and sedatives, was asked two different questions at the same time after a forty-three hour labor, this was the result:

Her father: "How does it feel?"

The medical receptionist: "What shall we name this beauty?"

Her mother's response: "It effin damn-well hurts, you bastard!"

Her father had finally learned to keep the pink thing in his mouth still, especially after his loving wife ripped out a handful of chest hair.

The medical receptionist sniffed: "You don't have to be so mean about it! I heard you just fine!"

Her mother: "What?"

The result: A tiny, beautiful little chocolate baby girl stuck with a name that would ensure future school fights and taunting for a lifetime.

And now, how Effin wished she had taken her mother's advice to heart, especially after she recalled how she got her name. But no! Effin Damnwell Hurtzs had to challenge fate and miscellaneous creatures by loudly declaring, "There are no such things as gremlins!" when her best friend confided that she was being plagued by a goodly tribe of them.

And what's even worse, she made her declaration on Friday, February thirteenth, black Friday, the unluckiest day of the year.

After ignoring her best friend Christa's horrified stare, she went home, had a nice mug of cocoa laced with a liberal shot of Cask & Cream Caramel Temptation, indulged in a nice hot bath, and retired to her boudoir to dream wonderful dreams of the blind date Christa had set her up with.

According to Christa, her date, Buster, was a CPA with an MBA and drove a BMW. The brother was supposed to be fine as hell, independent, didn't live with his mother, had a lucrative job that ensured he wouldn't be hitting her up for loans, and had impeccable social skills. That meant he had proper pronunciation and would say shrimp instead of scrimps, would chew with his mouth closed, would not brag about himself, and she would not suddenly determine that his ethnicity was actually Russian or Roman from the speed and accuracy of octopus hands.

Yes, Effin went to sleep with a smile on her face, her tummy warm and full, feeling sated and altogether pleased with herself.

Life was good, and tomorrow, Valentine's Day, it would only get better.

Chapter Two

"Good morning, starshine," Effin sang as she waltzed her way to her cozy, pale yellow kitchen. "The Earth says hello! You tinkle above us, we duck below!"

Then snickering at her adolescent behavior, she made her way to the coffeepot where her expensive cappuccino maker percolated happily. It had been a gift from her jealous tramp of a younger sister, Monika.

"Ah, Monika," she spoke softly to herself, used to the sound of her own voice in the mornings. After all, she was a bachelorette and lived in a huge house all alone. "Looks like you are over that childhood stuff and took classes in gift giving."

For as long as she could remember, her younger sister had been a tad bit jealous of her. Lord knew why.

Effin remembered when she was about three years old she'd peered into the cradle that had been handed down from generations of Hurtzses, amazed at the tiny being lying naked there, as her mother prepared to lift the baby into her first bath at home. Effin's huge brown eyes stared in awe at the perfect doll that her mommy said was her new sister.

She was filled with delight and joy at the prospect of nurturing this little creature, of protecting her and teaching her to play dollies, and to hug her whenever she was hurt or scared. Effin vowed to care for her precious baby sister -- right up until the first stinging spray of urine struck her right in her shining, emotion-filled eyeballs. She swore that her sibling snorted at her, gave her a warning glare, then turned her nose away as if to dismiss her.

And it had gotten worse from there. When they were older, Monika claimed that her parents loved Effin more, even with the dorky name, and sought to make her life a continuous hell by putting gum in her hair, mud in her bed, and bleach on her favorite dresses. Her dolls would disappear and mysteriously reappear headless and legless.

And it didn't stop there. When they were teenagers, Monika tried to steal her dates by dressing in very tight, low-cut, V-neck T-shirts whenever a boy came to take Effin out. She would spy, hide messages, eavesdrop on phone calls, and follow her on dates.

And finally as young ladies on the cusp of womanhood, Monika had the audacity to replace Effin's birth control pills with baby aspirin!

Good thing Effin didn't have a steady then, or she would have come down with a serious case of the nine-month stomach mumps. But she survived, went off to college, and matured enough to know to stay the hell away from that spawn Mother had whelped.

Monika seemed to mellow as well, trying to start a comfortable relationship with her older sister she had terrorized so, and slowly they were making it work.

But this fancy coffeemaker was the best gift her sister had given her in years.

And that meant Effin had survived years of purple and orange-striped fuzzy scarves, rap classics, CDs set to opera and zydeco, a fifteen-inch vibrator that looked more like a jackhammer than a sex toy, and a dozen pet mice in a broken cage because Monika thought Effin was lonely in her big house.

The glue traps were still in place to catch the last squeaker before it decided to become fruitful, multiply, fill her house, and reduce the dry goods in her pantry.

"Yes." Effin inhaled the rich aroma of her freshly ground imported coffee before taking her first sip of java heaven. "Things are moving along swimmingly."

Then the ceiling fell in.

Chapter Three

Masataka was not having a very good century.

He mewed, lifting one leg and eyeing his scrotum carefully. Nope, didn't need a tongue bath yet, he decided, lowering the leg, nose still twitching at the unfairness of his life. The only good thing about being stuck in this form was easy access to his balls. If he were in human form, he would never be able to twist his spine to essentially blow himself.

Of course, if he were in human form, he could find someone to do it for him.

But he was not in human form and it was all because of that bitch -- and he meant that literally -- who had ridden his cock like getting him off would save her life.

How was he to know that that luscious kitsune was already mated? *She* was the one to openly flirt with *him*.

How was he to know that it was her wedding day? Or that her chosen mate was a nine-tailed kitsune of great distinction?

The female fox-shifter had just smiled at him, licking her chops as her mate busted into the room, his *bi* -- his glowing foxfire power -- leading him directly to his mate and pulling her off him on the down stroke.

"One final bit of mischief," she explained to her irate mate, "before I settle down."

That was all well and good for her, Masataka had groused as she walked out of the room, but that left him with old Nine-tails to deal with.

"Look," Masataka tried to explain as he pulled the rumpled den sheets over his naked lap. His prick still stood erect and shiny, a testament to how well the female kitsune was getting off on her little ride. "I didn't know she was taken."

Twitching his nose, his eyes glowing in extreme anger, the thousand-year-old shifter pointed to the window behind Masataka's bed.

"Oh," Masa managed, blinking dumbly at what he saw. Despite the gently falling rain, the sun was shining brightly, the ancient sign that a female kitsune was getting ready for her wedding march. "I guess I never noticed," he muttered absently. "I mean, she followed me back here last night and we've been going at it since yesterday."

Masa smiled as he thought of the pale red head of the female kitsune, bobbing up and down in his lap as he held onto the bed sheets and prayed that his head wouldn't explode.

A stupid grin spread across his face as he wiggled his ass in remembrance.

"I mean," he continued, "have you ever seen such a fine ass on a female? Full and round, and high and tight -- an unusual thing in Asian women. Though I guess that she's not really Asian," Masa reasoned out loud. "I guess this means that she can take on any shape she wants..." His word trailed off as he took in the seriously pissed off look on the ancient kitsune's face. "Oh, dear." He slumped in his bed. "I should have guessed she was a kitsune when she swallowed my dick, fingered my balls, vibrated her neck muscles, and threw up that ball of light so I could see her work, huh?" Somehow this didn't make the nine-tailed fox-shifter smile. "This is going to cost me, isn't it?" The still silent fox-shifter nodded. "This is going to hurt me more than it could ever hurt you?" Again the fox-shifter nodded. "And I'm seriously not going to like it, am I?"

"It's not all your fault." The deep, rumbling voice of the elder fox-shifter radiated power. "Though if you paid a bit more attention to your surroundings, neko, this would have never happened."

"I am seriously regretting letting myself get picked up at that tavern," Masataka added, hoping that his ignorance would grant him a small reprieve.

No such luck, he realized as the fox glared at him.

"As a cat-shifter, you should be more observant. That is the one great trick of the neko that is unsurpassed by any other shifter. But I am thinking that maybe you are spending too much time in human form. It's dulling your catlike abilities. So, in order to help you, I am going to ensure that you get lots of time to work on your shortcomings."

As he spoke, a definite powerful glow began to surround him.

"You need to spend some time getting to know yourself better. And to do that, you really need to be in your cat form."

He waved his hand and a huge ball of brilliant white light formed before the ancient kitsune.

Masataka opened his mouth to speak, but the ball slammed into his chest, spreading fire throughout his system, forcing his body to transform. In the blink of an eye, Masataka's whole perception shrank and suddenly the world became a much larger place.

He opened his mouth to speak, but only a pitiful mew emerged.

"You are...cute like this." The kitsune chuckled as he stared at the small black cat who stared up at him with owlish amber eyes. "And to make sure you get lots of practice at being observant, I'm sending you to a place where no one will recognize you for what you are and try to take you in. Cat form you are, and in cat form you shall remain until you learn to be more observant and you use that to make someone wish for you to stay."

Masa screeched his disapproval and the kitsune laughed further. "You, my hapless friend, are going to America."

With his screech of denial still ringing in his ears, Masataka found himself flying through time and space to end up...in the lower section of Baltimore, Maryland. And for roughly a hundred years, here he remained, watching and observing the humans who were so different from the humans that populated his native Japan.

For the first few years, he hung around, picking up the language and learning culture. The next years were spent fighting off normal cats and animals, creating and marking his territory, and ensuring his safety.

After that, he spent his time observing these people and their strange ways.

And he discovered something about himself, too.

He was an ass man.

Kami, he loved a phat ass on a woman. Not a flabby or an out-of-shape one, but an ass that was round and high and tight, and partially the reason he was in this predicament in the first place.

Oh, he still hoped that fucking bitch of a kitsune gave her mate rabies or some other form of social disease. But after the amount of time he had spent in the US, his anger had faded dramatically.

Besides, here in this wonderfully liberated place, he got to experience a whole new class of ass.

There were the wide-hipped and curved at the bottom ass of most white women. In a way, it was similar to the Asian women he was used to. Then, there were women from India who had wide asses that were slightly rounded, but were hidden beneath the layers of clothing they wore. Native American women were few and far between here, but the few he managed to scope out had fine asses, both wide and full, but not that high. Latino women...Kami, he loved them because their asses were wide, full, and high. And the way they danced, hips winding, asses jiggling...Latino women knew how to work their hips. But that brought him to his most favored of asses, the black woman's ass.

They were round, high, tight, and full. They came in several shades and textures, and most came with the ability to do the most wonderful ass-jiggling dance moves he had ever seen.

They got low with it!

They shook it like salt and pepper shakers!

They worked that back, made that ass jiggle, ground it down and bumped that ass all around.

The sight of a well turned ass doing the butt jiggling dance of the hour made him retreat to the safety of his territory and lick like his dick was going out of style.

He loved asses of every ethnic group, savored the sight of each one, and relished each for their individual attributes and characteristics and style, but the asses of the black women were top among his favorites.

He studied women, observed their mannerisms, learned what turned them on and what turned them off. He was confident that he observed them so much, he could happily choose his mate from the selection this city offered alone.

Now, if only he could get out of this cursed cat form!

He had been licking himself for a hundred years and never really got any relief. He imagined when he turned human again he would have one grandiose case of blue balls.

He shuddered at that thought and shook himself out of his musings. He had things to do.

There was territory to defend, balls to lick, and asses to observe.

Being a cat wasn't all that bad, but damn, he sure missed pussy.

Chapter Four

"Why is this happening to me?" Effin wondered out loud as she absently scratched at the swollen and bumpy flesh that once made up her right cheek.

"Have you accepted Jesus as your personal savior?" the helpful tow truck driver asked, peering at her, trying to hold in a wince. "Prayer helps."

Effin rolled her eyes and tried not to pout; it made her swollen lips look all the more swollen.

"I pray," she groused. "Lately, I've been praying for death."

"Suicide is not the answer!" the large, greasy, stringy-haired, pale man snapped. "God has given you this wondrous life and you are planning on throwing it all away!"

"Whoa, God-boy," Effin shouted, throwing up one hand as if to shield herself from his glare of death that she was sure had to be patented in some death camp for prisoner torture. "I never said I was going to kill myself. It is just an expression."

"You need to express gratitude for your Lord and Savior!" the man growled back, making Effin discreetly turn her head away from his red-faced visage to check how far she was away from her home. If it was close enough, she was going to pop the door and make a run for it. This man had to be demented!

"I do!"

"By praying for death?" he growled, his three chins quivering in his indignation. "You are one ungrateful black child!"

What did he just say?

"What?" Suddenly, she was a lot less weary and a lot angrier. And her damn face was itching more as her ire built. "What did you just say to me?"

"I said that you are one ungrateful black child!" he fairly screamed, his eyes darting back and forth rapidly between her and the road.

"And I think that you are one greasy, overweight disgrace to the white race, you reject from a Southern Baptist prison camp! Me being black don't have shit to do with my bad day! You want to know about my bad day, you self-righteous asshole? It started with my ceiling falling in, my car not starting, and it seems to be ending with me having to deal with you, you overweight asshole! Don't you dare preach the Lord to me when you still use race to describe people! And what the fuck do you know about my prayer habits anyway? The good Lord is probably ashamed to have an asshole like you praying to him anyway, trying to tell me what I should and should not do! Well, fuck you!" she bellowed as she scratched at her face and arms, raising welts on the backs of her hands as her anger made her dig in deep with her nails.

"Get out!" the man hissed, jerking his wheel to the left and pulling over a few blocks away from her home. "Heathen! Blasphemer! Jezebel!"

"Your fucking mother!" Effin snarled, jerking the handle to the door of the tow truck and using her foot to kick the door open.

"Repent, you evil spawn of Satan!" he shouted at her as she hopped out of the large cab of the oversized, flatbed truck.

"You and the horse you rode in on!" she shouted back, slamming the door shut as hard as she could.

The driver took off with a squeal of his tires, and Effin began the two-block walk to her home, snarling as she recalled her morning.

First, her ceiling had fallen in, which was a surprise and a half, but that was not the worst of her problems. When she called the roofer who'd repaired the ceiling before she originally purchased the sixty-year-old federal house, she was told that he could be out sometime in the next week or two.

When she argued about the time, he pointed out that he would rather deal with the man of the house instead of a hormonal woman. After calling the roofer everything but a child of God and swearing that she would find a civilized, non-Neanderthal roofer, she discovered he was the only one in the area who dealt with slate roofs like the one she had.

So, she'd swallowed her pride, called him back, and tried not to cringe as he laughed and gave her a rough estimate for the size of her roof, if the warranty was not still valid -- the same warranty that he couldn't seem to find on file.

She was screwed.

But she was still going on a date with a handsome hunk of a brother and the evening would be magical. Magical, dammit, because she had earned it!

So pushing her anger aside -- besides, she had a copy of the warranty on file -- she washed her face with the wonderful soap from Monika and went to put on her shopping shoes! It was courtin' time and she was going to look her best in order to be courted properly.

But when she turned the key in her ignition, the engine wouldn't turn over.

She tried and tried, but the twelve-year-old Jeep would not start.

Finally, she was forced to call AAA, and even after they arrived an hour later than they promised, they could not get the Jeep started. They wound up sending a tow truck that took her battered baby to a dealership -- thankfully only a mile or so away from her home.

It took them fifteen minutes to tell her that her neutral ignition switch was busted and it was going to cost a whopping five hundred dollars to fix. But the good news was that they promised to have it done before two. Seeing that it was nearly eleven when she was leaving the shop, the timetable was a blessing.

"Thank you so much," she said with a sigh, shaking the mechanic's hand. But instead of responding in kind, the very attractive man winced and asked her what was wrong with her face.

"Nothing," she snapped, shocked that the man would comment on her beauty. Hell, she knew she was no runway supermodel, but she was not that bad looking.

But the man was looking at her weirdly and backing away from her, so she made her way to the ladies room and actually screamed at what she saw in the mirror.

What had been her face earlier in the day was now a mass of swollen, red skin and patches of bumps. Even her lips were swelling at an alarming rate, making her resemble a Fat Albert cartoon character.

"This is not happening," she managed and turned sharply when there came a great banging on the door.

She opened it to see the concerned face of the manager of the shop. The overweight, brown-skinned woman looked at her in pity.

"Our tow guy will take you home," she was informed. "You look like you are having a severe allergic reaction to something."

The only thing she could think of that would give her such a reaction was the soap that Monika brought her. The curse of the baby sister had struck again.

And then she had to deal with the driver and his overly zealous Christian reborn attitude...

She pulled herself out of her musings as she realized she was standing in front of her house. She smiled -- well, as much as she could with lips swollen to the size of soup bowls -- and basked in the warmth that came with knowing that safety was at hand.

She made her way to her house and immediately phoned her best friend Christa, and began her tale of woe as she searched through her cabinets for a bottle of Benadryl.

"And to top it all off," she added as she downed a few pills, paying no attention to the bright, pretty red nightlight that was emblazoned on the front of the bottle, "I still don't have anything to wear."

"Chill, girl." Christa laughed. "Go and look in your closet! I am sure that you bought something last week."

"Okay." Effin sighed. "I'll look, but if I can't find anything, I'm calling you back in an hour."

"One hour, girl," Christa agreed. "That is enough time for me to get my nails and toes done."

"Yeah," grumbled Effin, looking at the ravages of her face. "You just have got to have pretty feet."

After her phone conversation, she schlepped her way up to her walk-in closet and began contemplating her choices. Then a slow grin spread across her face as she recalled that she and Christa had picked out a perfect outfit for her, and at half off, too!

It was a stunning royal blue sheath that skimmed her figure and hugged all her curves in the right places. It took pounds off of her thighs, added inches to her bustline, and positively made her skin glow. She'd looked like royalty when she'd tried the dress on, drawn to it by the subtle beadwork that made her appear to be covered in sparkling fairy dust when the light hit it just so.

She sighed, a grin on her swollen face as she resisted the urge to scratch, and dug deep into the back of her closet, into the "when I have a relationship" section. Edging aside silky peignoirs, sleazy teddies on their padded hangers, and scads of fantasy wear, she reached for the "Total You" garment bag and...felt a note.

"What the hell?" she muttered, pulling the bag out to see what she had grabbed. Had she left a receipt on the thing? She didn't think so but...

The first thing she noticed was her sister's handwriting.

Squinting to read in the dim closet, Effin took a step back to better understand her sister's spidery print.

I saw this when I was borrowing the slinky spider priestess costume and couldn't resist.

Grant couldn't resist either.

Don't worry about the stains on the knees and the splatters on the front. I understand seltzer water can wash out protein stains.

Love you, Monika

"Just because your name is Monika don't mean you blow men in my blue dress!" Effin wailed, then screamed, "Eww!" She threw her beautiful, almost-perfect, one-of-a-kind dress back into her closet as she realized what the splatters had to be.

"Why do you hate me so?" Effin railed, looking up toward the heavens, then changing her mind quickly. The way her day was going, lightning might just fry her ass, and then where would she be?

Unable to pay for her new roof, unable to get her Jeep out of the shop, and fried too crisply to even contemplate wearing any of her fantasy outfits again.

Wait. Her sister was wearing her fantasy outfits, complete with thong undies?

"God, why me?" she wailed, racing to the kitchen for a huge contractor bag -- one of those garbage bags that was both heavy duty and hard to tear. She had some serious cleaning to do, after she called Christa so they could make a last-minute shopping trip. Maybe there was still something somewhere for her to buy and still make her date with the most handsome, well-rounded, put-together brother that she had ever heard of.

Right after she sat down for a moment, she decided. Running around the plaster on her kitchen floor had obviously made her tired. She would just sit on the comfy bed for a moment, close her eyes, and...zzzzzzzzz.

Chapter Five

Masataka rolled his eyes as he stared up at the heavens. It was beginning to rain again and that would mean the area beside the factories he called his home was going to get very muddy.

"I really need to get a life," the neko sighed, crawling into his makeshift home, an abandoned warehouse where he was protected from the rain and other elements.

The small black cat yawned, showing off razor-sharp white teeth, before making his way to the master bedroom. His master bedroom consisted of stolen cashmere scarves and baby blankets set near an exhaust vent that connected to the other nearby warehouses.

This building might be abandoned for the moment, but it still had heat and running water. The company probably was going to use it again, but until they did, Casa de la Ghetto was all his.

He sank into an uneasy lump of flesh and fur as he tried to decipher the restlessness that had overtaken him.

He knew that it couldn't be an attack of horny. His blue balls had been covered in fur for, like, forever! Frankly, he had grown kind of accustomed to the underlying hum of sexual energy that had been with him throughout the years since he'd been forced to assume this form.

It couldn't be the storm; hell, it had been raining off and on for days. It had been another typical Baltimore weather pattern and was something that never really bothered him in the past.

Could his biological clock be ticking? Did he want little kittens…um, babies to call his own and take over his nest?

He looked down at the baby blankets he was lying on and rolled his eyes. No. The sight of the little baby duckies and bears in diapers didn't even cause him one hint of longing.

So what was wrong with him?

As he peered out of one dirty window, he saw the workers leaving the factories for the day.

"Going to take the old ball and chain to dinner tonight," one rough-looking worker said with a chuckle. "Going to get me some tonight, too. It's Valentine's Day; she has to put out. It's an unspoken rule."

The man with him laughed and they parted ways, both making for their vehicles parked in the quickly emptying lot.

"Valentine's Day." Masa sighed. "That may be what it is. How could I have missed that?"

He pouted as much as his little kitty lips would allow and dropped his head onto his soft, pilfered bed linens.

"This is so depressing," he grumbled, then cut eyes at a plump brown mouse that had scurried out to stare at him. Before he could work up the energy or inclination to do as his cat body wished and pounce on the invader, he noticed a smaller gray mouse leaving the same hole. This mouse, the gray female, looked around, not noticing the predator staring at them, and nuzzled up to her mate, who squeaked affectionately at her.

It was so damn cute, Masa thought...as he ripped them limb from limb, tossing mouse guts all over his formerly pristine master bedroom.

"Fuck that cutesy shit," he growled, tossing the beheaded carcass out of his room and onto the cement floor below. "If I don't get laid, nobody gets laid."

Maybe he was just horny.

He purred as he licked the blood off his claws, waiting for the feeling of disquiet to leave. But it just got worse. And it had nothing to do with murdering the furry little pestilence that invaded his territory, though he thought that some small amount of guilt would be appropriate. No, the feeling of unease, of restlessness increased. He felt as if something were about to happen. The feeling built up in his chest, adding pressure around his heart, tightening his lungs until he felt that the whole warehouse was going to come tumbling down on him.

He had to get out.

Ignoring the rain and his comfortable bedding, Masa took off into the dimming day, hungering, searching for some unknown prey. He didn't know what was driving him, but he knew it was important. And Masa always followed his instincts.

Shaking his head at his own folly, he raced out into the rain, looking for something he could not name but driven toward it, all the same.

Chapter Six

It was the drool running down her chin that finally awoke Effin. It was a cold, wet feeling that pulled her out of her sleep faster than someone shouting fire. Groggy, she opened her eyes and absently wiped her chin, grimacing at the slimy feel of her own spit.

Definitely a shower was the first order of business.

But as she looked around her room and set her sights on her alarm clock, Effin let out a shriek of dismay. "It's six-forty-five!"

Then another thought hit her panicking mind. Christa was supposed to have come by to take her shopping!

Effin stumbled to her feet and landed flat on her stomach. Gasping for breath, she untangled herself and raced down the stairs, her steps unsteady as the last of the drugs worked its way out of her system.

When she got to the front door, there was a handwritten note tacked to the glass with a bit of gum.

*Came by and you didn't answer your door. I assume you
got a ride to the mall so I went to take a before-date nap.*
   Lubs ya,
   Christa

"No...no...no...NO!" Effin slammed the door shut,
tossing the note aside as she turned and raced back up the
stairs.

It was almost time for her date and she didn't have
anything to wear. She held in a sob at the injustice of it all.
And there was no way she could wear her work clothing on
a date. The business suits were as unfeminine as you could
get and still look like a woman. There had to be something
left!

Diving back into her closet, Effin eyed the sad remains
of her once proud costume collection, the only thing that
could even have a hope or a prayer of passing as dress
clothing.

And that meant there was only one thing in the hall of
horny fantasies that would pass.

The Spider Princess dress.

The Spider Princess was a costume she had bought a few
Halloweens back and never had the courage to wear. It was
extremely short and shot through with silver thread. The
bodice was almost completely lace and left very little to the
imagination. It was so tight she had to be careful what she
ate or she would look like a hippo! Uncomfortable, true, but

it was at least something that wouldn't make her look like she was turning tricks for a living.

Racing off to the shower, she was glad for once about her no nonsense hairstyle. A few strokes of a brush and her neatly shaved locks would fall into place.

After a quick shower, where she nicked her underarms on a dull razor blade, she ducked into her bedroom for some black silk undies. Then it was time to pull on the stockings.

The first pair of sheer, black silk stockings had a run.

That was a common enough problem and the reason she bought the sheer black hose by the dozen.

The next pair was shredded from top to toe.

The third pair was too small, the fourth too big, the fifth too long.

She was down to her sixth pair, which she eased on her feet...just in time for a fingernail to snag and tear a run right down the front of her right leg. The seventh pair went on perfectly, and, holding her breath, Effin eased her Spider Princess dress over her head.

It seemed to have shrunk since she'd last looked at it. The bottom of the dress barely touched the top of her thighs.

Before, it had been mid-thigh, but this was just indecent! Her ass was hanging out! Effin turned toward her mirror, only to hear a tearing sound. Lo and behold, the seventh pair of stockings bit the dust.

Effin stormed back to the bed and pulled off the ruined hosiery, glaring at it as if it were the cause of hunger, global warming, and her ceiling caving in!

The eighth pair went on just fine and Effin carefully tiptoed over to pull on a pair of high heels she thought of as date shoes.

But that just made the skirt even shorter!

"What the hell am I supposed to do?" She whimpered. "I look like five-dollar Fran!"

Then inspiration struck! Out of the corner of her eye, she noticed her hanging scarves. Effin loved long and flowing things, and scarves were among her favorite things to wear. She raced to the stand and quickly pulled out an extra long rectangle of black lace.

Yes! This would work!

She quickly folded and tied the scarf around her waist. Joy! It covered her ass! And it added a Latin flavor to her dress as well. Grinning, she gave a twirl before the mirror, and hissed as she heard that telltale tearing sound.

Her stockings had gotten caught up in the lace of the scarf and run.

The ninth pair of stockings was carefully pulled on while she sat at her vanity.

She would not move until she had to!

She carefully placed makeup on a face that was no longer swollen, but kind of itchy, and smiled at what she saw. She was beautiful! Perfect! She would knock her date dead.

And just in time too! She heard the sounds of a high-end European sports car stop in front of her house.

She walked over to the window and smiled at what she saw.

There was a fine-looking brother easing out of a Jag and making his way to her house. She plucked up a small, black silk purse, tossed in some cash, her house keys, and the all-important cell phone before meandering down the stairs, trying to control a heart that was beating a mile a minute in her chest.

After waiting until she heard the bell ring, Effin made her way to the front door and eased it open.

"My name is Buster and I am here to collect Effin Hurtzs for the evening."

Ohh! Polite, Effin thought. Things were definitely on the upswing.

"You have her." Effin smiled and stuck out her hand.

"Charmed." Buster grinned, looking handsome in his denim jeans and what appeared to be a silk shirt under his lightweight jacket.

It was unseasonably warm, so Effin just grabbed a light wrap.

"For you." He placed a kiss on the back of her hand and handed her some yellow roses.

"Beautiful," Effin breathed. "Thank you so much, Buster!"

Then he escorted her to the car.

This night was going to be a Valentine's night to remember. Effin smiled. She had a perfect date on a perfect night. She hoped it never ended!

Chapter Seven

Her date began to go downhill very quickly after he escorted her from her house.

The dozen beautiful yellow roses Buster handed to her just happened to be fake. The ends were covered in what she suspected was graveyard soil due to the RIP tag hanging from one ragged end.

Shaking her head at the oddity of it all, Effin rallied and made her way over to the Jaguar that was sitting in her driveway, trying to keep the ultra-high hemline covered with the huge black scarf she'd wrapped around her waist.

She stood by the door of the car and waited...and waited...and waited, until she noticed that Buster was already seated and tapping the steering wheel impatiently for her to get into the car.

"And wipe off your feet before you step in my ride," the man purred, eyeing Effin up and down like she was a side of beef ready for market.

Rolling her eyes, Effin halfheartedly scraped her feet on the curb before sliding into the cool, leather interior.

She turned to look at Buster, and what she saw eased her anger. Buster was a drop-dead gorgeous specimen of a black man. His hair was cropped close to his scalp, drawing attention to his caramel-colored eyes. Long, black lashes framed those amazing orbs and drew attention to his perfectly smooth, milk-chocolate skin.

His nose was a little broad and his nostrils flared as he scented her perfume. His lips were full and...was that lip gloss or a sheen of moisture from where he licked his lips while staring at her bosom?

Pulling her wrap close around her, she faced forward, waiting for him to start the engine and get them on the way.

"So, what's a fine mama like you doing, going on a blind date anyway?"

The question was unexpected, but was an interesting place to start a conversation.

"Well, Buster, I was asked to go on this date by my friend Christa. She says you are a wonderful person."

"Christa? The high yellow bit...chick with the high voice?"

"Excuse me?" Effin snarled, turning to glare at him with anger-filled eyes. What did he just attempt to cover up calling her best friend?

"Why? Did you fart or something? Don't be farting in my Jag."

"I...Uh..." Effin's eyes widened as she stared in disbelief at the man. "I most definitely did not pass gas, and if I did I would apologize for it. I was referring to what you almost called Christa."

"Don't worry about it." Buster smirked. "You not high yellow but you have a nice ass."

Before Effin could comment, Buster started the engine and set the huge car purring. Within seconds they were racing down the small street at breakneck speed and with an obvious disregard for any life forms stupid enough to get into Buster's path of destruction.

It only got worse from there.

The only music he would play was gangsta rap that glorified violence and gang life and contained so many curse words that if it were played on the radio all you would hear was one long continuous bleep. He made several loud, annoying cell phone calls to people named Murder Dog and Body Count, cut in front of no fewer than three tractor trailers, and flipped off a mother with two kids and a stroller after nearly running them down in a crosswalk.

Effin was ready to kiss the ground and thank the good Lord for helping her survive this trip.

But it got even worse.

* * *

House of Waffles was not her ideal choice of fine dining establishment.

Before he parked the car so they could enter the waffle house, he slipped off his jacket and pulled something that looked suspiciously like a semi-automatic weapon out of the glove box. He climbed out of the car without assisting Effin out, stuck the gun in his waistband, and gave a few of the dealers at the corners of the restaurant assessing looks before tossing up what had to be a gang sign and getting a nod of respect...which made Effin want to dive back into the dubious safety of the Jag's faux leather interior and its fiberglass exterior.

Fuck second thoughts. Effin was on fifth and sixth thoughts by the time they reached the restaurant doors.

Then, he wrapped his arm around her waist, pulling her close to the muscular body that would have looked lovely had he been wearing anything other than a pair of black jeans three sizes too big and a sleeveless silk muscle shirt two sizes too small. That jacket had hidden a lot, and what she'd thought was a tasteful outfit turned out to be more of a clown costume.

Effin forced a grin on her face as they took a seat at the sticky booth in the highly lit restaurant and a bored-looking, white-haired Asian man eyed them with a smirk before demanding to know what they wanted.

"Scrimps," Buster promptly stated with a smile wide enough to show Effin something she hadn't noticed before -- all the imitation platinum blingage around his front teeth. The word grill had never had such an exact meaning.

Effin resisted the urge to ask about health department certification and calmly began to examine the laminated menu. Before she could open her mouth, Buster began to order for her.

"It's *à la carte*, baby," he crowed. "Order what you want! In fact, she'll have the scrimps, too."

Then he grinned at her, the light glinting off his mouth metal so it seemed to twinkle with studio effects.

"I can order for myself," Effin gritted out, trying to smile because she wasn't dateless on Valentine's Day.

"I love me a independent woman." Buster laughed, slapping the table with his hand then staring at the spot where some syrup stuck to it, before shrugging it off. "Independent women are da bomb. She'll have the scrimps with extra ketchup and hot sauce. Gotta keep that booty clappin', girl."

Effin rolled her eyes and tried to remind herself that this date couldn't get any worse. She was wrong.

Somewhere between the water course -- apparently the substitute for an appetizer -- and Buster striking the bottom of the ketchup bottle and spattering it across the front of her black dress, the very same Murder and Body Count decided to join in their little Valentine celebration.

"My dawg!" Buster crowed, rising to his feet, arms extended in welcome.

It was then that Effin got her first glance at the friends Buster kept.

Murder was a tall, thin white man with a pencil-thin mustache and long, knotty locks. He was wearing a goose-down jacket with the name of some local sports team emblazoned across the front in bright purple. He had a joint tucked behind one ear and a dead expression in his slate-gray eyes.

"S'up," he nodded, then took a seat in the booth, pushing aside Effin with nary a glance.

Body Count was a short Hispanic man with a clean-shaven face and his hair buzzed short. He was wearing a hip-length black leather coat and a pair of overly large jeans with a belt buckle shaped like a gun. He looked over at Effin, then dismissed her as if she didn't exist.

"So...you down for tonight?" Body Count asked, giving Buster an unreadable look.

"Tonight, man? I'm on a date! Don't go messin' with my flow."

"Ditch the bitch and let's move," Murder insisted. He kept looking nervously around, observing the comings and goings of the other people in the room.

And of course, Effin took offense at his words.

"Excuse me, you troglodyte," she snapped. "I do have a name and I ain't nobody's bitch."

Body Count raised surprised eyes to her for a moment, before a slow grin spread across his mouth. "You got spunk. I like that, kid. But let me tell you that my man Buster ain't got no use for a mouthy woman. Why do you think we call him Buster?"

"Because that's the name his mama gave him?" Effin smarted back, common sense taking a back seat as she faced off against this man.

She was having one hell of a date, and that was meant in the harshest terms, and now these two yahoos were coming in and making things even worse. She had had enough. Something had to give!

"No." Body Count laughed. "We call him Buster because he busted a cap in the ass of the last woman who mouthed off at him. Bust her in the ass, if you want the whole name."

"Check, please!"

Effin raised her voice and her hand as soon as the words passed the man's mouth.

"Effin…" Buster began as his friends exploded into laughter. "It didn't happen like that, baby."

"Check!" Effin screamed, shoving at Murder to get him to move his skinny ass so she could leave. "Check and a cab!"

No fewer than three disreputable looking men rose to their feet and offered hack services, almost making Effin sit back down, but the desire to leave this place overruled all.

"Look, I'll take you home," Buster, or whatever the hell his name was, sighed. "Damn, dawgs," he grumbled as the Asian man returned, holding their orders in two brown paper bags. "Cock blocking 'n shit."

Wordlessly, Effin snatched one of the bags and made for the door, not caring that her scarf was slipping and that she was giving a wonderful view of her bouncing, irate ass as she made for the door.

"Damn, that ass is phat!" one of them -- maybe Murder -- said with a chuckle, and Effin increased her speed. This had positively been the date from hell. Christa would pay!

Chapter Eight

"Kami-sama, yeah!" Masa moaned...well, meowed as he found the perfect spot to rest and relax and relieve a little tension.

Who knew that sinking your cock into a warm, moist manhole cover was rather like getting a hot piece of tail? Okay, he was stretching it a bit. But who knew the warm heat and the moisture bellowing up from the small exhaust hole would feel so good to his kitty cock? It had been pure dumb luck that he chose to sit on the vent to warm his more delicate parts, but when the first blast of moist heat surrounded his sheathed cock and balls, his libido had flown through the roof. His cock had come out to play and he did what any self-respecting tom on the prowl would do. He took advantage of the situation.

He sighed as he bent his head to lap at his swollen pink organ and his tiny, fuzzy balls. How the mighty had fallen, he thought for a moment, and then bent to work again, lapping at his rapidly swelling and throbbing cock.

He had no idea what had driven him to this spot, but now that he had found some form of entertainment, he was determined to stick around for a while and enjoy it. He slitted his eyes as the feelings began to swamp his body -- familiar feelings that made him tingle and shiver.

His tail lashed wildly and his breathing increased as little kitty mews left his throat.

Yeah, there was nothing like being able to give himself head. The heat and moisture of the vent gave him the sexual stimulation his cat's body needed to actually achieve an erection for other than cleaning purposes, and he cleaned himself thoroughly. Constantly. He had the cleanest kitty cock in existence!

But this was a rare treat and might even drive him toward orgasm! It had been how many years?

But thoughts like that would take his mind away from reaching that ultimate pleasure, so he stopped thinking about history and started thinking about the present...the present orgasm that was building.

He flexed his toes and marveled that his right leg never got tired being hitched up to the sky.

But the sexual tension in his body began to tie him into knots. He felt his tail begin to tingle, his whiskers twitch, and his balls burn as his tongue lashed over the pink head of his throbbing cock. Some part of his mind marveled that he had achieved a full erection. The furry sheath that protected his cock in this form was fully retracted, allowing him full access to the head and shaft, access that he instantly took advantage of, using both the moist heat from the grate and his rough tongue.

Faster and faster he lapped, licking away the precum that made his cockhead glisten, stimulating the whole of his cock until he felt his body stiffen, his back arch, and white lights began to dance behind his eyes.

Letting out a mewl of desire, Masa's head arched backwards, his body going rigid as the first drips of milky seed exploded from his cock.

His body spasmed convulsively at the first release he'd experienced in ages.

Breathless and panting, Masa rode the waves of release until his body lost its rigid stance and settled onto the warm grate.

Exciting, he thought to himself, as he allowed his eyes to close. Deep purrs emerged from his chest. *Not as good as it is with a partner, but damn fine indeed.*

Sighing deeply, Masataka relaxed and rolled beside the vent, a slow purr rumbling through his chest as he let the afterglow take him. He would wait here until the warm, lazy feelings eased and then he would head home. The pressure in his chest had relaxed a bit, and he decided that it had been an attack of horny, after all.

With one final, muffled meow, Masa closed his eyes and waited for the lethargy to lessen. This was not exactly the life, but it was better now that he'd had his first orgasm in Kami-sama knew how many years.

* * *

"I'm sorry about the guys," Buster -- whatever the strange man she was out with was really named -- stated. "They just don't know how to treat a lady."

Effin didn't say a word, but she reached for the radio on switch and she noticed that the car didn't have a cigarette lighter.

"The guys are always kidding, and they just picked the wrong time to show up. I wish I didn't tell them we were going for chicken and waffles."

Was that a no smoking sticker on the dash?

Effin was beginning to suspect that she was in a rental.

"So... What is it that you do again, Bus...man?" There wasn't a friggin' cigarette lighter!! Only rentals and preachers' cars and taxis... "I understand you work with Christa."

"Understand," he chuckled. "I love an intelligent bit-- lady. I am in stocks."

"You play the market?" she asked, arching an eyebrow as she examined the creature she had been running around with. She was beginning to feel uneasy. She turned the radio on in hopes of finding something decent to talk about.

"The only market I play in is Pantry Pride. I work in stocks, as in the stock room."

Effin smiled at the creature with a smile that showed all of her teeth.

Then she reached into her purse for her cell.

Still grinning at the stock boy, she pressed speed dial, instantly getting Christa's cell.

The stock boy opened his mouth to speak, but Effin held up one hand to halt his words.

"Christa?" she purred. "I am having a won... I am having a time with Buster the bitch slayer, and I want you to know that I will thank you personally for this one."

"Not now, girl! I'm on a date!" Christa's voice was almost drowned out by music and the sound of cutlery clanking against real glass plates. "It's rude to speak while at dinner."

"But..." Effin tried not to scream and call her best friend some horrible names.

"Later, girl! Henry might propose!"

Then, her best friend unceremoniously hung up on her.

Effin turned a sick smile to the oblivious Buster the Stock Boy and turned up the radio just in time to hear the newscast.

"Police are looking for a black male about six feet tall with dark brown eyes and black hair, driving a rented Jaguar. Baxter Collingsworth is wanted for questioning in the brutal shooting deaths of several Baltimore women. Police believe that he may be a serial killer and could be trolling for his next victim. The suspect can be identified by his extreme amount of platinum teeth."

Before Effin could hear more, Buster, the alleged woman slayer, quickly changed the station.

"News bores me, baby." He chuckled nervously.

"Um, is this a rental?" Effin asked, easing toward the door as she noticed that they were heading away from her house and going toward the warehouse district in Dundulk, Maryland.

"Why? You checking out my pocket book? You need to be like J-Lo, Effin. Her love didn't cost a thing."

"Just a wedding ring, a ceremony and subsequent divorce settlement. Where are we going?"

"Just for a little spin, to get to get know one another."

"I want to go home."

"Don't be like that, baby."

"Don't 'baby' me. I want to go home!"

Effin was getting really nervous now. The lights of civilization were spinning away from view and the dark shapes of the warehouses loomed darkly before her.

"Why? You too good to go out with a stock boy?" Buster sneered, beginning to look every bit as menacing as his comrades in arms.

"No, but because I like life, I want out of this vehicle."

Effin reached for the handle of the Jag, tugging unobtrusively while Mr. Serial Killer kept his eyes on the winding roads.

"If I wanted to hurt you, you would be dead by now."

With that, Effin opened her mouth and began to scream. Loud, piercing wails left her throat as she pulled on the handle.

"God, I take it back! I don't want to die!" she screamed, fearful eyes on Buster.

"Hey...hey!" Buster tried to calm her. "I was just kidding! I was playing!" He reached out to calm Effin, but she screamed even louder as she popped her seatbelt open and began to push frantically at the door.

As Buster made another attempt to reach out to her, the door swung open. Seeing her chance, Effin dove out of the slow-moving car, and rolled several times, screaming at the top of her lungs.

"Stupid bitch!" Buster bellowed, before hitting the gas and taking off for parts unknown, leaving Effin safe, but dreadfully lost and alone.

* * *

Lost, alone, with no cab in sight, wearing the best in hooch wear, Effin sat on the side of the road and let the tears flow.

"What the hell did I ever do to deserve this?" she wailed. "Gremlins, I'm so sorry I doubted you! God, please stop punishing me for the death comments. I'll even bake the tow truck guy cookies! Christa, you set me up with an alleged serial killer! Please, somebody make it go away!"

In desperation, she reached for her cell phone, then winced as she discovered her cute little black purse was now a torn, wretched silk sack which contained the remains of her cell.

Sniffing, she realized that she still had cash, but no way to call a cab.

"It's hopeless." She sniffled and dropped her head in defeat. "Nothing else is left to go wrong."

Then it started to rain.

* * *

Masataka watched the car screech by and the saw the body come tumbling out. Female, he determined, from the sounds of her wailing and the way she rolled.

She landed almost on her face before she pulled herself together and sat down on the most delicious rump he had ever seen.

The female was black, stacked, and apparently having one hell of a day. He listened to her litany of sobbing and self-recriminations before he pulled himself from his hidey-hole and went to investigate further.

He was a cat, and damned if he wasn't a curious creature.

* * *

Effin looked up at the sky and sighed.

The rain could not do any worse! She was dressed in organic hooch wear, her long lace scarf barely clinging to her ass; her only viable means to communicate that she needed help was trashed, and now it was raining on her.

Resigned, she stopped her sniffles, rose to her feet, and started the long trek toward the lights of the city.

If she were lucky -- and up to this point she would have to say the only luck she'd had was Murphy's -- she wouldn't be mugged, shot, raped, or beaten to within a inch of her life for her cute little shoes.

She took one step, then tripped over something once again, and found herself windmilling her arms to no avail. Her legs went out from underneath her and she landed once again flat on her ass.

"Ouch, dammit!" she grumbled, looking around to see what she had tripped over, after assessing that the damage was only to her pride.

Looking down, she spied the most amazingly cute thing -- a small black cat looking up at her.

"Damn, baby." She giggled, "You look like you are having a day like I am."

Masataka said nothing, but he edged closer to the female, feeling drawn to her. He hadn't meant to make her fall onto such a delicious ass, but he had to get another look at this female.

Maybe she would take him home if he played his cards right.

So he looked up at her with almost-human, liquid eyes, making them as large as he could while offering up a pitiful mew.

"Poor baby," Effin purred, then plucked the small kitten up from the cold ground.

His fur was damp but soft as she nestled the little...guy? She lifted its tail and peered underneath, ignoring the indignant squawk, and saw that he was indeed a guy.

"You got big balls for a kitten." She chuckled, righting the spitting kitten and soothing the fur he had raised over his body in protest at her peeping.

"I'm sorry, but I have to know what to call you. Anaconda would be appropriate." She snickered before cuddling the cat close and got a purr out of the deal. "You and I are castaways, apparently. And you know what? I'm going to spend the rest of my night with you."

Looking at her watch, she was pleased to see the crystal wasn't shattered and she could still see the time.

"It's almost midnight, kitty. That lovely man and scenic ride took longer than I thought."

Sighing, she rose to her feet, kitty in arms, as she began her trek toward the lights again.

"You see, I didn't want to spend Valentine's Day alone, pretty kitty. I wanted to go out on a date with a fine brother who had it together. Instead, I got a reject from Boyz in the Hood, along with his supporting cast of assholes."

She winced as she began to climb up the embankment she had rolled down, praying that the rain would not make her trip more difficult than it already was. But she made it to the top with no trouble at all, her new friend purring contentedly in her arms.

"You must be a good luck kitty."

Masataka rolled his eyes. She had no idea.

"Kitty, I am going to take you home with me and then I won't spend the rest of this wretched day alone."

She began her walk up the road that Buster, the forty-year-old stock boy, had driven down. "I wish you were a man, little pretty kitty. With that package, you would definitely be something scary in bed." She smirked at that wicked thought. "Then I would have caught and claimed a male of my own and I wouldn't be alone."

Masataka could relate. He mewed quietly and reached up to lick the tears from her face.

"Thank you, pretty kitty." Effin felt a boost in her self-confidence. Maybe owning a pet would be good therapy. First, though, she'd have to get him fixed...

Those thought were interrupted by the lights of a vehicle shining through light drizzle. She made ready to leap if it was a black rented Jag, getting a firm grip on her bag and her kitty. Instead of Buster and the obnoxious gang out for revenge, she spied the warm comfort of a Yellow Cab.

"Yes!" she shrieked, jumping up and down, waving one arm in the air.

For a moment, she thought the cab was going to pass her by, but her kitty yowled along with her and suddenly the cab stopped.

Effin ran to the passenger side window and tapped the glass. "Please tell me that you are taking fares?" she asked, all but dancing in her hope.

"Lady, you shouldn't be out here dressed like that," the cabbie, an older lady, admonished. "People will think you are a hooker. Besides, there is a serial killer on the loose."

"Let's just say it was a bad date, gone even worse," Effin said with a sigh. "More like a Greek tragedy. So, are you taking fares?"

The cabbie was about to answer when Masataka mewed.

"What a pretty little kitten. Did ya find him here?" she asked. Her tired eyes, which had appeared more cynical than Effin's, widened with glee.

"Someone tossed the little guy away so I am taking him home. Best thing to happen to me since this morning." She cuddled Masa against her cheek.

"Get in."

"Pretty kitty," Effin purred, after she settled in the back seat and gave the cabbie her address. "You must be good luck."

Looking down at her watch, she saw that it was midnight exactly.

"I survived the St. Valentine's Day Date Massacre." She looked down as her kitty began to purr. "Happy Valentine's Day, kitty. May tomorrow be a hell of a lot better than today."

Chapter Nine

Effin carried her shivering yet precious burden into her house. Her kitty immediately began to show more signs of life, leaping out of her arms and going off to explore his new environment.

Somewhere in the back of her mind, she hoped he wouldn't spray to mark his territory. She decided to make an appointment to get him neutered. Hell, if she had to rely on cats for companionship -- and it certainly seemed like her future would be filled with a string of unproductive dates if this one was anything to go by -- she wanted to ensure that she didn't have a house filled with cats. One was enough. Besides, she didn't want to look like the stereotypical old lady with a bunch of cats and no other meaningful relationships at all.

Since she was still a bit keyed up after all that had happened, she decided to clean up some of the plaster that had fallen. She made her way into the kitchen, hoping against hope that there wouldn't be a soggy mess for her to take care of, but to her surprise, the kitchen was dry, albeit dusty.

So she spent a good thirty minutes picking up plaster and sweeping up the worst of the mess.

That done, and feeling more grody than ever, Effin decided to make for the bathtub. First, though, she needed to create her kitty a makeshift litter box until she could get to a store tomorrow and pick something up.

But, to her surprise, she found an indignant kitty squatting over the toilet when she pushed open the bathroom door.

"Somebody trained you right, puss." She nodded in approval, then left he room as the cat continued to glare at her.

Soon, she heard the flush of the toilet and Effin returned to see the cat looking up at her smugly.

"Well, that kills the need for a kitty litter box." She remembered all those stories about people training their cats to use the john. "I guess the hype was true."

That settled, Effin peeled herself out of her damp, clinging clothes and tossed them directly into the garbage.

"I could never wear them again without the memories," she explained to the cat, who watched her every move. She assumed that he was learning her personality, never noticing how the cat almost fell off his paws when she stripped out of her undies and tossed them, too. In fact, she never noticed the pained yowl or the eyes that glazed over as they watched her ass sway back and forth as she moved around, collecting things for her bath.

* * *

Masa thought he was in heaven!

First thing he did, after detecting the scent of teasing gremlins, was to have a discussion with them.

His female, as he now thought of that cute human with the great body who had brought him home with her, had said some unthinking things and had annoyed this clan of gremlins. Masataka could understand defending your pride and self-esteem -- he was a good luck neko, after all -- but he couldn't allow the harassment to continue. To ignore it would fly in the face of all he was, even if a fellow preternatural creature was seeking justice.

So, he ran off the gremlins and sent a warm wave of good luck throughout her home, undoing a lot of nasty pranks that the gremlins had set for her.

Then he went off to find the facilities. He hated digging latrines to take care of his personal needs, and found the comforts of a toilet an indulgence he'd never expected to use again.

But then his female interrupted him. At least she had enough sense to give him privacy to finish his business before she entered again.

He was looking rather smug at her shocked expression before she began to undress before him. Then it was all he could do to stop himself from hiking that leg back in the air and giving the cock a good old cleaning.

Effin, as she had named herself, was one hot female!

She was built like he loved them, all curves and long legs. Her bustline was average, but her breasts were firm and high, perfect for licking and suckling.

But it was her ass that almost knocked him off any claim to sanity he still possessed. Effin's ass was high and round and tight, and jiggly! It was perfect! Those globes of dark flesh rubbed together as she walked, teasing him as they slid together in a hypnotic way.

Then, as she bent over, he almost bit his tongue off, seeing the shadow of a delicate cleft between her thighs. As she bent lower, playing with the water settings in the tub, her cheeks gaped open, just a bit, giving him a teasing glimpse of her tiny rosebud, and beyond that, the milky, pink wink of her clit. Even her cone-shaped breasts swaying slightly as she added some kind of oil to her water made his eyes water with the sheer perfection of this creature!

He never realized he was purring out loud, his head swaying with her actions as she rose up and turned to look at him.

* * *

"Oh, does the kitty want a bath?" Effin asked, noticing that her cat seemed to be staring at the tub. "Kitty want to be clean? You are one weird kitty, liking water the way you do." Effin giggled as she picked up her cat tentatively and eased into the tub. She expected him to hiss and spit, but was surprised when he just glowered at her. "I used lavender oil," she whispered as she settled into the tub, gently placing her kitty at her feet, laughing as he continued to stare indignantly up at her. Sighing, she reached for him and placed him on the rim of her tub, watching as he stared intently at her and dipped his paws into the warm water.

She quickly bathed, dried off, and fluff-dried her kitty before climbing into bed with her new friend, gently stroking his head in contentment. The day's events quickly caught up and they both drifted off to sleep.

* * *

Last night had been a nightmare of unbelievable proportions, from the blind date from hell to getting dumped in the middle of nowhere.

Finding a poor, defenseless kitty abandoned on the side of the road was where her luck had begun to change.

First, the cabbie refused payment for the trip, calling it a Valentine's Day gift, and then the rain had completely stopped.

But that was last night and now she was having this delicious dream!

* * *

Effin moaned as teasing warmth ran over her thighs, a tantalizing brush of silk and satin. *This was one hell of a dream*, she decided, as her mind began to function, one dream that she didn't want to wake from.

She stretched, opening her legs wider, hoping for more of that slick, warm sensation.

Those silky caresses and gentle touches had taken advantage of her open legs, and now a wet tongue gently circled her clit.

"Mmm," she moaned...then jerked up as the feeling became all too real!

But it was too late; that burning touch was now crawling up her stomach, teeth nipping, a tongue teasing a navel that had never been erogenous before.

Before she could open her eyes fully, she screamed in pleasure as a set of warm lips latched onto a turgid nipple, licking and biting, and sending pure sensation shooting down deep within her core.

There was more of that silky glide -- hair, she assumed -- and then her other nipple was equally attacked, sucked, laved.

While she was trying to wrap her mind around this, she felt the soft fingers dip and begin to explore her.

Her widespread legs gave easy access as those curious fingers tickled the insides of her thighs.

"I can feel you...you are so wet," a voice breathed against one heaving breast before she was arching back and shivering.

Those fingers had traveled up through her slick wetness to gently graze her hungry labia, shooting sparks through her body.

Her thighs trembling with the sheer joy of the unfamiliar caress, Effin spread her legs wider, lost on a sea of pleasure as her labia were delicately parted.

"So hot..." he breathed, and then that head dropped lower, licking a path from her tingling, burning nipples to the thatch of trimmed hair at the top of her groin.

"I wonder how you taste..."

That was her only warning before those fingers spread her labia apart, exposing her swollen flesh.

Hot breath wafted over her delicate inner flesh, her hooded clit, and then a tongue gently sampled her juices, then delved deeper between her folds.

"So long...been so long!" that voice groaned before firm lips wrapped around her clit, suckling and teasing with the tip of a wiggling tongue.

"Oh, God!" Effin moaned, her hands reaching out to her sides, fisting in her bedclothes. "Lick it harder!"

Eager to obey, that tongue pressed harder, flicking her clit back and forth before dipping lower to the entrance of her body.

It wiggled inside as a softly pointed nose nudged her clit.

"Yes!" Effin screamed, her thighs jerking up to lock around that head that was giving her such pleasure, the hair a silky glide against her overly stimulated flesh.

Then he was sucking the juices out of her, the fingers easing away from their hold on her labia to dip inside her body.

Effin screamed, her hips bucking as her nerves were stimulated.

Her head whipped from side to side as sounds like a wounded animal flowed from her throat.

God, this was good, so damn good!

Then two fingers were added, and they were thrusting, stroking her, a tongue flying in between, catching all of her spilled cream.

Then that mouth was again wrapping around her clit, sucking, pulling, that tongue flicking around the excited clit.

Effin felt a coil of tension winding up in the center of her body.

"Oh Godohgodohgodohgod…" she chanted, unable to control the words pouring from her mouth. "More," she panted. "God, more!"

The fingers thrust harder, crooking upwards to stroke the top of her quivering sheath.

The second hand dropped low, running through the slick essence that poured from her eager pussy along her ass. A finger ran through that moisture, using it as lubricant as he began to circle her wrinkled pink rosebud.

"What…God, harder!"

Effin wanted to be filled, wanted more in her pussy, more in her ass, just more! She needed to be penetrated, to be taken, and taken fast and hard!

Her body arched up higher and she let out a wail as the tip of that finger slipped into her ass.

Colors exploded behind her closed eyelids as the coil inside her snapped, lashing out in pure ecstasy as her body convulsed underneath the ministrations of fingers and mouth.

"Fuck, yes!" she wailed, her hands reaching down to tear at silky hair, holding that head closer, riding that face like it was her way out of purgatory.

And the orgasms kept coming!

Her tormenter forced her through a never ending wave, those fingers never stopping their thrusting, that mouth never relenting, that evil tongue lashing at her clit over and over.

She climaxed again as he began to purr deep in his throat, the vibrations traveling from his mouth to her clit, increasing the intensity of her climax.

Finally her over stimulated body shut down and floated back to the mattress, her grip on the mystery man easing.

"Oh...oh...ohhh." she moaned, relaxing into the covers, shuddering as that wicked mouth gave her one final lick.

Then the man rose up, tossing the bedcovers back and pulling his hands from her body.

Her gaze met with a pair of almond-shaped onyx eyes framed by femininely long lashes. His skin was a creamy gold, his hair long, black, and flowing over her body like a blanket as he crawled from between her thighs, licking his lips.

His bottom lip was full and swollen from the oral attention he had given her.

The muscular chest rising above hers was nothing to sneer at.

The man was absolutely gorgeous and obviously Asian.

But as he rose to his knees, Effin was met with the reality of his swollen, uncut, unfulfilled cock, which was twelve inches long, if not longer, and looked to be so thick her hand would barely fit around it. That, coupled with his sexy little leer, made her realize that she really wasn't dreaming! There was a naked Asian man in her bed, and he had just gone down on her.

Effin's siren-like squeal lingered long after she slammed the bathroom door, leaving a shocked Masataka wondering how she'd managed to get out of the bed and across the room so quickly.

"My God!" Effin mumbled to herself as she clicked the lock in place for good measure! There was a naked Asian man in her bed giving out orgasms like he was the satisfying-sex fairy!

How had he gotten in? Who was he? Why was he going down on her? Where was her cat?

"Oh, my God!" Effin panted, repeating herself as she stood staring at the door in shock. "There is a naked Asian dude in my bedroom doling out orgasms!"

The ridiculousness of that statement momentarily stopped the fear that threatened to flood her mind and drive her to insane acts, like jumping out of a window.

"Let me explain," a gravelly, almost purring voice called through the door to her. "I can explain this."

"Explain how you got into my house, you son of a bitch!" Effin screeched, the fear flooding back and making her eyes dart around the room, searching out something to use to defend herself.

"I am your cat!"

Would a pulsating showerhead deter a pervert that claimed to be a cat?

"I've got water and I'm not afraid to use it!"

"I'm not afraid of water, Effin," Masataka purred. "I am rather fond of it, myself."

"How did you get into my house?" she shrieked. She looked around and saw her salvation -- a toilet brush. Gripping her makeshift weapon tightly, she kicked at her door. "Go away!"

"Can't." Masa smirked "Besides, you brought me here; you are the only one who can send me back."

"I don't recall asking for a short Asian man to eat my pussy!" Effin screamed.

"No, but you wished for someone to spend your Valentine's Day with! You wished that your little black pussy was a real man while railing at the fates for giving you the worst date ever!"

Effin froze at that.

"H-how did you know?"

"I was there." Masataka grinned. "You may call me Masataka, but Masa will do."

"Masata... I don't believe it! Get out of my house!"

"I guess it's going to come to this." Masa sighed, and then the room went silent.

"Come to what?" Effin asked, voice husky as she tried to contemplate what "this" was. "What is this? You are not going to burn my house down, are you?"

The silence was nerve wracking.

"Hello? Asian man?"

There was no response from the bedroom, but there was a tapping at her window.

Effin looked up to see her pretty black kitty.

"Kitty!" she whispered, easing her way over to the window and opening it a crack.

Effin grinned as the sleek kitty made his way into her bathroom, safe and sound.

She closed the window and turned to cuddle her kitty, but her kitty was no longer standing there. Without any sound or light effects, her kitty was gone and in his place was her orgasm-giving Asian man.

First she looked toward the closed door, then to the man who was grinning at her choice of weapons. Where the hell had he come from?

"Meow!"

"ACK!" the toilet brush went flying in one direction, and Effin went in the other, trying to get away.

Just when she was doing a great impression of a cat climbing the walls, all the while keeping her wide eyes on the man who'd invaded her bathroom, the man in question disappeared.

"What...?" Effin pulled her fake nails out of the wall and stared at the kitty who had taken the man's place.

One minute man, next minute he had achieved kitten-tude!

"How the hell...!"

Then just as quickly, there was the naked Asian man again.

"You have a foul mouth," Masataka pointed out. "And you have an excess of useless emotion."

"But you were a cat!"

"I am a neko, to be precise."

"A neko?"

Effin felt a bit faint, so she took a seat on the throne and stared at the stranger who, moments before, had had his hand between her legs.

"Yes. I am a cat spirit and I was trapped in my cat form until your wish released me."

"But you are Chinese!"

"I am Japanese," Masataka corrected. "Neko is Japanese for cat. A spiteful kitsune -- that is Japanese for fox -- trapped me in that cat form."

"And I thought my luck was bad." Effin was still dazed, her mouth working on autopilot while her mind struggled to catch up.

"No, your bad luck was caused by gremlins."

"Um..." Effin pulled her gaze away from the nothing she had been closely contemplating to stare at the man. "Gremlins are real?"

"Yes, and you had an infestation of unhappy ones. But seeing that nekos are lucky creatures, they have all fled the premises with the promise not to return for a time."

"You couldn't keep them away?" Effin asked, amazed that the question came from her mouth. Did she believe in gremlins? Well, she did believe that there was a neko cat person standing in her bathroom so stranger things had been known to happen. Well...okay. There was a strange neko cat person in her bathroom.

"No one can keep them away forever, especially if you make comments that invite mischief."

That shut Effin up.

There had been too many shocks, and it seemed that she had invited her troubles in. Hell, she'd invited the neko in and taken him into her bed. She was just reaping what she sowed.

"So, are you going to kill me or curse me or something?" she asked, just wanting to get all the shocks over with.

"No." He laughed as he took a step in her direction. His eyes flashed gold, and Effin was reminded of how good he felt suckling at her clit and fingering her pussy. "I'm going to finish what I started and eat you."

Effin's nostrils flared as she inhaled deeply, drawing in the wild scent of the man.

"But I don't even know you!" she wailed as she felt her wetness spread between her thighs and her inner walls throb. "What are you, the big bad wolf?"

"That will come later," Masa assured her. "Calling us a wolf is insulting."

"Oh," was all that Effin could say as his hands reached out and drew her to her feet.

"Do you want this?" Masataka asked. "I can smell your heat, taste it on the air around you, but if you say no, then I will take my leave of this room and allow you time to compose yourself."

Then Effin had a decision to make. Would she take the gift that she had been offered, the man that she herself had wished for, or would she turn tail and run?

She looked into his eyes, amazed to find that they were the same height. He seemed so much bigger when he was doing that cat shift boogie.

But that was neither here nor there. She had a decision to make. She could take what she had wished for and received: a well-endowed Japanese man with a talented tongue and an ability to keep her house mouse free. Or she could run and hide, let this go, not take what she wanted like she normally did.

Fuck it!

She wanted!

So, she took…or rather, she gave.

"I want this, Masataka," she whispered, as she stepped closer to him, invading his personal space. "I want this!"

"Good, then when you cum, call me Masa!"

* * *

"Masa!"

Effin swore she saw Pluto as Masataka, the neko, eased his thick, hot cock deep within her body.

She was leaning over the sink, holding onto the cold porcelain for dear life as Masa slowly sank his thick girth into her.

She moaned as inch after inch of preternatural cock made its way inside, striking all her nerve endings, hitting every erogenous zone in her pussy.

When he hit bottom, his cool balls gently slapping against the backs of her thighs, she let out a moan that came from the depths of her soul.

Masataka had played her body like no one ever had before. In between thrusts, he told her a story of lust and deception, of nekos and their more powerful cousins the kitsune, and all about how he had become trapped within his cat form.

All the while, his fingers flicked at her nipples, his thumb rubbed on her clit, teased both her ass and her pussy until she was a writhing mass on the bathroom sink.

"Look," he breathed, as his long nails trailed over her back. "Look and see us together, Effin. We are beautiful."

Effin slowly lifted her head and blinked her eyes, forcing them to focus as she stared into the mirror above the sink. It was not a medicine cabinet, but a large, wrought iron-framed mirror that showed a good three-quarters of a person's body.

Within that mirror, Effin watched a long-haired, golden-skinned man, a feral smile on his lips exposing his fangs, lower his head and nip at a woman's neck.

But not any woman; this woman's eyes were dazed, her mouth slack with lust, her darker, naked body a perfect foil for the golden male who hovered dominantly behind her.

Effin realized, with some shock, that the beautiful woman was her.

She watched as her neko gripped her hips in his broad hands, his nails tickling her tingly flesh, and pulled back, dragging his cock out of her clinging heat.

Effin let out a sharp groan as Masa plunged back inside, frissons of fire leaping from the place where cock joined pussy, making her back arch toward her man and her whole body shiver.

Effin watched as her neko took her, each thrust powerful, sending her breasts swaying and forcing her up onto her toes. The pleasure she received from that thick cock, that hot, muscular body, from the silky hair that rippled over his shoulders and across her back... She couldn't take her eyes away.

If felt so wicked, like she was a voyeur watching someone being taken, yet she knew it was herself and her neko. She felt every moment as her pussy clenched around him so tightly she could feel his heartbeat deep within.

His hot, bare flesh felt so good! Bare, because he was preternatural, and that there would be no disease or pregnancy. Bare, because she felt wicked and decadent and daring, wanting to feel his hot cream when he exploded deep inside her.

Her wish had come true, had brought this magnificent man to her bed, and she was going to enjoy each second of it, no matter how long this thing lasted.

Moaning, she let one hand release its grip on the sink to travel back underneath his long hair to grip one firm cheek of his ass, pulling him in tighter, trying to force him to move faster.

"Slow, Effin," Masa breathed. "If I go any faster, this will end before it truly begins."

He closed his eyes, his breath rasping as his ass flexed underneath her hand.

Her body began to jerk and quiver. Beads of sweat rolled from his body, making him glisten, making his hair stick to his body, almost tiger striping him in his silky locks.

But his hips began to move faster, to drive harder, his breath rasping faster as he angled his thrusts to strike a bundle of nerves deep within her sheath.

"Masa," she moaned again, closing her eyes as waves of sensation flowed over her body. "Mmm."

She bit her lower lip as tremors shook her body. The things he was making her feel!

Then one of his hands released her hip and dipped low, sinking between her spread thighs to press into the swollen flesh around her clit.

A small scream erupted from Effin's mouth as a thumb came into play, flicking at her clit.

Then he was slamming into her harder, driving the air out of her lungs, attempting to climb his way into her body.

It was too much!

The room began to spin and Effin was screaming uncontrollably as her body tensed in preparation for her release.

"Masataka!" Effin shrieked as that thick piece of meat slammed repeatedly over her G-spot, sending her nerves singing in pleasure as her vaginal walls tensed.

"I'm..." She panted. "I can't!"

"You can!" he growled into her ear before he nipped it.

"I...I...I'm gonna..."

"Cum for me!" he hissed, the hand tormenting her pussy lifting and delivering a small slap to her clit. "Cum for me!"

He repeated the stinging caress and then Effin saw white!

"Masa!" she roared as her pussy clenched around his cock, milking it, wringing every ounce of pleasure she could out of that thick shaft.

"Effin!" Masa groaned, his eyes fluttering as his breath hissed from between his teeth. He thrust twice, deeply, and then he froze, his cock jerking and jumping within her pussy.

Then Effin was flooded by his scalding heat. His cream rushed forth in spurts, sizzling her insides, sending another orgasm tearing through her body.

"Masataka," she moaned, going limp as his weight settled onto her.

Together, they relearned how to breathe before Masa rose up and eased his still swollen cock out of her flesh.

"That was enlightening," he purred, the sound rumbling through his chest as he lowered his head to lick at the salty flesh of her neck. "Now we have to do it in the shower and then in the bed. I have a lot to show you, my dearest Effin, about how nekos love."

"I've created a monster," Effin moaned, but moved eagerly to start the shower and begin these new games.

Cats so love to play, Effin decided, watching as Masa ran his hands over his body as if still amazed that this human form was once again his. And playing was much more fun with two.

Chapter Ten

"Effin, baby!" the feminine voice called merrily as she burst into the kitchen, a huge grin one her face. "Guess what? Evan has asked me to take... Well, well, well. What do we have here?"

Masataka had just left Effin to her shower and had gone to investigate his new surroundings. Curious as a cat, he'd donned a pair of her sweatpants and explored every inch of her abode, delighting in the personal touches that made her home unique.

He had just settled down to make breakfast when the obnoxious female voice assaulted his ears.

Turning from his perusal of the refrigerator, he spied the female in question.

She looked somewhat like his female, but there was something that sent his senses negative vibes.

"Aren't you a little cutie," she purred, and instantly Masa recognized another predator.

"No," he corrected. "I am a man. And you are...?" He arched one eyebrow and waited for her to make the next move.

"I'm all woman, baby." She smiled, taking a step closer to him and running one finger down his bare chest, a finger that was surrounded by a mass of diamonds and gold.

"Yes, you smell of a woman who is fresh from another man's bed, yet you are flirting with me."

Again he awaited her response.

"I..." Monika sniffed as she stared at the man dressed in her sister's old sweats. He wasn't like the usual creatures Effin brought home. This one didn't look easily manipulated.

It was Monika's goal in life to torment her sister.

She didn't know when it had started or how to end it, but from the moment she could recognize those dark blobs hanging over her as human, the sight of her sister had set her teeth on edge.

It wasn't like Effin was prettier than she, though she was a bit taller and had more feminine curves. It wasn't that Effin had a better career, though she obviously had the better paying job as an accountant. It wasn't even that her sister had a better name. Whoever heard of calling a child Effin, anyway?

But there was something unexplainable about her sister that made her want to prove that she was the better woman.

In the past she had ruined her clothes and makeup, she had sneaked into her bedroom and cut her hair while she was sleeping, and read her diaries, but that was childish stuff. And as time went by and childish things were laid to rest, so did Monika lay aside her childish torments for assaults of the more sophisticated kind.

She again sabotaged her sister's makeup, adding chemicals and agents she knew her sister was allergic to. She stole her boyfriends right from under her sister's nose, proving that she was the better woman at keeping a man. She even found herself reading through her sister's mail, invading her house when she was at work, and prying into her private affairs.

But now that her sister's old flame Evan had proposed, Monika felt that the rivalry, one-sided at that because her sister always forgave her, could come to an end.

But those thoughts went right out the door when she walked into her sister's house and saw the hunk of man standing there in front of her refrigerator amid plaster dust and what appeared to be fragments of ceiling.

Any thought of letting this game end died a sudden death as she examined the man.

Formidable would be the word to describe him.

He didn't react to her presence at all. In fact, he acted as if he had the right to be there and she didn't! He was not impressed by her words or her caresses; flirting seemed to roll right off his back.

He was a challenge.

Her sister couldn't handle a man like this. This was the type of man *she* liked, one that took time to break before he came when she crooked her pinky.

She smiled her most seductive smile and narrowed her eyes at him.

"I know where I've been, darling. Now, I was wondering where *you* have been, you naughty boy. You just crawl out of my sister's bed? Did you give it to her good? Did she scream?"

Around this time Effin, done with her shower and dressed in a casual running suit, made her way downstairs to clean her kitchen and make a bit of breakfast for her and her neko.

She was wondering what nekos ate when she noticed the voices coming from the kitchen.

She stepped into the hall outside of the messy, dust-covered room, and heard her sister's comments.

Indignant, she was about to step in there and put her sister in her place, when Masa began to speak again.

"And why is it important for you to know?" he asked, stepping back from the offending hand and eyeing this female coldly. "Perhaps you are envious of your sister and mean to emulate her. Perhaps you feel you are inadequate and need practice with many different males like a dog in heat. Or is it that your sister now possesses something that you will never have the skill or strength to possess?"

"And I assume you mean you?" Monika hissed, not liking the way this was going at all. He was not playing the game right!

"Indeed, I was not referring to myself. You sister possesses a bright spirit forged in misery, a misery that I can easily see comes partly from you. For shame, to come into your sister's territory and try to stake claim to what she obviously possesses. Your sister can claim integrity, as well as beauty and an indomitable spirit. Can you say the same?"

Monika's mouth opened, and her jaws flapped for a moment before she could think of anything to say.

Had this man just rebuked and rejected her? *Her?* Monika Hurtzs, the most beautiful and desirable woman in this backwoods, jerkwater town?

"I believe you are insulting me!" Monika hissed, anger showing on her face and taking away some of that beauty she was proud of. It made her look like a spitting raccoon.

"Then there is nothing wrong with your thought processes." Masataka sniffed. "And if you are insulted, you indeed know where the door you entered through is, and know that it can be utilized in the opposite manner, as well."

"Are you telling me to get out? To get out of my sister's home?"

"Yes, you are quite bright, after all. And I was thinking that you were a total idiot!"

"Tell my sister I shall return," Monika gritted out as she turned on her heel and made for the door, leaving in a huff.

Shrugging, Masataka turned back to the refrigerator and began to examine the contents again.

"You know, if you put her in her place, she will leave you alone," Masa commented, and Effin gave a surprised gasp as she stepped into the kitchen.

"You knew I was there?"

"Of course, koi." Masa chuckled. "I have scent-marked you. I could smell you if you were three miles away."

Effin made a face at that. "That doesn't sound too pleasant." Then she thought about what he called her. "Koi? As in fish?"

"You smell of musk and vanilla," Masa assured her, before turning to face her. "And koi is a shortened term of endearment."

The grin that spread across his face told of a need to have another shower if she didn't say something to distract him quickly.

"Um, food?"

"Did I ever tell you that I love your ass?" he purred.

Effin gulped and took a step back, wishing the figure-skimming velour suit didn't hug her curves quite so much.

"Your ass is round and high and tight, an ass any man can appreciate."

"Um, thanks." Effin blushed, the rose color highlighting her cheekbones.

"I would love to sink my tongue between the cheeks of that ass and watch it jiggle as you squirm on your back."

"Um, food?" Effin tried again.

It was getting hot, she decided, as her clothing became more of an irritant. In fact, if he kept this up she would be forced to change because of a wet crotch.

"I want to feast on you, to spread your wet, pink labia and feast on the tender flesh there. Are you wet for me, Effin? Is your body hungry for my touch?"

Effin whimpered as she took another step back and froze as her back thumped into the wall.

Her eyes gleamed, liquid and bright, the pupils dilating as she inhaled the sweet musk of him. She licked her bottom lip, her breath coming faster as she stared into his deep, dark eyes.

There was only one answer she could give.

"Yes."

Effin gasped as his hands went to her shirt, the warm backs of his fingers caressing her skin as he whisked it over her head, carelessly tossing it aside.

"Yes," he repeated, leaning in close enough so that his breath brushed against lips hastily wetted with a quivering tongue.

He leaned in, nuzzling her, running his nose against her neck and cheek, inhaling her scent as he let his chest press close to hers, flattening her breasts, sending shivers of lust down her spine.

Her thighs trembled and her breath hitched as her arms dropped to her sides, her sweaty palms pressing against the wall.

The sudden lash of his tongue against her neck made her body tremble and her voice squeak, much to his amusement.

"Masa!"

"I love it when you scream my name," he growled out, his eyelids dropping to half-mast. As he spoke, he began to sink to his knees, his nose nuzzling down her neck, between her breasts still bound in their black lace bra. He paused as his nose nuzzled her crotch.

"You smell of you and me and sex and seed."

"Seed?" For a moment, Effin had nightmares of giving birth to a litter of black furred kids with kitty ears and tails!

"No," he breathed, inhaling deeply of the scents that came from her most private of places. "To reproduce, I would need another neko. With you, there is no danger of disease or pregnancy. I am immune and you are not compatible."

Effin sank again the wall in relief, but gasped again as his teeth snagged the waistband of her pants.

Her gaze dropped to his and locked as he slowly pulled her pants down to her knees.

He looked so delicious kneeling there, all golden skin and long black hair, his eyes shining with mischief.

Effin couldn't contain a moan of hunger.

Grinning, as if he knew her thoughts, Masa rose to his feet, his fingers skimming across her thighs, brushing lightly at her throbbing groin before continuing up her stomach to cup her breasts. His thumbs rubbed at her nipples as he lowered his head to her full, soft lips.

The first brush of his tongue against her bottom lip was delicate, like a fairy's kiss or an angel's wings. It was soft and sweet and pure. His tongue ran along the seam of her lips, gently parting them and insinuating itself between them, pushing into the warm, wet cavern of her mouth.

Effin's hands fisted as the electricity in that kiss seared her very being. She tilted her head to the side, trying to get more of his tongue within her mouth to suckle, to take in his flavor and delight in the firm texture of it. She inhaled deeply, taking in the spicy scent of him mixed with that magical musk that made her senses reel. Her arms rose slowly, her fingers unclenching to run through the cool silk of his hair.

His groan of pleasure was enough to make her knees give way, so she clutched at him blindly, her eyes closed, lost in the sensation of his kiss.

His tongue danced in her mouth, running over her teeth and exploring her, learning her taste and ensuring that she remembered his. Masa moved closer, the kiss changing, dominating her now as he began a slow fucking motion with his tongue, the same motions that he repeated as he ground his hips into her, letting her feel the swollen erection beneath his soft sweatpants, an erection born of want of her precious body.

His hands dropped to her thighs, lifting one to slide even closer into the vee of her crotch, pressing right up against her pussy, forcing her to feel his need.

Effin's whimpering response was immediate as her hands went to his shoulders, clung to them as she tore her mouth free of his to pant her pleasure to the heavens.

Surely, this man was some kind of god, to make her feel the things she was feeling.

Joy, pleasure, excitement, a taste of the exotic -- all of these things made up the man called Masataka, who was now grinding between her legs, letting her feel all twelve of those powerful inches as he pressed her harder into the wall.

"But I want to taste you, little koi," he purred, before he released her and spun her around. "Damn, what an ass," he managed as his eyes grew wide at what he saw.

Effin was now facing the wall, leaning against it for support as Masa took in the little surprise she had for him.

Masa felt a tear well up as he eyed the tiny black thong that parted the full, rounded cheeks of Effin's ass. Never had there been a more perfect division of full, well-rounded ass globes!

Her skin was soft and lightly scented from her lotion, and as she breathed, the round melons of her ass cheeks quivered.

He couldn't help himself. He raised one hand and let it fall sharply on the right cheek, then chortled gleefully as her ass jiggled so perfectly.

"Shake it, baby," he breathed, leaning forward to drop kisses along her neck and shoulders. "Shake that ass for me."

Feeling a bit self-conscious, Effin nevertheless bent her knees and swung her hips a little, feeling gravity take effect as her booty made a small clapping sound as her cheeks moved. She peered over her shoulder, and the stunned look on Masataka's face was enough to make her close her eyes and pretend she was in a music video. She shook her ass, then bent her knees, dropped toward the ground, and rolled her hips in circles, all the while letting her ass jiggle madly.

Masa moaned audibly at the sight, one hand going to the now tight sweatpants as he stroked himself slowly, his eyes never leaving the erotic sight of his Effin doing stripper-pole moves without a pole.

Her ass swayed as her hips moved from side to side, enticing him, making him drool with the sheer beauty of it. Then she squatted low, one hand on the wall for support, the other caressing her widespread thighs as she bobbed her ass, making her ass cheeks clap louder.

"Fuck!"

Effin jumped at the shouted explicative, but that was all she had time to do as Masa made his move.

Reaching down, he wrapped both hands around her waist, pulling her up straight, and then tore the tiny thong from her ass.

Before she could protest the treatment of her clothing, his lips seared the warm mounds of her ass with kisses and licks.

"Beautiful," he breathed. "More than I ever expected...than I ever hoped!"

Then his hands parted her cheeks, his tongue darting out to lave the soft skin from her ass crack to her perineum.

"Masa!" Effin wailed, realizing that she was being rimmed and that she really liked it.

His tongue danced over her asshole, tickling it before his kisses began to rise up over her back to her neck.

One of his hands reached for the cooking oil on a nearby counter, the fingers scrambling as he dropped low to plunge two fingers of his free hand into her wet pussy, drawing a primal scream from her throat.

"God, yes! Fill me!"

Masa grunted as his hand connected with the oil, and he brought it to his mouth using his teeth to rip open the top as his teasing hand plunged rhythmically in her pussy.

Effin screamed and rode those two fingers, begging for more as she felt the warm oil trickle down her crack and asshole.

Masa tossed the bottle aside and then eased his fingers along the trail of warm oil, rubbing in circles, massaging the oil into the skin of her rosebud, teasing the puckered entrance and drawing more screams and cries from her.

Then one finger sank into her ass, slowly working its way in, rotating and caressing her inner walls.

"Is it too much?" he rasped in his ear, and was rewarded with a low, steady moan.

The fingers that teased her cunt pulled out a bit and searched for her clit, finding the erect button and firmly pressing it.

"Fuck me, dammit!" Effin wailed, arching toward both touches, begging for more. The sensations in her ass and her pussy... God, she was on fire! She needed penetration, she needed to feel full and complete, like the missing part of her had been found.

She didn't care where he did it, but Effin wanted Masa within her body, plunging into her heat and slaking the thirst he created within her.

Tension and anticipation built, driving her onward, making her arousal stronger, making her need for release all consuming.

Masa added a second finger to her ass, scissoring within and stretching her. She humped and arched madly against him.

Her muscles strained, her back tingled; pleasure spilled from her every orifice so strongly she had to scream.

Then there were three fingers, and Effin was barely coherent, a slave to the driving needs of her body, Masa a tool to end the erotic torment that he devised.

"Now, Masa!" Her voice broke as she fought to breathe; sweat sheened her body, her muscles quivering with the effort to stay on her feet. "Fuck me now!'

Masa pulled his fingers from her ass and quickly placed the head of his cock at her backdoor. He ran the head in small circles along her rosebud, coating it with excess oil before slowly pressing into her.

"Effin!" he cried out, the heat and tightness of the ring of muscles encasing his cock almost his undoing. He pulled his fingers from her pussy to grip the base of his cock, halting his orgasm before he lost control.

"Masa... God, Masa!"

"Kami-sama!" Masataka ground out from between clenched teeth as he fought to control his body. His every instinct demanded that he thrust forward, that he bury himself fully into her wet heat, that he take what was his.

But his human side and his common sense dictated that he be careful, that he cherish this treasure that was so tantalizingly spread out before him. So he eased himself forward slowly, stopping when she tensed, then continuing as her body relaxed around his.

It was so slow and exhausting and fulfilling, and just so damn good that he began to purr.

"God, this feels so good," Effin whimpered. "Fuck my ass, Masa! Fuck me!"

Slowly he pulled out, his free hand reaching around her to stroke her clit and swollen labia as his other hand anchored him to her by gripping her hip.

Slowly he began to move back and forth, his ass clenching on every forward thrust, his balls lightly slapping her pussy as he bottomed out inside her.

They started a long, slow rhythm that sent ice-cold shivers up his spine and red-hot fire shooting through her body.

The nerves in her ass sizzled as pleasure flooded her every pore. Effin had become a creature of need, a slave to the man-cat Masataka, who was taking her on a journey she had never imagined she'd take.

The kitchen was filled with the slick sounds of bodies sliding against each other, Effin's whimpering gasps, and Masa's purrs as they began to move faster.

His fingers plucked at her clit, feeling the tension in her rise. His cock felt the walls of her ass tighten in preparation for her orgasm.

"God, just a little bit more!" Effin gasped. "I'm almost there! Just a little bit more! God, faster, Masa! Move faster! Harder! Deeper! Masataka!"

"Ride it, baby." He nipped her neck, the small pain adding to her pleasure. "Ride it out, koi! Cum for me!"

Then he changed from a thrusting motion to a grinding one and Effin began to scream!

"Fuck, Masa! I'm cumming! God, I'm cumming! I can't... I can't...Ican'tIcan'tIcan't...Ohh! Ohh! Masa!"

White lights flashed before her eyes as her ass spasmed around his hard cock. Her eyes rolled to the back of her head as her whole body stiffened. "Ohhhmmm," she moaned, tears flooding her eyes as her clit burned and itched, and delivered a climax that shook the very rafters of her soul. "Masa!"

"Mmmm... Ahhhh! Effin!" Masa roared as the rhythmic tightening of her rear passage walls forcing the cum right out of his cock. "Kami, Effin! You are perfection. ???"

Sweating and heaving, her body pressed against the wall. His soft, silky black hair covered her shoulders. Effin could only smile as she felt Masa settle against her back and began to lick the sweat from her shoulders.

She had never done anything like that before. Now, after having done it, she felt so liberated, so complete. Who knew anal sex could be so intense?

"Now," Masa whispered, giving one last lap to her shivering skin. "I'm hungry for food. Feed me."

Effin looked over her shoulder to see Masa giving her sad kitty eyes, even though he looked like a cat basking in the sun.

"Pretty kitty." Effin winked at him. "I just fed you."

"And my appetite is sated on the feast of desire you have created. But man cannot live on sensual delights alone, and I fear my physical being needs sustenance to keep up with your...sensual side."

The last words were said on a satisfied growl that had Effin laughing. Slowly they disengaged, and Masa pulled Effin up into his arms.

They would shower, and Masa would get to explore more of her lovely body. Masataka, for once, felt like a lucky neko!

Now if he could get her to jiggle her ass again...

Chapter Eleven

Two hours later, a sated and content Effin walked beside Masa as they casually strolled into a Japanese restaurant.

It was a good thing that Masa was about the same size as Effin because he nicely fit into a pair of her newer sweats and trainers. He actually looked rather nice in her clothing. A team throwback with a black fleece jacket completed his look for the moment.

As it was Sunday, Effin decided to drag Masa to the local mall via local bus, and to outfit him in some new duds. But before they shopped, Masa insisted that they eat.

Having no money, his kitty treasures hoarded back in the warehouse, he was forced to depend on Effin's kindness for their first meal as neko and female.

It was here, while walking into a Japanese restaurant, when the first odd looks started.

A group of well-dressed Japanese American elders began whispering amongst themselves as soon as Effin and Masa were seated.

When Masataka began to order in what she later learned was high-caste Japanese, the odd looks became openly hostile.

At one point a man rose to his feet and began to engage Masataka in rapid-fire Japanese before blanching, turning, and walking away.

"And what exactly was that all about?" Effin asked, watching as the man collected his coat and left.

"A difference of opinion. Nothing more," Masa was quick to point out before looking down at his menu.

"About what, Masa?" Effin was curious and Masataka found that trait endearing, close to his own personality.

"About the person that I, someone of obvious high breeding, choose to be with."

"What?" Now Effin was getting pissed! Her faced flushed with anger and she turned to stare at the people in the room, noticing how eyes dropped when hers met theirs.

"I hope you told him to kiss my shiny black ass!" Effin hissed, leaning across the table and shooting the people in the room dirty looks.

"I told him that it showed very poor breeding to interrupt your betters at mealtime, and that it was a reflection on his family how poorly raised their child was."

"In essence, you said, 'Yo mama.'" Effin chuckled at that.

"Yes, and I told him that he should be ashamed of his actions."

Smirking, Effin sat back and smiled as the waiter approached, and Masa fired off more Japanese, impressing the hell out of their server.

Within seconds, an older woman and the impressed waiter returned, both bearing tea trays filled with its accoutrements.

With a bow, the woman began to serve the tea in what appeared to Effin's eyes to be an elaborate ceremony. Then with another bow, the woman began to speak. She had only uttered the first words when Masataka cut her off.

"Please, Grandmother, in English. I wish not to be rude to my guest."

Smiling, the woman nodded and began again. "Honored neko. I ask that you place a blessing upon this establishment, that you grant us luck and prosperity for the coming years."

Masataka sat up straighter and grinned at the older woman.

"You know who I am?"

"Yes." The lady smiled back. "I have good English, but I still remember the old tales I heard when growing up in Edo. You are a neko. Your stance, your hair, the way you move and speak -- they are all clues if one but looks and believes."

Masa's smile made him look like the cat who not only swallowed the canary, but got away with a few goldfish, as well.

"I would be honored to place a blessing upon this establishment," he said formally, then rose to his feet, bobbing the flat of his hand up and down in Effin's direction, almost as if he was waving bye-bye.

Raising one eyebrow, Effin looked at his hand, then at up at his face, confused. What did he want?

"Oh!" Masa grinned. "Cultural differences. Waving my hand this way means 'come on.'"

He waved again, and a chuckling Effin rose to her feet to follow.

"Cultural differences?"

"Yes," Masa said as they both followed the old lady and the waiter, who they soon learned was her grandson. As they passed, many employees -- family members, they later discovered, that had moved with them when they moved their restaurant businesses from Edo to America, bowed their heads in a show of respect as Masa passed by.

As he walked to all four corners of the restaurant, a light current of air, sweetly scented, followed in his wake.

Masa began to chant slowly under his breath, his eyes nearly glowing as he mumbled words in Japanese. They made the circuit three times. The fourth time, Masa made flinging motions with his arms, as if casting out something, and damned if the air didn't begin to smell sweeter, to feel cleaner, to just become better.

Sniffing, Masa gave a small mew as if to say good riddance, before he returned to his table, Effin in tow.

"I cannot thank you enough," the old lady began, but Masataka waved her thanks away.

"It is what nekos were created for, Grandmother. And your establishment will be fine. I would suggest getting a Kaso expert to do a more thorough cleansing and help place your furniture for positive spiritual flow."

Nodding, the old woman turned and began to walk away, but paused for a moment.

"Was there something here?"

"Something wanted in," Masa told her truthfully. "But it will not find your business one that can be easily cast into ruin."

Nodding, the older woman left with her grandson, who returned in short order with a tray filled with soups and dishes that Effin had never before seen.

"But we didn't order --"

"Bah!" Masa rolled his eyes. "Americanized Japanese food. This is authentic, Effin, what the owner would serve her own family. It is a treat that I have not indulged in for many a year."

"And the woman didn't mind that I am obviously not Japanese?"

"That good woman had sense enough to know that a good luck neko would only be with someone of impeccable breeding and refinement."

"In other words, you told her to mind her own business and you knew what you were doing, although not in so many words." Effin grinned. Masataka seemed to be a man who let nothing get in the way of what he wanted.

Of course, they were not presented with a bill, and Masa took that as his due.

Nodding to the old lady, who walked them to the door, Masa and Effin strolled out into the mall.

"You know, I really enjoyed that." Effin smiled and Masa gave her a grin. "And now, it's time to indulge in an American custom that I love."

"And that would be?" Masa asked, curious as a cat, eyes glowing as he watched her. In response, Effin reached down and grabbed his hand to pull him through the crowded mall.

"Power shopping! What else?"

* * *

Three hours later and loaded down with bags, Masa finally put his foot down.

"Enough, female! I am not a doll to be dressed for your amusement," he groused as Effin ran her fingers through his long hair, caressing the leather thong she'd purchased to tie back his inky-black, silky locks.

"But dressing you is almost as fun as undressing you."

The wicked grin she gave him was enough to make Masa's cock twitch with interest.

Looking down at his reacting cock, he shook his head, thankful that he'd found a woman just as sexually insatiable as he.

"Undress me, Effin," he breathed, pulling her close, ignoring the bags that dropped at their feet.

They were a few feet away from the exit, close to the bus stop that would let them off a block from her home.

"The bus…"

"Leaves in forty minuets," he reminded her, glancing down at the kitty face watch she'd insisted he buy, then back into her eager, hungry eyes. "And there is a family bathroom just over there." He tossed his head in the direction of the empty bathroom area set up for families of multiple genders and needs. Beside the two bathrooms, there was a room set aside for nursing mothers that had a large comfortable couch and chairs.

"But... It would be so wrong."

"I am a neko! It is not wrong in my culture. What is the moral standard here?" He gave her a sly grin, daring her to find a reason for them to stop.

"Um, not to do it in public?" Effin offered, squirming as she contemplated him riding high and hard between her thighs.

"Public! Ha! There is a door, Effin, a door with a lock."

"But, Masataka..."

"I am so hungry," he whispered, bending down to lap at her lips. "Feed me."

And she was lost.

* * *

"Touch yourself for me."

Masa's command was soft and throaty as he placed his naked female on top of the padded counter and took a step back.

"Show me how much you want me."

Moaning in pleasure, Effin placed both of her feet on the edge of the padded counter, spreading her legs wide and exposing all of her secrets to her wicked little neko.

"You have to kiss where I touch," she whispered as she blushed a bit, looking up at Masa from beneath her lashes.

From the moment they'd entered the room, Masa had wasted no time in stripping off her clothing.

The small family restroom was warm and carpeted, complete with a chaise lounge and a recliner for nursing moms. There was a reinforced padded counter for changing babies and toddlers, along with two separate bathroom stalls.

"I want to kiss and lick every part of you, Effin," Masa breathed. "Doing this would be no hardship."

Then he peeled off his pants, letting them drop to his knees before shuffling back a step, watching with serious cat's eyes.

Effin closed her eyes and tried to envision where her man would touch first.

She started by cupping her breasts in both hands, pinching at her nipples and caressing the sensitive skin that surrounded them.

Her hands trailed lightly over her chest, her fingers fluttering as they hit sensitive spots on her sides.

A small moan rolled up from her throat as she lingered there, letting her fingers reach up and caress the bottom of her aching breasts.

Her nipples felt full under Masa's intense gaze and she couldn't help but be reminded of the times his lips had feasted there.

Moving on, she splayed her hands over her thighs, caressing the soft skin of her inner thighs that led to her swelling labia.

Her breath hissed from between dry lips as she raised one hand to pinch at her nipples while the other gently ran over her clit.

"Part yourself for me; show me where it aches."

His whispered command made her body tremble. The wickedness of touching herself while Masataka watched was turning her on almost as much as the caresses themselves.

Obediently, Effin spread her legs further and allowed her finger to first dip slightly into her body. Collecting some of the spilled juices, she used that wet finger to tease at her slit, circling it gently while she teased herself with that one wet finger.

Effin hissed at the sensation. With the overhead lights on, she felt as if she were putting on a show for the man she desired, that this small counter was a stage, and she was the sole performer.

So she spread her legs even wider, and with two fingers spread her lower lips, allowing Masa to see all of her tingling, wet pink flesh.

"Beautiful," he whispered, taking a step closer and dropping to his knees, examining her closely. "Show me more."

Growling under her breath, Effin arched her hips and allowed her fingers to dip low, to sink into her own body, gasping at the wet heat she found.

"Do you feel this when you are pounding inside me?" she breathed, her eyes blazing with passion. "Do I grip your cock like I do my fingers?"

"Kami-sama, yes," he panted feeling her heat. "Your lips are so wet."

He gently ran a finger over her labia, touching the moisture before leaning forward and lapping at the slick fluid with his tongue.

Effin groaned, her whole body shuddering at the sheer eroticism of the act. Then Masa pulled back enough to lick his own finger, lubricating it enough to slide in between her penetrating digits.

"Maaaasaaaaa..." Effin moaned, nibbling at her bottom lip as the slight stretching sensations filled her, made her tremble. Her head rolled back on her shoulders as she fought to hold her hips still.

But Masa was not done yet.

Thrusting his finger in alongside hers, he brought his free hand to his mouth to thoroughly slick it with saliva before he allowed it to roam down further, pressing between her cheeks.

"Ah!" Effin's reaction was loud and instantaneous when he touched those sensitive nerves.

Masa grinned at her reaction and stroked faster, allowing the tip of a finger to breach her rosebud.

"More!" Effin breathed, and Masa gladly dropped his head again, this time lapping at the juices running down their fingers while he wiggled that other finger deeper into her asshole.

By then, Effin was riding both hands, wanting those fingers in deeper, wanting the pleasure to never end. Her low, breathy moans filled the small room with a sexual soundtrack.

"Someone will be coming soon." Masa pulled back after lapping at her clit a bit, shooting fire though her groin. "We have to be fast."

Then he pulled her hand free with a slick, popping sound and drew it into his mouth. He purred around the taste of her even as his finger stroked the soft folds of her anal passage.

He rose to his feet, keeping in contact with her always, before retracting the foreskin and positioning his cock at her weeping entrance.

"Say my name," he rasped, running the thick, uncut head against her glistening flesh.

"Mmm... MMMassssaaa."

Masataka closed his eyes as his female submitted and moaned his name in such a delightful manner.

He growled in response, pushing forward to breach her just a bit. The feel of her vaginal mouth slipping over the head of his cock was enough to weaken his knees. Hissing, he pushed forward suddenly, slamming himself in to the hilt.

Effin's hands reached around his shoulders, scrambling for purchase as she was suddenly filled. It was such an amazing sensation, the feel of his thick prick invading her and filling her to overflowing, the heat of his body pressed close to hers, that finger tickling her through her ass!

Effin closed her eyes and held on for a good, fast ride.

Closing his eyes also, Masa gave in to the feelings seeping through his body: want, desire, need. They all combined to send him into a state of sexual ecstasy he had never experienced before.

He actually cared about this female, so stubborn and vulnerable yet proud and strong.

He breathed in their combined scents, felt the press of her inadequate claws bite into his skin, felt the desperation that clung to her skin like an aura.

His Effin needed him, she wanted him, she was letting herself go! And he was so very lucky to be the neko that shared the journey with her.

Pulling his hips back, he thrust harder, faster, stronger, slamming their bodies together until the wet sound of slapping flesh could be heard over their constant moans.

Suddenly, Effin was there, her body stiffening as her muscles went wild around his cock and the finger buried in her ass.

Effin let out a small screech that he quickly took into his mouth as he invaded it with a savage, demanding tongue.

Then he was calling out his pleasure into her mouth, muffling the sound as he felt his essence spurt into her milking body.

Breathing heavily, he lifted his head as Effin suddenly exploded into helpless giggles.

"What?" he asked, a purr rolling throughout his body at the contentment he felt at the moment.

"You are a good luck neko," she chortled. "When I'm around you, I'm always getting lucky!"

Masataka snorted, rolling his eyes as he gently disengaged himself from her still twitching body.

Reaching for the stack of nearby tissues, he gently wiped his Effin as clean as he could get her, then felt around for her panties.

"I can do it," she protested, beginning to dress herself as he also wiped himself as clean as he could and pulled his pants up.

"You know," he explained, "I could turn myself into my neko form and simply cleanse my cock the old-fashioned way."

Effin grimaced at the sound of that and shot him an incredulous look.

"Besides, I like the way we taste mixed together." He mewed at her cutely, grinning and showing his fangs.

"Damn nekos." Effin chuckled as she opened the door and peered around the corner to see if anyone noticed them.

Masa snatched up the bags and exited, dragging a blushing Effin with him.

"You ain't seen nothing yet," he promised. "Let me tell you about Japanese knot tying."

Chapter Twelve

Monday morning was a revelation.

Effin awoke with a smile on her face and a spring in her step.

Good sex will do that for you, she decided, as she rushed off to take a shower.

Before leaving for the day, she woke Masa to tell him some things she thought he should know.

"Don't let anybody into the house," was her first order. "The roofing people may show up. I'll deal with them later. And if any gremlins make their way back into my life, tell them that I am most sorry and that I humbly apologize for insulting them. Got it?"

Masataka slowly blinked up at her with sleepy cat's eyes and curled back into the comfortable bed.

"You are such a cat." Effin chuckled and left for the day. She was getting a cab to the dealership and then heading off to work to deal with a certain best friend. Life was sweet.

As for Masataka, he closed his eyes and took a little snooze. Delivering orgasms by the busload was hard work. If he was in heat, Effin would be carrying his litter by now.

But things were as he told her. He was unable to get her pregnant or pass on any diseases. He was a preternatural creature, after all.

But he went to sleep with images of Effin swollen and heavy with his child.

The image woke him up and he tried to puzzle through its meaning. It was probably just him getting over twenty-five plus years of celibacy. Snorting at his own fancifulness, he snuggled into the covers again and resumed sleep.

Sleep lasted until there was a distinct knocking at the door.

Growling under his breath, Masa pulled himself from his warm nest of blankets and made for the front door, disregarding all that Effin had told him.

After all, he was a neko, and nothing, barring vengeful kitsune, could harm him.

He swung the door open, yawning wide to show his long fangs, and absently scratched at his bare chest as he glared at the person standing there.

The man, if someone that gave off that much negative aura could still be considered a man, blinked as if surprised to see him there.

"Can I help you?" Masa finally asked, growing weary of being closely examined by the short, hairy human.

"Um… I'm here to look at a roof for a little lady?"

"Effin Hurtzs."

"Yes." The man grinned. "I thought she didn't have a husband."

"I am not a husband." Masa rolled his eyes.

"Oh, she's like that, is she?" The man leered.

"Like what?" Masa narrowed his eyes as his dislike of the man began to grow into something much darker.

"You know, one of those independent types who does without a man…unless she pays for him." The man winked and nudged Masa with a flannel-clad elbow.

"Pays for a man?" Masa was drawing several conclusions, and he didn't like any of them.

"That or is she the easy type."

"Easy…" Suddenly the sleep left Masa's mind and his protective instincts flooded his being. "Are you calling my female a ho?"

Masa's voice raised several octaves as he realized what the dark-haired human was saying.

"Well, is she any good?" The man leered again.

When his boss sent him out to assess the damage, he had warned him that Effin was an extremely independent woman. In his world, that meant gay or easy. And since a half-naked man answered the door, despite the fact he looked kind of girlie, that meant she was easy.

"Where is the little heifer? I would love to meet her, if you know what I mean."

"Yes." Masa purred, flexing his fingers as his milky-white claws slowly took the place of his fingernails. "Please come in. I am sure I have many great things to tell you about Effin."

Sixty-nine and one-half minutes later, a blubbering roofer shakily signed papers that stated all the repair work that had been done was under warranty, and that the roof would be completed by the end of the week.

"I...I didn't know that you creatures existed," the man sniffled as Masa, in his cat form, calmly licked the blood off his once pristine claws.

There were various slash marks and bites covering the man's face and neck and a suspicious tear right around the crotch of his pants.

"Please, I never meant any offense to Ms. Hurtzs. I never knew she had a pet demon for protection! I am so sorry! Please don't kill me!"

Rolling his eyes, Masataka assumed his human form again, glaring at the creature who looked as if he would soil his pants any moment.

"Oh, God!" the man wailed, watching as Masa went from cat to human in less than a blink of an eye and tugged on a pair of sweatpants that hadn't stayed on his body when he changed.

"Human, remember. I can track you wherever you go. I know about the three females you are sleeping with, and I also know that you are doing much more than sleep." He tsked as he shook his head.

"My wife..."

"Will do more harm than I." Masa sneered. "And all I have to do is go to your home and tell her."

"Oh, God!" The man looked ready to cry as well as defeated, as Masa picked up the signed papers and shooed the man toward the door.

"Do the work you are supposed to and never mention Effin's name again. We guardian demons can hear a whisper on the wind."

With that little piece of information, even if it was entirely untrue, the man turned tail and ran.

Satisfied, Masa shut the door and waved his hands, sending a cleansing wave of air around the areas where that man had walked before being attacked by his cat demon.

Shaking his head at the stupidity of humanity, he placed the signed papers on the kitchen table and went to take a nap. This defending the territory stuff was hard when in human form, but damn near exhausting when doing it as a cat.

Within seconds, Masa had made his way back to bed and climbed in, too tired to even remove his pants. Almost instantly, he was lost in a dream, his hands twitching and small mewls coming from his throat as he dreamed.

* * *

It was unfortunate that Masa was such a deep sleeper, because no sooner had he drifted off than trouble arrived.

Monika waltzed into Effin's house as if she owned it, pocketing the spare key Effin swore she'd lost and promptly replaced, never knowing her sister had run off with it.

At the time she stole the key, Monika claimed she was doing it out of sisterly concern. After all, if there was a fire or something and Effin was trapped, how would she get out?

It was this same twisted logic that led Monika to once again invade her sister's home, on the off-chance that she could find more information about the Asian dude that hadn't given her any attention when she'd made her entrance into the kitchen the day before.

It was her chance to do some snooping, and if there was something that Monika was good at, it was being nosy.

She silently made her way into the kitchen, noting that it had been cleaned up and that there were repair invoices on the table.

Monika sniffed at that and went searching through the first floor.

Other than signs of sex, a few containers of lube placed in convenient areas, there was no sign that a man was cohabiting with her sister. Maybe it was a weekend thing?

Wrinkling her nose in disappointment, Monika made her way to the top floor, hoping to find something good and juicy before her sister got home.

And she found something rather big and juicy.

There was a naked Asian man in her sister's bed, and damned if the boy wasn't delicious.

He was all golden-toned skin and muscles, like he was a martial artist. His long hair was spread out over the bed in silky waves; his breathing was deep and even, making those perfect pecs rise and fall rhythmically.

Her sister was keeping secrets, Monika thought. And it wasn't good of Effin not to share.

Before she could investigate further, there was the telltale sound of her sister's engine, the vintage Jeep sounding like no other as it pulled into her driveway.

A wicked grin spread across Monika's face as she began to rip off her clothing, her body moving before her mind could assess if this was a good idea or not.

Without making a sound, she slipped into bed beside Masa, grinning as she thought of the trouble this encounter would cause. Effin was sure to be pissed and maybe even cry! The thought was so tasty she had to hold in a giggle. Effin would never know what had hit her.

* * *

Effin giggled as she walked into her house, gabbing on her cell to Christa.

"You can say you are sorry all you want," she mock-growled. "You set me up with a serial killer!"

"Alleged!" Christa was quick to remind her.

"And I would be doing my Jason impersonation on your ass if I hadn't met the most amazing guy." She sighed as she placed the take-out lunch she'd brought home for her and Masa to share on the kitchen table.

She looked at the paperwork spread out. Somehow, Masa had let the roofers in and had gotten the work order signed and sealed.

How great a man was that?

"I've got to go, girl." She grinned, her mind going on ways to thank him. Maybe a little "afternoon delight" before she had to go back to work. "Masa is waiting."

"Did you just call that man master?" Christa gasped. "Are you into some kinky BDSM stuff?"

"No!" Effin gasped, rolling her eyes. "His name is Masataka. He's Japanese."

"Ohhh!" Christa moaned. "Effin's playing hide the rainbow roll with Bruce Lee!"

"Japanese!" Effin corrected. "Bruce was from China. And girl, it's more like hide the torpedo!"

"I want details!" Christa laughed. "Later! After you go and get your ship sunk!"

Laughing, the two friends disconnected the call and Effin went in search of her Asian treat.

"Masa!" she called, walking up the stairs to her bedroom. "Masa? Where are you hiding, my handsome neko?"

Spying a lump in the bed, she walked over and yanked the comforter off.

"You lazy kitty -- What the fuck!?"

Effin's eyes almost popped out of her head as she saw her sister's naked body lying next to Masa's.

"Mmm," Monika groaned as she opened her eyes in feigned surprise. "Oh, Effin!" Then pretending modesty, she pulled the top sheet over her exposed breasts. "I...I'm so embarrassed..."

But before any more words could pass her lips, Effin attacked.

Growling like an angry lion, she pounced on the bed, claw-like nails extended, her teeth bared in her fury.

But instead of attacking Masa, she went straight for the bane of her existence.

"You stupid bitch!"

Then Monika and her perfectly naked body went flying across the room.

The screaming woke Masa, who looked around him with sleepy eyes, trying to figure out what was going on.

"Effin?" he asked, as he smelled his female...and an oddly similar feminine scent.

But Effin was paying no attention.

She was sitting on her sister's naked chest, delivering round after round of open-handed slaps to Monika's cheeks while delivering the sermon of a lifetime.

"You do not touch my things, you bitch!" she bellowed, her face a mask of fury. "You do not flirt with my man! You do not *ever* come into this house again, or I will fucking kill you!"

She grabbed a fistful of her sister's hair, avoiding the flying fists and drumming feet to slam Monika's head back onto the carpeted floor.

"Do you understand me?"

On the second bang, the hair extensions, so carefully sewn in, fell apart, leaving Effin with a handful of treated hair tracks and a surprised look.

But her amazement only lasted a second as her screeching sister tried to fight back.

"Oh, no!" Effin snarled. "Not this time!"

Her anger giving her strength, Effin rolled over to sit on the floor, dragging her sister across her lap, her naked ass wiggling in the air.

"You act like a spoiled brat, so I'm going to treat you like one!"

She raised her hand and delivered the first of many stinging blows to her sister's backside. She didn't stop swinging until her sister was a limp, sobbing piece of human flesh across her lap, her ass a bright red to match her eyes, from which her tears continuously flowed.

"I'm sorry!" she hiccupped, sniffing at her humiliation. "I'm sorry!"

"Yeah, you are a sorry piece of shit, Monika!" Effin growled, shoving her sister off her lap. "Now get the fuck out of my face and don't expect a Christmas card this year!"

Monika didn't waste any time gathering up her clothes and racing from the room like a scalded cat.

In minutes there was the sound of the front door slamming shut and Monika's car racing away.

Taking a deep breath, Effin now turned to take care of the last of her unfinished business.

"Masataka? We need to talk!"

* * *

"Why?"

"Why what?" Masataka was confused. Not that he hadn't enjoyed the female's deserved punishment, but what was his woman asking?

"Why did you sleep with my sister?"

"I didn't sleep with your sister!" Now the confusion fled as Masataka took in the situation. "You think that that underhanded female and I cavorted?"

"She was naked in my bed with you, Masa! What the hell am I to think?"

Effin rose to her feet and stormed over to the foot of the bed, glaring down at the man she had trusted.

Growling, Masa rose to his feet, hitching his sweatpants as he glared at his female.

"How dare you accuse me of such duplicity? I would never…"

"But you slept with that kitsune's bride!" Effin reminded him coldly. "That is why you were stuck in your cat form."

"I was tricked into sleeping with her," Masa growled, his eyes glowing in his anger. "I had no idea what she was doing or who she was. She was just…"

"Another lay," Effin cut him off. "Apparently, like I am."

Those words hurt to say, but Effin knew in her heart that she was not good enough for a royal neko. Hell, the man was preternatural! He could have any woman he wanted! Why would he want a plain Jane like her?

"You are not just another lay, Effin. You are growing into a part of me!"

"Yeah, and the part's between your thighs and bumps into your sac with regularity!" Effin growled, turning her back to the man she had been making whoopee like mad with for the past weekend.

"Effin, if I wanted sex, I could have it anywhere and with anyone. But I chose you!"

"Because I freed you!" Effin snapped. "God, it's happened again! I start to open my heart up to a man and he shits all over it!"

"I have done nothing to warrant this attack!" Masa snapped back, growing angry himself.

"Then what was my naked sister doing in your bed?"

"I have no idea!"

Spinning around to face him, Effin rolled her eyes in disbelief. "So a naked woman crawls into your bed and you don't even notice?"

"I was asleep, Effin!" Masa's voice rose, as did his ire. "I was in a deep sleep replenishing my energy for you!"

"Bullshit!" Effin sneered. "You can smell me from the basement, and you never even notice a naked woman climbing into your bed?"

"I made a commitment to you!" Masataka roared, inflamed at having his word, his honor, questioned.

"Fuck you!" Effin screamed back. "I was just a convenient lay! Admit it, you bastard!"

Masataka reached for her, wanting to draw her close and bring an end to the arguments, but Effin snatched away, fearful that the longing in her heart would overcome her reason and she would forgive him.

"Don't touch me, you damned neko! I wish you were still a cat! I wish I had never brought you home to hurt me!"

Masa's eyes widened in amazed hurt, but before he could utter a single word, he was sucked into his cat form.

"Holy shit!" Effin breathed, knowing that Masataka had not wanted this change. "Masa…"

But then those all too human cat's eyes were glaring at her in hurt and betrayal. Then before she could take a step to reach him, to right what her anger had wrought, Masa bounded across the room and out of the window, leaving behind sweatpants and a devastated Effin.

"Masa," she cried, tears welling up in her eyes. "I'm sorry."

But it was too late. Her lucky neko was gone.

Chapter Thirteen

The storm that suddenly rolled in fit her mood exactly.

Effin lethargically began to strip her sheets, her mind not really on the task at hand, but on the words she'd spat and could not take back.

But her reaction had been a knee-jerk, "hurt them before they hurt you further."

And after her sister's ultimate betrayal and her violent reaction, she began to distrust everyone around her. It was a defense mechanism, but it was one that had saved her from hurt in the past.

Only this time, it didn't quite go as planned.

Sure, her sister was guilty of some duplicity or another -- she always was. But it wasn't until she watched her pretty kitty race out of the window that she really opened her eyes and looked around her.

Her kitty had climbed out of a pair of sweatpants.

You can't have the kind of sex that would put you out for hours and still remember to put on sweatpants before you slept.

Masa was innocent of any wrongdoing, but still...

They were just so different!

She recalled why he was trapped in the neko form! He had slept with another preternatural creature.

Sure, she had tricked him into it, but she was an exotic creature filled with beauty and light. How could Effin compete with that?

Sure, Effin had freed him from his curse and had given him the only sex he'd had in years, but she was only human.

Effin sighed as she sat on her unmade bed, her thoughts going back to what she and Masa had done together.

God, she loved to hear him talk about her ass!

She snickered as she remembered the way he would caress it, lick it...fuck it. That was really exciting and taboo, and had just about put her down for the count.

Masataka had always made her feel special and protected.

He'd rejected her sister when he'd first met Monika, when her sister had been riding high from her glorious date with Effin's ex, and...

He had rejected her sister, her beautiful and perfect sister!

He hadn't bothered to look at another woman the whole time they were together; in fact, he'd clung to her more as he saw the females that were out on the street.

He didn't care if she couldn't bring the rain or have any powers.

He appreciated her for what she was. And what she was, was an idiot!

"Nuts to this," Effin breathed as she rose to her feet. One quick phone call to her office and she had the next two days off.

Then she threw on some old jeans and a sweater, grabbing her umbrella on her way out the door.

She was going to find her man!

She was going to apologize and get him back to his human self, if she had to take on the very Japanese gods themselves!

Her neko was not going to get away!

And if she couldn't make him human again... Gods, that thought hurt. But if she couldn't get him human again, she would see to it that he lived like a king.

And not because he was a good luck neko or because he doled out orgasms like the Easter bunny gave out chocolates, but because he made her feel like a queen, he always made sure she came first. He'd showed her that she mattered. And that was good enough for her.

She nodded, her confidence coming back as she made for her Jeep, thankful that it had four-wheel drive as she was pounded by the deluge. She was going to get her neko, come hell or high water, and nothing had better stand in her way.

Chapter Fourteen

Effin cursed as her Jeep rumbled over the wet roads in Dundulk, looking for a landmark of any kind that would remind her where she had met her pretty kitty.

She knew it was near some warehouses and that there were vents around, but she was not sure, and the darkness brought on by the rain was not helping matters any.

Finally, she drove to a spot that looked familiar, hoping that her kitty had made his way back here. Hell, she hoped that this was the place he called home.

Pulling off to the side of the road, she extended her umbrella, hoping it would block out some of the driving rain and improve her view, as she began climbing down the steep embankment.

"Masa!" she called as she searched the ground, every ditch and under every scraggly bush. "Masa! Where are you?"

She was so intent in her search, moving further and further away from the safety of the road, that she never even noticed the purr of a high performance European car pulling up beside her Jeep.

* * *

Masataka sulked.

Okay, maybe sulked was too childish a word.

He brooded.

Masataka, lost in a nest of his castoff baby blankets, stared indolently out at the rain and wondered what had happened.

Things had been going so well! He had found his female, he was having sex, he was in human form, and then all of a sudden, poof! It was all gone!

It made no sense.

And it was entirely that stupid sister's fault!

Effin's sister was so good at playing games she could be a kitsune. If the bitch weren't so sneaky, then none of this would have happened.

Masa knew that Effin's attitude sprang from years of abuse at her sister's hands, and a low self-esteem that apparently her jealous sister had helped create. A weekend with him was not going to change how she felt about herself very much.

But Effin needed to realize that there was more to her than the dependable accountant, the sister who was all forgiving, the friend who was a pushover, and a lover that was easily cast aside.

He had watched as the scars on her soul had begun to heal, and he'd watched as her sister's actions had torn all those wounds open again.

He sighed as he burrowed deeper into his nest, realizing that it was not as comfortable as the comforter Effin kept on her bed. He'd seen the moment that she'd made her damning wish, saw the shock and desire to take those words back, but it had been too late.

Without any fanfare or outward display, Masataka was back in his neko form, and mad as hell.

He felt betrayed, felt as if he were being punished for someone else's misdeeds. It wasn't fair! He knew that Effin was not a hateful person, nor a person to wish ill upon someone. Still, the moment he had been forced into this shape again, he had seen red.

In anger, he had fled Effin's home, not allowing her to take the wish back or make a new wish, or even explain herself. He'd seen regret in her eyes, knew that she didn't mean it, but what if he was stuck in this form forever? Sure, it gave him the ability to lick his own cock, but unless Effin was into diminutive bestiality, there was no way a relationship between the two of them could work.

And he was really getting to like her, too.

He could still picture her, heavy with his kittens down the road, and he sighed, depressed as he realized that that half-formed dream would never even have a chance of becoming a reality.

So, he'd returned to his territory and his warehouse, climbed in his warm blankets still by the exhaust vent on the second level, and brooded.

Maybe if he brooded long enough, an idea would come to him.

Snorting at his own fancifulness, he closed his eyes and tried to blot out the sound of the storm raging above. Before, he'd had a reason to dislike the rain. Now, he absolutely hated it.

* * *

Effin, ass up and nose to the ground, followed a path around a bush near a warehouse that didn't look like it was in too much disarray.

She had hoped that her kitty would hear her call and come out to meet her...or attack her. Either way, she could get his little kitty tail out of this storm and explain what had happened.

She was about to move back to her Jeep and travel a bit further up the road to search anew when she bumped into something hard and warm.

Jumping up, she turned and realized that she was looking at Buster the stock boy with a duffle held over his shoulder.

"Buster, what are you doing here?"

She rolled her eyes as she backed away from the man.

After talking to Christa, she was sure that the yahoo was nothing more than a wannabe gangsta with delusions of grandeur. There was no way that he could be the killer they were looking for. She was sure that the "Buster cap her in her ass" was contrived to make her feel uncomfortable and him big.

But one could never be too cautious. She backed up and started to move around him, never taking her eyes off his body.

"Who the fuck is Buster, lady?"

"Whatever," Effin groaned, still backing away. "What did you do, Buster, raid the stockpile at the office and get a stolen load of staplers?"

She took a step back and Buster took a step forward, dropping the duffle off his shoulder as it if were meaningless.

The muffled grunt that came from the bag, however, sent shivers of fear down Effin's spine.

Lightning flashed, and for a moment she could clearly see that this man was not poor, deluded Buster! This man had a darker visage, an evil menace that surrounded him.

"Holy shit!" Effin breathed. "You're the serial killer!"

His response was a slow grin that froze the blood in her veins.

Tossing reason to the wind and her umbrella at his face, Effin turned tail and ran.

She tried to make it back to her Jeep, but Psycho ran around in front of her, trying to knock her to the ground, cutting off that avenue of escape.

"What you gonna do now, bitch?" he growled.

In reaction, Effin let out a shrill, piercing scream and took off in the opposite direction.

Uncaring of the rain or what she was running through, Effin's fight-or-flight mechanism took her racing toward the warehouses, hoping against hope that she could lose him in the maze of buildings.

* * *

Masa jumped, sure he'd heard his female's voice.

She sounded like she was upset about something.

But that couldn't be right. His Effin was supposed to be at home, snuggled up in her big comfortable bed, doing whatever women did when they kicked their lovers out in the cold.

He hoped that she had celebrated at least a little about kicking her sister's ass; the hooch deserved it.

He closed his eyes, thinking that maybe it was his imagination, when he heard her voice again. And this time she sounded scared.

Climbing to his feet and leaving his nest of blankets, Masataka made for the side exit of his home, peering out into the rain to see what was going on. Curiosity was the one trait he had, human or neko, and his whiskers were buzzing with the need to investigate.

He stalked outside, ears cocked to the side, listening and hearing only pouring rain, when the scream came.

Shit! It was his Effin! And she was in danger!

Taking off through the rain, he lifted his nose, cursing the liquid falling from the sky as it attempted to mask her scent. But her adrenaline was racing so much that it was easy for him to track her.

Leaping over rocks and abandoned machine parts, Masataka saw something that nearly cost him one of his cat's reported nine lives. There was a huge man chasing his female, and the scent the man gave off was pure evil!

Knowing that he was virtually powerless in this form and that teeth and claw would not work well against his evil, Masa suddenly came up with an idea.

His heart raced as he zipped through the buildings, keeping his ear out for his female as he raced to intercept her.

* * *

Effin raced ahead, trying to keep her screams at bay as she heard death following her.

She was growing desperate and tired, soaked to the skin, her breath rasping, her heart slamming in her chest. She was beginning to slow, a stitch developing in her side, when she saw what had to be a cat's form keeping stride.

The cat separated from the shadows and nearly clipped her, but it paused to lift his paw and kind of wave at her, then it was off.

Cultural differences! That "come on" wave was the one that Masa had showed her!

Her pretty kitty was alive and trying to save her!

Instantly putting her trust in the neko, Effin changed directions and followed the cat through the shadows of the tall warehouses.

Around and around he led her, scrambling under fences and around boxes until they reached a brick wall, literally.

"Damn it, Masa! This is no time for revenge!" she panted as she lost sight of the black cat in the shadows the wall cast, even in the rain.

There was a little mew to her right, and Effin realized she had to get low and wiggle into some kind of crawlspace her kitty had found.

No sooner had she squeezed into the small access chute than her cat was off and running.

Effin watched in horror as he leapt onto the psycho's head, scratching and spitting, before he leapt off, leading the man in the opposite direction.

"Masa!" she breathed, but could not leave the safety he had led her to. She hoped that he knew what he was doing, that he would not be hurt, and she prayed to God that her kitty would not die before she had a chance to apologize.

* * *

"Patooie!" Masa hissed as he tried to spit the taste of the serial killer out of his mouth, along with a portion of the psycho's ear.

But his little love bites had done what he'd intended; the maniac was following him instead of chasing Effin.

And now that the bastard was pounding in the mud behind him, it was time to let his luck come into play.

Twisting in mid-jump, in a move of astounding aerial acrobatics, Masataka reversed his position and headed for a warehouse that he knew stored dangerous chemicals.

Knowing that the psycho would follow, seeking revenge for his ravaged ear, made it childishly easy to lead the menace right into the laser eye that ran across the doors at what would be considered human height and trip the silent alarm.

That done, he just had to keep the son of a bitch occupied long enough for the cops to get there.

Gotta love paranoid chemical companies that produced bleach and ammonia cleaning compounds. They were so terrorist shy that they'd recently redone all the alarms, both audible and silent.

His little kitty whiskers trembling in excitement, Masa made another pass at the psycho, this time raking razor-sharp nails across his chest, forcing a roar of rage from the killer's throat.

This was almost fun.

Masataka danced around the man, getting his strikes in where needed and amusing himself as the hunter never realized that he had become the prey.

So lost in his play was he that he never saw the shadow that crawled out from behind some boxes and started toward the serial killer and the cat.

* * *

"Effin, you are a coward!" Effin berated herself as she listened while the crazed lunatic chased after her neko. He had led her to safety and then led the monster away from her.

She was such a fool.

Masa would never risk his life if she was just a casual fuck, and she knew he was at risk with his smaller size.

She gritted her teeth as she heard a roar of pain and blanched at the thought of the man actually getting his hands on her Masataka! The monster would kill him, and then go back for whoever was in the bag.

It was not right, Masataka risking his life for the woman who'd trapped him in this form and for a victim he didn't even know about.

A second roar reached her ears, and with that, her hands stopped trembling and her resolve firmed.

Effin crawled from her hidey-hole and followed the sounds of struggle. After running around several buildings, Effin saw something that would have taken at least one of her lives if she had been a cat.

Her neko was leaping and tearing bits out of the serial killer, leaving the man running in circles as he attempted to catch the attack cat.

Seeing that the man was distracted, Effin picked up a huge rock in both hands and tried to sneak up behind him.

She was about to slam the rock on his head, when he turned and grabbed her by the neck.

"Call off the cat, bitch!" he growled, shaking her roughly and making her drop her makeshift weapon. He noticed that the cat paused in its frenzied attack.

"Call it off or I will snap your neck."

Masa! Effin screamed in her head as she watched her kitty stare worriedly up at her.

"So, sic a cat on me, will you? I'll teach you to play games." The man leered as one hand left her neck to cup her right breast through her sopping wet sweater. He grinned evilly as he let his hand trail upwards, over her jaw, his fingers fanning over her cheeks. He gently wiped the water from around her blinking right eye. "You cost me an ear, so I'm going to take an eye."

Before he could move, Effin was shrieking, "No! Masa!"

The man turned to see a ball of black fury hurtling through the air toward his face.

Instinctively, he let Effin go to shield his neck and eyes, and that's when the police lights hit him full in the face.

"This is the police! We have you surrounded! Get your hands up and keep them where we can see them!"

Effin wilted, literally sinking to her knees as police swarmed the area. A helicopter suddenly appeared, shining lights overhead, and several deputy U.S. Marshals raced onto the scene.

Before Effin could blink, someone wrapped her in a blanket and began leading her away.

"Wait!" she called out, before she could get too far. "Where's my cat?"

Before people began to think that maybe the strain of being attacked was too much for her, a small, bedraggled black kitty leapt into view and into Effin's arms.

"What were you doing out here?" a police officer asked as she was led to an ambulance and swaddled in towels.

"I…I was looking for my cat." Effin looked down at her neko and swore she could read relief in his little kitty eyes. "I got mad at him about something stupid and he got out. I was coming to get him before he got hurt."

Hearing that, Masa began to purr and nuzzle under her chin. A grinning paramedic handed her a towel to dry her kitty.

"Hold onto that kitty." The police officer reached out a hand to stroke Masataka's head. "He saved your life. He made mincemeat out of the perp and…"

Just then, the perp in question was led away in cuffs, cursing and screaming about demon cats and witch women who control them.

"He is special," Effin agreed. "I just got him, but I think I can easily fall in love with him."

Smiling, the cop walked away, presumably to begin filling out reports, and Effin was left to answer questions.

When she told the cops about the body that had grunted in the bag, they backtracked to her car and began to search the area. They found the bag, but no body inside. They chalked it up to the victim freeing herself and making haste away while the attack cat dealt with the serial killer.

Finally, Effin was released, told to not leave town, and allowed to take her Jeep home. She and her kitty had a lot to discuss.

Chapter Fifteen

"Pretty kitty," Effin purred as she wrapped her favorite pussy in a thick plush towel and gently patted his fuzzy coat dry.

The first order of business was for her to get her pussy clean and dry.

Masa hadn't protested the bath, seeming to love the cleansing wash that she had given him in lightly scented water.

He especially loved the fact that she was naked in the tub with him.

But thoughts of kitty sex were too much even for Effin, and the bath was strictly for warming and cleansing.

Now, they both sat on Effin's huge bed surrounded by the little odds and ends that Masa had brought to her bedroom as small tokens of his esteem.

"I was so jealous." Effin began to softly talk to Masa as she stroked her kitty dry, knowing that she owed the neko an explanation.

"You see, my sister always gets what I want. If it is mine, she takes it. Hell, her past boyfriend was mine first. And when I saw her with you, I just snapped."

A huffing sort of meow followed and Effin had the grace to blush.

"I know you wouldn't cheat on me, but I was reacting on useless emotion as you would say. But I wasn't thinking. All I saw was my sister taking something again that I had claimed as my own. And you are a neko, Masataka. I looked it up, you know. You guys are known for catting around."

She got a huff of amusement that made her lift his small, fuzzy body and press a kiss to his vanilla-scented head.

"But then I started to get scared, Masa." She sighed and cuddled her kitty before laying him back on her lap.

He gave her a questioning mew and looked up at her with his serious liquid eyes.

"I was scared because we are so different, Masa. I mean the racial difference is one thing, but you spend half your time as a cat! What if you want to, you know, get it on kitty style or something? I am nothing exotic or beautiful like you, Masa. And I kind of got scared that you would find someone else more appealing."

She sighed, knowing that half her problem was her sorry self-esteem. She dropped her head and sighed again.

But then a small, soft paw pressed against her cheek, and a rough little tongue lapped at her face, taking away invisible tears that she refused to shed.

"You think I'm beautiful." She chuckled. "I got the message, and a loofa to exfoliate, Masa."

She looked down at her kitty and noticed the very un-catlike leer on his face.

"Well, we both know I appreciate that rough little tongue of yours in some situations, but this ain't one of them, bub."

Then she hugged him to her bosom, squeezing him gently.

"I don't know what I'm gonna do, Masa! It's like the old saying: you never know what you have until it's gone. You are gone and…"

She sniffed as she desperately tried to hold in the tears that threatened to fall.

"And I miss you so much."

She dropped her head to the kitty's, sniffling as he tried to mew comfortingly to her, but it only made her cry harder.

"Masa…Masa-Masa-taka!" She closed her eyes as the hot tears flooded her face. "Masataka I-I m-miss you s-so much."

Her breath hitched as she tried to inhale, but the grief that filled her heart needed a release before she went mad. Her sobs were wrenching and loud and childishly undisciplined as she gave in to her sorrow, knowing that it was all her own fault. "I-I w-wish you were hum-hum-human again!"

Then she curled into a ball around her pretty kitty, hiding them both in the world underneath her huge soft comforter, the small body wiggling in her neck offering some comfort to her.

But guilt kept her sobbing far into the night. She knew she had cursed Masataka to spend an eternity in his cat body, and that through her own fears and lack of self-confidence, she had condemned herself to a life without him, or worse, a life with him as a cat.

"Masataka," she sniffled, eyes swollen and nose clogged from her crying. "I am so sorry. And I was beginning to love you so much."

Then she closed her aching eyes and tried to lose herself in sleep, cuddling the tear-soaked fur that smelled sweetly of vanilla and the faintest scent of the man that Masataka had once been.

* * *

A tickling warmth woke Effin the next morning, a soft glide of silk between her legs that had her instinctively spreading her legs apart.

She moaned at the feel of a rough tongue laving her skin.

She shuddered, her hands reaching down to draw that mouth up past her nipples when…

"Masa?" she queried. Then her sleepy eyes blinked. "Masa, you better be a man in my bed or so help me God I'll…"

The tongue that invaded her mouth stopped any further speech.

Effin tangled her hair in long yards of silk as she opened her mouth wider. Her tongue slipped out to tease at the one invading her, playing with it and trying to hold back her moans.

She would know that taste anywhere! Masataka was back.

"But how?" she asked as they finally broke for air.

She lay over a reclining Masa as if she were his favorite blanket, her hands gently tangling in his hair. "You were a cat and…"

"Your sincerity wished me back," Masa purred, his own hands stroking softly up and down Effin's back, then cupping the ass he loved so much.

"Is that all it took?" She lifted her head to stare at him intently.

"That, and I had learned my lesson, it would seem. I used my ability to observe more than carnal seduction, though that is always fun."

He leered at his female as she exploded into laughter.

"I thought I had cursed you, Masa," she breathed. "I was so scared and disappointed in myself. I thought that you would hate me."

"You still do not really know me, Effin, yet you are beginning to trust me. Otherwise, you would have never followed me. And you are beginning to trust yourself, to stand up for yourself, to demand the respect that you deserve."

"You mean I spanked my sister's ass," Effin drawled.

"And a very entertaining show that was."

Effin sighed and laid her head back on her fleshly pillow. "So now what?" she asked.

"Now," Masa purred, "now you decide how you want me and I give you pleasure that you have only dreamed of. Then we let the future take care of itself. I am, after all, a lucky neko, Effin! Everything will turn out exactly as it should."

And Effin had to agree. She was about to get very lucky again, right now.

* * *

"Touch yourself, Effin."

Masataka's voice dropped as his hands gripped his female's waist. His mouth near her nipple blew a puff of warm air before the tip of his tongue flicked around her throbbing flesh.

"Masa!" Effin gasped, her hands tangling in his long, silky hair as she forced her body down, taking all of his cock deep within her clinging pussy.

Her labia spread impossibly wide, the full thickness of him forced itself balls deep within her as Effin shuddered.

They had started this session with Masa giving her her first taste of uncut meat, as he called it.

He had been so thick and hot in her mouth! She had only been able to get a quarter of his length buried within her orifice, but she worked those inches over with teeth and tongue until Masa was a mewling mass of flesh begging for mercy.

She had lapped at his balls until they threatened to rise up and expel their load when he pulled himself from her mouth and took her lips in a powerful kiss.

Then he flipped her over onto her back and spread her legs as wide as he could get them. Almost salivating at the thought of her sweet taste, Masa buried his head between her legs and proceeded to suck her dry.

Her nipples were nibbled, her clit laved, her labia stroked in long, hard licks. He tongue fucked her pussy until she was screaming his name and begging for mercy. Then he had done something new.

He lifted her ass high in the air, stuck a pillow beneath her hips and covered her rosebud with gentle kisses and licks.

Effin went mad, her legs scissoring and kicking as a pleasure so great filled her she had to move or go mad as he fucked her ass with his tongue.

Finally, placing her fingers around her opening, he sank his cock deep into her, letting her feel each inch that delved deep into her body.

"Touch yourself for me, Effin," he repeated, and leaned back, her legs around the bends of his arms as he watched her worry her clit and pull on her nipples.

The sight was breathtaking and his eyes glowed in passion as he observed his female bringing herself more pleasure.

His slow, even thrusts began to speed up as his whole body demanded release from the tension that was building as he tried to fuck his female through the mattress.

"Harder!" Effin screamed, her whole face flushed in passion, her lips parted and her breathing rough. "Fuck me harder! Faster, Masa!"

Eager to comply, Masataka increased the speed and depths of his thrusts, angling his hips so that the broad head of his cock stroked each and every inch of her sheath.

The two moved like a well-oiled machine, pistoning each other, giving their all and striving to share the passion with their partner.

Mewls, growls, and cries were flowing from Masa's mouth as he shook sweat-soaked hair from his eyes.

"Now, Effin," he breathed, feeling the tension in her about to snap. "Cum, beloved. Cum for me!"

Then she was there, screaming as her body exploded, as her mind flew away, as pure sensation took over. Her pussy grabbed at Masa's cock, demanding more pleasure, deriving more as her sensitive walls clenched around his hardened length.

Then Masa slammed four times deeply into his female, and held still as his balls slammed into the base of his cock and his seed exploded from his body in spurts.

"Effin!" he chanted. "Kami-sama, Effin!"

Then his muscles relaxed and he found himself sinking into the waiting arms of his female.

"This thing we have," Effin breathed as she gently stroked his hair, bringing him down from his orgasmic high as her world slipped back into something like normalcy. "This thing, whatever it is, it may not last forever."

"But it is here now." Masa licked at the salty flesh of her neck, a purr deep in his chest for his female. "It is what we have for now, and I think we were both lucky to find it."

Effin agreed as she closed her eyes and just drifted.

The sun was rising and today would be a new day.

Funny, she never realized how beautiful a sunrise was, until she shared it with someone she cared for. She looked over at the dozing neko and had to agree.

They may not have forever, but they had now...and it was very fine indeed.

Kittylogue

Outside the window the next morning, a tall, dark figure that looked remarkably like Buster prowled, smiling as he observed the scene.

"Now my debt is paid, neko." The deep, masculine voice began to change, growing lighter as a bright flash of light hid the tall man from view.

In a blink of an eye, the well-formed black man was gone, and in his place stood a tall, pale feminine figure...with three tails. "And now that my deceit and trickery has been forgiven, I can obtain my fourth tail and finally have my wedding."

"And you learned not to go fucking around with stray nekos," a droll masculine voice said.

The female kitsune looked back at her nine-tailed mate and grinned. "Though you almost messed it up by leading her to an area where a serial killer was hunting. It was not comfortable being in that bag."

The male kitsune rolled his eyes as he called back his foxfire, the same foxfire used to form the shapes of Murder and Body Count, Buster's ghetto-fabulous sidekicks.

"Well," she purred as her body began to glow in a wash of pale foxfire magic. "At least not fucking them literally." She almost purred. "And our little neko used his skills of observation for more than getting laid and stealing stuff."

With a chuckle, the female kitsune flashed away, her bemused mate following suit.

"Now will you forgive me?"

"That remains to be seen." The male nine-tailed kitsune chuckled. "But in the meantime, let's go fuck with some humans."

"Perfect idea," the female agreed, and they both shared a mischievous grin.

Yup, there were many ways to fuck with humans, in a nonsexual manner. The only problem was figuring out which way would be most amusing.

A gentle rain began to fall, though the sun was shining brightly, and that too went unnoticed by the lovers inside.

~ ♥ ~

Stephanie Burke

Stephanie Burke, known as Flash, is just your typical housewife who keeps a collection of slave-type males in her attic, leather and bondage gear in her living room, dimensional portals in the downstairs bathroom, and a few dozen worlds in the basement where they tend to collect dust and require vacuuming every now and again.

Stephanie has no pets; she has a husband and two little ones instead, gardens when weather permits, forces family members and loved ones to pose for her paintings, and has an unfounded reputation for assaulting waiters! (Big untruth! No one has documented proof!)

In between maintaining her own little piece of the universe (the sky really is magenta there), she writes constantly, travels to conventions, is actually paid to give lectures (go figure), and devises new ways to try and push the envelope, any envelope, just a little bit further. Find Flash's chat group at groups.yahoo.com/group/FlameKeeper or contact her at Flashycat2004@aol.com.

* * *

INTO TEMPTATION

Lena Matthews

Dedication

To Leo ~ My Funny Little Valentine

Thanks for showing this lifelong pessimist that true love really exists. I love you.

~ Lena

Chapter One

"Fuck Cupid."

Startled, Billie Fowler looked up from her desk and into the beaming face of her co-worker, Jenna Fields, with amazement. She couldn't have heard what she just thought she did. "Excuse me?"

"Fuck Cupid," Jenna repeated with a smile as she jiggled an envelope in her hand. "That's the theme this year for my annual Anti-Valentine's Day Party. Fuck Cupid."

Billie winced again. The obscenity grew louder every time Jenna said it. Quickly standing, she snatched the invitation out of Jenna's hand and looked around over the walls of her gray cubical, hoping no one else had heard her insane colleague. "All right, girl, I heard you the first time. I was just hoping I hadn't."

"Oh, you heard me, all right." Waggling her eyebrows, Jenna grinned. Decorum wasn't a word in the extroverted woman's dictionary. She was all about shock factor, the dirtier the better, but at eleven o'clock in the morning, it felt like a bit much. "So are you going to come to my party?"

Jenna's parties were legendary around the office -- hell, around the whole city. To the petite blonde, bashes were a way of life. No matter how much Billie tried, she couldn't get Jenna to stop inviting her. It wasn't that she didn't like Jenna, because she did. Billie just didn't have the energy for the *Sex in the City* lifestyle that suited Jenna.

A girl had to sleep sometimes.

"I don't know what my plans are yet," Billie lied, trying her best to politely refuse. She knew exactly what her plans were. They included sweatpants, a Lean Cuisine, and her *Dirty Dancing* DVD.

A quiet, safe Valentine's Day, where the only heart that could possibly be broken was her heart-shaped candy dish.

"Don't give me that 'maybe' stuff. I want you front and center this year. There are going to be a lot of single people there, and no one is allowed to bring dates. It's a get-laid-palooza. Even you can't screw it up."

"Thanks," Billie scoffed. *Was that supposed to be a selling point?* It was a good thing Jenna was her friend, not her enemy. Lord only knew what she might say.

Jenna had the grace to look a bit embarrassed. "Ahh, come on, you know what I mean."

Billie had a pretty good idea. "That I'm a hopeless shut-in with no future for a mate."

"Not even. I'm just saying that it's time you need to get out there. You know, embrace your inner wild child. Free your alternate you…"

"Shave my legs."

"Exactly." Jenna beamed, missing Billie's sarcasm altogether. "So you'll be there tomorrow night. Oh, wear red."

Billie watched Jenna stroll away, bemused. Apparently *no* wasn't in her dictionary, either. Looked as if Billie might be going to a party after all, whether she wanted to or not.

Shaking her head, Billie pulled the scarlet invite out and almost swallowed her tongue. The party theme was spelled out in large, bold, black letters, with a picture of Cupid being sodomized on the cover. Unfortunately, the wide-eyed cherub didn't seem to be enjoying the plundering all that much. It was obscene, offensive...and so *Jenna* that it was downright hilarious.

"Jenna has a way with visual aids, wouldn't you say, Holiday?"

Billie smiled as she began to place the invitation back in the envelope. The play on her name and the smooth Latin accent could only mean one person. "I agree; I think Levin should put her in charge of the ad department."

"Somehow I don't think that's a good idea." At his soul-deep chuckle, Billie looked up. As usual, when she was next to her handsome co-worker, Tomás Mendez, her heart did a silly little pitter-patter in her chest. It was sickening how drawn to him she was.

The uncomfortable silence between them lengthened as they stared at one another, both seemingly looking for something to say. Not that words were always a necessity; Billie was quite at ease with sharing stolen moments of peace with him as the world at large whizzed by them.

Unfortunately, in her moment of bliss, Billie didn't realize she hadn't put the card up completely and the dirty picture caught Tomás's eye. "So can I see the whole picture, or am I just to look at the large...member?"

Tapping her finger against the card, Billie eyed him in amusement. She wouldn't have classified Tomás as conservative or anything, but he did seem a bit above bawdy bathroom humor. "I don't know. It's a bit graphic."

Her words came off more like a challenge, not at all what she had been intending. "If you can see it, Holiday, I think I can take it."

"Suit yourself, Tomás, but don't say I didn't warn you."

Raising a brow arrogantly, he took the card from her outstretched hand. Their fingers brushed as he pulled the card away. The contact, although brief, led to them looking into each other's eyes. One stared questioningly, the other surprised.

Of course the second he pulled the card out of the envelope, all unasked questions were forgotten.

"Oh, my God!" He choked on his laughter as he studied the card. As she watched him, Billie realized she was such a goner.

She couldn't help it. Tomás Mendez was the total package. With wavy dark hair and smooth skin blessed with a natural tan, Tomás was the quintessential Latin heartthrob. He was handsome, charming, and successful -- everything a woman could possibly want, and then some.

The only problem was, when she wanted to drool over him, she had to get in line. In the seven months he'd been there, he'd had the entire female staff -- and some of the male staff as well -- panting after him.

Where the other women were audacious about their wants, Billie was more comfortable with just sitting back and playing the cards where they lay.

She would never approach him in any way that wouldn't be deemed friendly. She just wasn't that type of person. And it was probably one of the reasons Tomás sought her out. He saw her as friend, someone he could speak to over coffee breaks with no risk of injury to his posterior.

"You'd think she'd have something better to do." Shaking his head, Tomás shoved the invitation back into the envelope and handed it back to Billie, who was wearing an *I told you so* expression on her face. "What's the deal with the Anti-Valentine's Day party?"

"It's a bitter single woman thing. You wouldn't understand," she replied, as she tucked the invitation into her purse.

"You're assuming I wouldn't understand, why?"

Leaning against her desk, she wondered where he was going with this. "Because you're not bitter or a woman."

"But I *am* single."

That was good to know. "I'm sure Jenna has every intention of inviting you."

"Should that scare me or make me feel better?"

"Now, that is the real question."

Tomás leaned against the wall of her cubical and crossed his arms. "So you're not bitter, but you are a woman, and single; are you going to rearrange your Valentine's Day plans so you can go?"

Billie liked the way he didn't assume she didn't have plans. "I haven't decided yet. What about you? You have a big night planned?"

"I'm still pretty new to the area. A little too new to have a Valentine."

"I've been here for five years, and my big competing plans involve a frozen dinner and an old movie."

"Sounds like it might be a hard decision to make."

"It is my favorite frozen dinner and movie."

"I guess it would be kind of hard to compete with the two of them."

"It is." She tsked. "Lesser men have tried."

"That's the whole problem right there, Holiday." A slow, sensual smile spilled across the fullness of his mouth. "Lesser men. Not real men."

*   *   *

No matter how much he warned himself to take things slow with Billie, Tomás couldn't help the need he felt to put his mark on her and make her his. He'd only known the dark beauty for a short while, but time didn't matter with affairs of the heart.

From the first moment they had been introduced, Tomás had been taken in by her warm personality. Her laughter was infectious. Her voice could make him hard from a hundred yards away. She was beautiful, sexy, and a fun person to be around, but the "just friends" vibe she was sending him was about to kill him.

Billie held her hands up to her cheeks, as if trying to keep her embarrassment at bay. "Damn, you're smooth. Do you practice these lines in front of the mirror before you say them, or do they just come naturally?"

"Blame it on Cupid. The frisky little devil is up to no good."

"Do you echo Jenna's sentiments?"

"Oh, no." He shook his head as he walked further into her cubical. Stopping a breath away from her, Tomás leaned against her desk, letting his arm brush against hers. "I believe in *el amor*. All Latin men do."

"I thought that was Frenchmen."

Tomás scoffed. "The French think love is pretty words and flowery gestures. Real love is dirty, hot, and overwhelming. There is nothing pretty about it."

"Wow." Billie's hands slipped from her face as her large, doe eyes stared up at him in wonder. Despite the wall of friendship she had erected between them, Billie wasn't immune to him. "That was..."

"Real."

"Real's a word for it, all right." Her nervous chuckle stirred Tomás.

Then again, everything about her stirred him. From her coffee-tinged skin, so dark and smooth like a clear, starless night, to her thick, wavy hair that she wore twisted into spirals springing around her oval face.

She was the epitome of beauty; exotic, breathtaking, damn near irresistible. Just standing here next to her, breathing in her sweet scent, was giving him ideas that he didn't need, especially at work.

"Are you going to go to the party?"

"I wasn't planning on it."

"I think you should go."

"You do?"

"Oh, yes." There weren't enough words to express how much he wanted to see her out of the office. Out of her clothing and stretched out on his bed would have been even better, but he would settle for what he could get.

"I don't know," she teased, her full lips spreading into a welcoming smile. "I'm not really into violating Cupid."

"We could go together, as friends of course." He added the last part just to ease her mind. The last thing Tomás wanted was for her to say no.

For a second it seemed like her warm smile slipped a bit, but before he could question it, Jenna came back towards them.

"Tomás, just the man I was looking for."

"If you know what's good for you, you'll run," Billie whispered teasingly.

"Too late."

Hurrying to where they stood, Jenna thrust an envelope with his name scrawled on top, out at him, "I was going to leave your invitation on your desk, but I wanted to hand it to you personally."

Tomás was pretty sure the invitation wasn't the only thing Jenna wanted to give him personally, but the perky blonde was a bit too much for him. "I was just discussing the party with Billie. She was just saying how much she couldn't wait to go."

From the corner of his eye, Tomás saw the *thanks a lot* look Billie shot him and grinned. There was no way he was going to a bitter woman's party without her.

"Really?" Jenna shimmered with excitement. "That's wonderful. You're going to come too, right? I just won't take no for an answer."

"Then I better say yes."

"There are going to be a lot of happy women tomorrow night."

"Why, are you going to spike his drink?" Billie asked, tongue in cheek.

It took all of Tomás's hard-won control not to burst into laughter. He was well aware of the come hither looks some of the women on the staff tossed his way. Their behavior was something he was used to Billie teasing him about; she just didn't normally do it in front of people.

"Billie!" Jenna's phony gasp was as transparent as her white blouse.

"Jenna!" Billie mocked back. "Come on, Tomás knows he's a hottie. He can feel the stares on his cute derrière as he walks."

Tomás looked at Billie with a grin of his own. "Cute, huh?"

"Downright adorable." Her brown eyes twinkled with amusement. Tomás was going to have to pull her across his lap and teach her a little lesson. She was such a little hellion.

Wait a minute...spanking her...the thought had merit. Just the word *spanking* in the same sentence with *Billie* was causing an upheaval in Tomás's body. It had been a long time since he had been with a woman, and even longer since he'd wanted someone as much as he did Billie.

If -- no, *when* he got her under him...

"Well, I'm off." Jenna's nagging voice broke through Tomás's lust-clouded brain. "I have a few more invites to pass out."

Startled, Tomás turned his head back to look at her. *She was still there.* "Okay."

Jenna eyed them with interest before walking away. There was something very predatory-like in her stare, only further driving home the point that Tomás didn't want to be caught alone in a room with her.

"I think she likes you," Billie teased. "Word to the wise, don't drink the Kool-Aid."

"I'd think I'd be wise not to drink the water either."

"It must be nice to be the belle of her ball."

Tomás lowered his voice, so they wouldn't be overheard. "I have no desire to ball anything of hers."

Billie's sharp laughter drew several stares in their direction from people passing by. But the curious glances were all worth it just to see her smile. Glancing around at the attention they were receiving, Billie stepped away from him with a cautious smile. "You are going to get me fired."

"Then I'd have no reason to come to work." With a wink, Tomás stood up. On his way out of her cubical, he stopped and turned back to her. "Will you be there tomorrow night?"

"Do you want me to come?"

Talk about a loaded question. With an inner groan, Tomás willed his cock to stay down. "Most definitely."

Chapter Two

With a gleeful squeal, the front door burst open before the last note of the doorbell had rung. It happened so fast it almost gave Billie a heart attack. One moment her finger had been on the glowing dot and the next she was standing like a deer frozen in the headlights. She hadn't even had time to get her phony smile in place before Jenna was standing in front of her.

"You came." The overwhelming mixture of Cashmere Mist and Peach Schnapps engulfed Billie as Jenna pulled her into a hug. Wide-eyed, Billie clumsily patted her on the back, unsure of what her role was in this embrace. She hadn't known she and Jenna were on a hugging basis.

When Jenna released her, Billie pasted a fake smile on her face, trying her best to look like she wasn't dying slowly on the inside. "I made it."

"Great, now we can really get the party started." The words were hardly out of her mouth before a giggling couple bumped into them on their way out the door.

From the looks of the seemingly inebriated people stumbling by, Billie was more than sure the party had started without her.

"Follow me," Jenna instructed loudly as she turned and headed down the hallway.

Eighties' power ballads blared from the speaker, sending a chill down Billie's spine as she trailed Jenna through the packed house. This party was going to be worse than she thought. Billie wasn't one for faceless crowds, and she definitely wasn't someone who enjoyed hair bands.

"So what do you think?" Jenna stopped in the middle of the room and spread her arms out wide, like a demented Vanna White.

What did she think? Was she kidding?

It was horrible. "A woman scorned" couldn't begin to describe the vibes the room was sending out. Little cupids strummed down from the ceiling, hung from red velvet nooses. Broken hearts were tacked to the walls, and the room was adorned in more red than a western whorehouse. Although it could have been worse, Billie supposed; Jenna could have had cocks bobbing in and out of the cupid dolls.

"Festive." *If she was going for the brothel in hell look.*

"I know. I love it."

Billie just smiled, not surprised at all. With Jenna appeased, Billie followed her hostess through the house. She nodded to the people she knew, not taking time to stop and chat. She was there for one reason, and she didn't see him anywhere.

If he had flaked out on her, come Monday he was a dead man.

As they passed through the hallway, Billie caught sight of Tomás ahead of them. Dressed in black slacks and a red pullover shirt, he looked entirely too tempting for her own good. His dark hair, normally pulled back into a ponytail at his nape, was flowing loosely around his shoulders. The crimson material of his shirt was pulled taut across his muscular chest, showing off a set of matching pecs that Billie had never noticed before.

Damn, was she glad she'd shaved!

Billie walked by him without making eye contact or saying a word. She wasn't trying to play coy; it was just a bit difficult to approach him with the entourage of cleavage surrounding him.

With a self-deprecating sigh, Billie continued on to the dining room with Jenna, cursing the blonde's very existence. Maybe she had read his signals wrong yesterday at work. Maybe he did just want to be friends. Maybe she should have stayed home after all.

"Name badges." Jenna's voice brought Billie's attention swinging right back to her. "Because you're late, you won't get the cream of the crop, but I'm sure we can find one for you."

Name badges. That cinched it. There was no maybe it about, Billie should have stayed home.

"You know, I don't really need a name badge. I know a few people here and…"

"Oh don't be silly. They don't have your name on them. They have the evil things love makes us do on them."

Wow, they had officially passed Bitterville's off ramp an exit ago. "Is there a painful breakup you want to share with me?"

Jenna laughed stiffly. "Please, I don't get my heart broken. I break hearts."

Looking around with a sympathetic grimace at the room and the party theme in general, Billie somehow didn't quite believe her.

"Oh, here's one," Jenna squealed happily. She held the heart out towards Billie, gesturing for her to take it.

With a resounding sigh, Billie reached out and pulled the cut-out heart towards her. This was such a bad idea, much worse than wearing the stupid heart thong she had on. All traces of her good humor vanished when she saw the two words printed on top of red paper.

"Sex Slave." *Not just no, but hell no!* "I don't think so, Jenna."

"Why?"

Was she kidding? "Because I make it a point to never wear anything that says slave on it. Call it a black thing."

"Oh, come on Billie, it's not that kind of slave."

"Yes, because a slave that's forced to have sex is so much better than one forced to work." *How the hell had she let herself get talked into coming to this stupid party in the first place?*

"Holiday, you made it," Tomás called from behind them, strolling to where they were with a large grin on his handsome face.

Oh yeah, that's how.

"She's not playing fair." Jenna pouted. "She won't wear her name badge."

"It says *Sex Slave*," Billie repeated again, hoping this time the idiocy of the whole damn thing might sink into Jenna's vapid head. "*Sex Slave*."

Tomás winced as if he understood her plight, but Jenna continued to stare at Billie as if she had two heads. "I know what it says. What's the big deal?"

Blanching, Billie turned pleading eyes to Tomás, who looked as if he was trying his best not to laugh. He wasn't going to be much help. "The deal is, walking around with *Sex Slave* on my dress in a room full of people I don't know is like taking out a blatant billboard for freaky-deaky sexual deviants."

Jenna's blank expression didn't change.

"Did I mention it had slave on it?" Billie's voice faded out as she looked from Tomás's grinning face to Jenna's confused one. "Oh, forget it."

"Great." The doorbell rang, prompting Jenna to clap her hands in happiness like a toy monkey. "I'll be right back."

Jenna was gone in an instant, leaving Billie and Tomás staring after her. "Is there a back door to this place?"

"Not planning on leaving me so soon, are you?" Tomás's breath brushed Billie's ear as he leaned in close to speak.

Billie looked up at him with a raised brow. "It didn't look like you were lacking for company when I came in."

"Is that why you didn't come over to say hello?"

"I didn't think you'd notice."

"There's very little about you I don't notice."

If he didn't know better, Tomás would think Billie was jealous. It was a sentiment he could truly relate to. From the moment she walked into the room dressed in a short black dress, Tomás had wanted to hustle her out of the party so no one else would have a chance to look at her lovely legs.

"You look lovely." The word "lovely" didn't quite do her justice. Unlike everyone else at the party, Billie wasn't wearing red, and instead of standing out like an anomaly, she appeared like a rare orchid in a field of daisies.

"Pretty words aren't going to change the fact that you made me come to this horrible party."

"You came for me?" he teased, wanting her to admit it.

Billie smiled. "I didn't come for the candy hearts and degrading name badges."

Ignoring her last comment, Tomás focused more on what she didn't say, instead of what she did say. "I like that you came just for me."

His words were lower than he intended, giving away the hunger in his voice. Billie's gaze locked with his for a moment. The space between them appeared to shrink as the heat level rose.

"I like that you like it." Billie brushed against him as she walked over to the table bearing the name badges.

The touch had been brief but the effect on his body was anything but. His cock stirred to life at the simple touch of her body against his, and Tomás wasn't the only one who knew it. A knowing little smile had flitted across her lips as she'd passed by. The little vixen knew exactly what she was doing to him.

So much for keeping things light and friendly. "So are you going to put on your name badge?"

"You're not going to start now too, are you?" Billie glanced over her shoulder at him and frowned.

With a slight smile, Tomás walked over to her. "Come on, it's all in good humor."

"*Alpha jerk.*" Billie snorted as she flicked his name badge. "Of course you don't see a problem. Yours is an attitude. Mine is…"

"Just a joke. Yours no more fits your personality than mine fits me." Although his was a bit closer to his own personality than Tomás cared to admit. He didn't like to think of himself as a jerk, but Tomás knew he could be very controlling when it came to certain things, the bedroom especially.

"So you don't see me as a *Sex Slave?*"

Tilting his head to the side, Tomás pretended to study her, when in all reality it was just giving him ample time to feast his gaze upon her. "Sex slave no, sex kitten, yes."

"*Sex Kitten?*" Billie's brows creased. "You look at me and see *Sex Kitten?*"

From the storm brewing in her hazel eyes, Tomás knew he had to explain. And fast. "Yes and no. When I look at you,

I see a very beautiful woman who knows that she's lovely but doesn't hide behind it. I see a sexy lady that I would love to get to know better. But most importantly, I see Billie, the single most interesting person I've been blessed to meet since I came here to this city. I want to see more of her."

For once, Billie had nothing to say. The surprise swimming in her eyes said it all, encouraging Tomás to continue.

"The kitten part comes from your playful attitude. The way you laugh. It's like a deep purr that caresses my skin, making me want to risk your wrath by running my hands up your shoulders to caress your neck with my fingers, then my lips."

The air thickened between them, and Tomás found it hard to concentrate on what he was saying. Enough with the word play. He was ready to move on to the foreplay and more. "Beautiful, strong, playful, sexy; whether you want to admit it or not. So yeah, *Sex Kitten*."

The quiet room burst forth with laughter as people strolled in and went to the bar. The moment, no matter how much he hated it, was lost. Stepping back from him, Billie gave a nervous little laugh, brushing her hair behind her ear.

The pearl-pink tip of her tongue slipped out and moistened her lips. "You think she'll get upset if I change my heart?"

Clearing his throat, Tomás tried to lighten the mood. "I think Jenna's a bit unstable with the whole Valentine thing. She might try to take you out."

They both laughed at the absurdity and the truth in his words. With a sigh, Billie reluctantly pinned the heart to her blouse. "I look like a tool."

"You look perfect."

"Yes, perfectly ripe for the plucking."

"No one will come near you tonight." Or any other night, if Tomás had a say in it. "You'll be my 'Sex Slave' tonight, and I'll be your 'Alpha Jerk.'"

Her brow rose teasingly. "You know you'll be breaking hearts left and right, if you keep me fastened to your side."

"Or I could be making two hearts very happy."

The words lay between them for a moment, neither one of them willing to ruin the mood by talking.

"Can you believe this shit?"

Startled, Tomás and Billie turned to face the stranger who had abruptly broken into their conversation. One second they were semi-alone in the dining room; the next thing Tomás knew, a large blond guy was peering at them.

He wasn't large as in weight-wise, but in height and body mass-wise. He was a Viking-looking giant. Too pale for the beaches, yet too blond to come from a bottle. There was a childlike quality about his face, but it was the only childlike thing about him. Especially his language.

His large arms extended out as he shook his head in disgust. "This is some fucked-up shit right here."

"What?" Billie asked, standing a little too close to the crazed man for Tomás's peace of mind.

"This whole bunk-ass party. 'Fuck Cupid.' That's just fucked up."

"You mind watching your language, son? There's a lady present."

Billie shot him an amused looked before mouthing, "Lady," to him. Tomás ignored her amusement. She *was* a lady, and he wasn't going to put up with anyone talking rudely in front of her.

"Oh, I'm sorry, where are my manners?" Beefy boy shoved his large hand at Billie. "Name's Eros."

"Billie, and my overprotective friend is…"

"Tomás, yeah I know." Quickly releasing Billie's hand, he grabbed Tomás's in a bone-crunching grip. "Sorry about earlier, but you can see how this party might throw a man off."

"I guess," Tomás agreed, reaching out and snagging Billie's arm, bringing her closer to him. Tomás didn't know how this Eros guy knew his name, and he didn't care. All he knew was he didn't want him touching Billie again. Big or not, Tomás would take him to the ground.

"I mean, how insulting is this?" Eros pulled out the invitation, waving the sodomized cupid in the air like a flag. "It's sacrilegious."

"Technically, Cupid isn't a deity, in the essence of worshipping. So I don't think it's sacrilegious. Just in very poor taste."

"The poorest," he growled. "When I get my hands on Jenna…"

"Do you know her?" Tomás interrupted. This was all so David Lynch. None of it made any sense. Especially the anger Eros was expressing.

"Know her? There are days when she is the *only* person I know. And the one night of the year when I have to work, she has a pity party. But dammit, this year she's taking it too far. They're all laughing at me."

"Someone's laughing at you?" The awe in Billie's voice echoed inside of Tomás's head. Stepping slightly in front of her, he positioned himself to protect her in case Eros got violent.

"They won't be for long. I'll show her." Turning, the beefy man made to exit the room, but stopped and turned back around to face them. "But I knew I was right about you two. Looking good."

With that parting comment, he was gone, leaving as quickly as he had entered.

Tomás kept her at his back until the guy stormed from the room. He didn't know who he was, or what he was, but Tomás wasn't letting him within an inch of Billie. "Do you know him?"

"He seemed familiar to me."

"Like he might work with us?"

"No, I think I would remember that." Billie clasped her arms around herself as if warding off a chill. "Let's get out of here."

"Good idea." Tomás placed his hand on her lower back and led her from the room to the porch.

The bass of the music could be heard from behind the closed door. Billie strolled over to the fence of the deck then turned so she was leaning back against it. Following out behind her, Tomás stopped in front of her and looked down into her upturned face. The cool night air simmered around them, not so cold that they needed to go in, but not too warm either.

Slipping his hand between them, he traced the heart pinned to her chest. Slowly allowing his finger to graze against the abundance of her breasts, he looked deeply into her eyes, "I think I'm growing attached to this badge."

"Then you should wear it."

"Oh, no, Holiday." He smiled. Although he was done tracing the heart, he kept his fingers resting on her breast. "It looks so much better on you."

"I disagree; I have an image of you wearing it, and not much else. I have to tell you, it's so working for me."

"I'm up for a little role playing." Leaning forward, he placed one hand on either side of her body, trapping Billie within his embrace.

"I don't want to play, Tomás. Unless we're playing for keeps."

"We are of like minds." Tomás couldn't resist brushing his hand against her cheek.

"What do you want?" Her whispered words stimulated him.

"I just want you."

Chapter Three

So maybe the party wasn't that bad, after all. It wasn't every day that a girl's dream man professed he wanted her. For Billie, it was a first. So new, in fact, that it left her speechless.

In the wake of her silence at his comment, Tomás brushed his thumb against her bottom lip. "Cat got your tongue?"

His touch, though fleeting, caused a chain reaction to go off in her body. Her hands were sweaty, her nerves were wracked. Billie's heart began to beat a tattoo so loudly she thought it might overpower the subdued beat blaring behind the closed door. Her pleasure felt juvenile to her. All of this because she was standing close to Tomás.

In an action telling of her nervousness, Billie moistened her lips again, as she tried to think of what to say. "Fuck me, you big Latin stud," came to mind, but thankfully, the words froze on her lips.

She was bold but not psychotic.

Tomás, on the other hand, didn't seem to be suffering from the same nervous dilemma. Stationed over her, he peered down into her eyes, as if trying to see into her soul. His gaze was probing. His body, large and looming, made her feel delicate in comparison, and he smelled damn good.

How the hell was she supposed to think when she could hardly breathe?

"I don't think I've ever seen you this quiet before, Holiday."

"We've never been this close before," she countered, feeling even more foolish for her sudden shyness. What the hell was wrong with her? He was just a guy. A really good-looking, great smelling, nipple-hardening, panty-dampening guy, but a guy, nevertheless.

"Not from lack of desire on my part."

"What do you expect me to say when you say things like that?"

"That you want me too."

Billie laughed softly. "Do you really need me to tell you that?"

"Need? No," he replied with a quiet laugh of his own. "But it would be nice."

"What happens when I say that?"

"I take you in my arms and never let you go."

Her stomach dropped to her feet. *Was he for real?*

Men didn't really talk like that. Not in real life. There was probably a reason for it. There were only so many condoms Trojan could make in a year. His simple words had her salivating like a rabid dog, primed to jump him at his command. Either she was incredibly horny, or he was damn good.

Maybe it was a wicked combination of the two. "You're working awfully hard to get me into your bed."

"I don't just want you in my bed, Billie." He used her first name, something he hardly ever did. "If I thought sex could purge you from my soul and mind, I would have moved quickly to make love to you. But it's just not sexual desire between us, is it?"

"I don't know." Her voice was husky with desire. "The desire is pretty potent. At least on my part."

Tomás chuckled harshly. "It's not just on your part. But there's more, isn't there, *querida?*"

Billie wasn't quit sure what *querida* meant, but she liked the way it sounded. "Much more."

She couldn't lie to herself any more than she could lie to him. He was right. If it was just a sexual attraction, they could have easily taken care of it at any time. They were both consenting adults who didn't need to fool themselves or each other with talk of a future just to bed one another. Yet here they were.

"I want you, Billie, but it won't be just for tonight."

Was that supposed to sound like a threat? Because it sounded damn good to her. "You move awfully fast."

"Seven months is fast to you?"

"It is when this is the first time you've spoken of it."

"I had to wait until you would let me in."

"You're not in yet," she teased.

The sensual smile that she loved so much spread across his face. "Yet?"

"You know you're getting some." Reaching out, Billie slid her hands up his chest, loving the feel of his muscular torso under her fingers. The slick cotton added to the pleasure, and she imagined how nice his shirt would look on her bedroom floor.

Tomás's breathing deepened under her wandering hands, but he never made a move to touch her. Simply allowed her to go at her own speed, familiarizing herself with his body.

Not wanting to go into forbidden territory, Billie kept her hands above his belt buckle, although she did drift by occasionally to run her finger over the leather.

"You're a lot a bigger than I thought you would be." The second she said the words, Billie wished she could have recalled them.

Even Tomás, who had been on his best behavior, burst out laughing at her comment. "Trust me, *querida*, you haven't seen anything yet."

With his dare thrown down between them like a gauntlet, Billie wrapped her arms around his neck and leaned into him. "Show me, Tomás. Show me everything you have to offer."

Tomás moved quickly, scooping her up into his embrace. "I warned you before this won't be for just one night."

"That's what I'm counting on."

They pressed even closer to one another. Eyes slightly parted, lips moist and ready. Then just when Billie tilted her head up to receive the kiss she'd been dying to have, the back door flew open, startling them into jerking apart.

Tomás set her down and away from him as Holly, another co-worker, burst out of the house, her eyes wide with shock. "We have to call the police."

Tomás stepped towards her with his hand extended. "What's going on?"

"The phones in the house aren't working. Actually, hardly any of the electrical devices are working. There's like a big surge of energy screwing with everything."

"A surge?" Billie questioned, confused. What had they missed?

"Yes. Jenna and this huge guy, who I think is her ex-boyfriend or something, are screaming the house down." Looking between the two of them curiously, she added, "I'm surprised that you two haven't heard anything."

"We were having a party of our own." Tomás reached into his pants' pocket to retrieve his cell phone. "Let me see if I can get a signal."

"Do you think she's in danger?" Billie looked into the open doorway with a concerned expression on her face.

"It's hard to tell. I mean, he's mad, but I don't think he'll hurt her."

"Damn," Tomás muttered, slamming his phone closed. "I've got nothing."

A loud crash broke their conversation up; all three of them raced back into the kitchen to see what was going on.

* * *

Eros was there and as angry as ever, yet his towering frame and menacing fury didn't seem to faze Jenna at all.

Hands on her hips, toe to toe, she was giving just as much as she was taking in the argument. Tomás couldn't tell exactly who was winning, or why.

"As if the stupid nooses weren't bad enough, did you really have to sodomize my baby picture on your disgusting invitations?"

Jenna gasped in outrage. "They're not disgusting. They're humorous."

"To pedophiles and really fucked-up people."

"Your mother helped me make them." She had a smug look on her face as she dropped that little tidbit.

Her cool words stopped the raging man short. Startled, he stepped back as if dodging a blow. "My mother! You brought my mother into this?"

Red blotches marred the mask of anger Eros's face had taken on, but it only seemed to spur Jenna on further. An evil gleam appeared in her sparkling eyes as she said with a smirk, "The themed party was her idea."

With a thunderous yell, Eros tossed his hands up in the air, defeated. "You're trying to drive me crazy."

The air between them crackled like lightning. Not just figuratively, but literally. Or at least Tomás thought it did. Maybe Jenna had spiked his drink after all, because to him it seemed like the room vibrated with color. It was the weirdest thing Tomás had ever seen, and he officially went from trying to be a quiet observer to being full out nosy.

Who the hell was this guy, and what the hell was going on?

"Psst...move...scoot over." Nudging him with her shoulder, Billie pushed her way past the other observing partygoers, and leaned in against Tomás. "What's going on?"

"I have no idea," he whispered back, although a whisper wasn't necessary. No one in the room was remotely trying to pretend the party was going on anymore.

The music had died down. So did the chatter. All eyes were focused on the drama being carried out front and center. The small room was packed full with everyone staring at the arguing duo.

"You're demented!" Eros roared. His anger was so tangible it was almost hard to watch.

"I married you, didn't I?"

Married? Tomás looked down at Billie, who was staring up at him with an openmouthed expression of shock. Apparently, he wasn't the only person who hadn't known that.

"This has got to stop." Cheeks red with rage, Eros stomped over to the table where a few heart name badges remained. Everyone in his path backed up as the fuming man glared down at the table. With a guttural cruse, Eros swept his hand across the counter, grabbing the remaining hearts in his grasp. "What's with the stupid name badges, Psyche?"

"My name isn't Psyche anymore. I left that name when I thought I left you." Storming over to him, Jenna snatched the crumpled hearts from his hand. "And it's not stupid. See, this is our problem Eros, this right here. You think everything I do is stupid. You don't support me. You ruin everything."

"I'm not the one throwing an Anti-Valentine's Day Party, defiling the only day of love for people. *You* are."

"What do you know about love? It's not all fairy tales and happy endings. Love," with her hand on her hip, Jenna edged closer to the irate man, "hurts. It turns people into sniveling, crying, possessive binge-eaters. For once, I wish you would come down off your gold lamé pedestal so you could get a firsthand visual of what love does to people."

This was getting ugly fast. There was no way in hell Tomás wanted to be anywhere near the party when the cops came.

"Billie," he whispered from the side of his mouth, grasping her hand in his. "I think it's time we left."

Eyes wide, she nodded. "You ain't never lied."

They hadn't even gotten a step away before Eros spoke again. "Is that what you want, Psyche?"

"Yes, it is."

"Wish granted, my love." Out the corner of his eye, Tomás saw Eros reach under the back of his shirt and pull out a weapon.

"He's got a gun!" someone yelled from across the room, as everyone hit the floor.

Fearing for Billie's safety, Tomás pulled her to the floor, covering her body with his own. But it wasn't a gun Eros was brandishing. It was a golden bow with an arrow.

What the fuck!

"Put that down Eros, now!" Jenna demanded, sounding more peeved than worried.

"Your name badges. Your version of my love. Your friends. Have a happy Valentine's Day."

The arrow whizzing by was almost drowned out by the screams of terror filling the room. By the time the arrow landed across the room into the wall, Eros had vanished.

Jenna stomped her foot in frustration. "Get back here now!"

Pushing up from Billie's trembling body, Tomás looked around the room in shock.

Get back here, where did he go?

People just didn't disappear from crowded rooms into thin air. They also normally didn't carry gold-plated archery weapons, either, but that was neither here nor there.

This was the strangest party he'd ever gone to.

The screams silenced almost as quickly as Eros had disappeared, and the room took on an eerie silence.

"See, this is why I left you." Jenna dropped the hearts to the ground and stomped out of the room as Tomás looked on, bewildered.

What the fuck was she into?

"We're leaving now!" he ordered, pulling away from Billie. To his surprise, instead of letting him get up, Billie grabbed hold of his arm and held him on top of her.

"There's no need to leave just yet."

Startled, Tomás looked down into her face, and the look of lust in her eyes nearly took his breath away. "Billie, what's wrong with you?"

"Nothing," Leaning up on her elbows, she smiled seductively at him. "In fact, I've never felt better. Make love to me, Tomás."

Chapter Four

The second the words left her mouth, Billie jerked back in shock. Did she really just stay that? From the dumbfounded look on Tomás's face, the answer was more than obvious.

"Billie..."

"Oh, my God," Billie's mouth was agape in horror. "Did I just ask you to..."

Tomás cleared his throat roughly, "To make love to you, yeah."

"I didn't mean it."

"You didn't mean it?"

Did she? "Let me up."

"I would but..." Tomás looked down pointedly at her hands, which were still grasping his arms.

"Oh." Heat filled her cheeks as she followed his gaze, but she didn't let go. She couldn't. Not before she tasted every inch of his skin.

Billie's mouth watered with the desire to lick him, nibble at his flesh until every inch of his body was covered with the imprint of her teeth. She wanted to roll him under her and stretch her tingling body over his.

"Billie, don't." Her fingers were digging into the taut flesh of his arm and the hoarse sound of Tomás's voice brought her eyes back to his.

At least he could talk. Her mouth felt drier than the Sahara, but it was the only part of her body that was dry. Her skin was damp with perspiration, and her vagina was wet with need.

"What's wrong, baby?"

"I have no idea." With an inner strength Billie didn't know she possessed, she forced her hands to release their grip on Tomás's arm, and lay back on the floor. But the minute she stopped touching him was the instant her body began to ache. "Something's wrong, Tomás."

"What's wrong?" With eyes clouded over with worry, Tomás peered down at her. Leaning towards her, he ran his hand over her damp brow. "*Mierda*, you're burning up."

"Tell me about it." Licking her lips, Billie let out a dry chuckle. She was on fire, and it wasn't just on the outside. Pushing her head into his hand, she whimpered at the feel of his touch on her heated flesh. "I need…"

"What do you need?"

"I need you." Moving quickly, Billie wrapped her hands around his neck and brought his face down next to hers, but just before their lips touched, a loud shriek came from the corner of the room.

"Why doesn't he love me?" a woman cried as she ran from the room.

The wail was a like a dose of cold water on her heated flesh. Billie released her hold on Tomás and pushed him away as she sat up.

Un-fucking-believable.

The room had erupted into an emotional pity party. It was like a scene out of the worse chick flick ever. There was someone sitting Indian style on the buffet table stuffing her mouth as tears streamed down her cheeks. Another woman was yelling into her cell phone as two men shoved into each other, fists raised.

As they looked around the room, a man walked over to them and touched Billie on her shoulder. "What's going on here?"

But before Billie could reply, Tomás grabbed the guy by his shirt collar and tossed him into the wall. "Don't touch her. Don't you ever touch her!"

Gasping, Billie grabbed at his arms. "Tomás, let him go."

"What's the deal, man?" Eyes bulging, the man dug at Tomás ' hands, his face going red from exertion.

"The deal is she's mine."

"Tomás!" Billie had never seen anyone so upset before. Tomás'sface was set into cold lines of fury, his dark eyes were piercing, his skin flushed with anger.

It was like looking at a monster. Someone she didn't know. He had turned so fast...almost as fast as she had turned into a horny leg-humper.

What the hell was going on here?

"Tomás, let him go," she ordered again, this time keeping her voice level and cool. Billie didn't want him to redirect his anger in her direction; she just wanted him to let the man free so they could figure out what was going on. "Tomás."

"He shouldn't have touched you."

"No, he shouldn't, but now the big bad man knows that." Easing her way into his line of sight, Billie cupped his cheeks in her hands, and forcefully turned his blazing eyes in her direction. "He's not touching me now. No one is."

Her words seemed to cap the fuse that had imploded inside of him. But unfortunately for her, it also relit the fire inside of her. Billie's pulse sped up, and her nipples hardened, all from a single touch.

Tomás's fingers unclenched from the stranger's neck, forcing him to quickly crumple down the wall and gasp for breath.

"Get out of here," Tomás warned, taking a step back from the wheezing puddle of flesh.

Warily, Billie leaned against the wall the man had just vacated, trying her best to avoid Tomás's touch. "I'm sure once he can breathe again he will."

"Come here?"

Billie raised a brow at his tone. "I think it's best that I stay right where I am."

"Now, Billie," he snarled, stepping over the man, who had yet to get up from the floor. "Don't make me tell you twice."

"Listen, caveman, I know some women get off on..." The second the words left her mouth, inspiration dawned inside of her bright and clear. "Oh, my God, Tomás. You're acting like a caveman."

"I heard you the first time," he growled, stepping towards her menacingly. His domineering glare had her quivering and aching in all the right places. Billie's nipples tingled in awareness, and her mound ached to be filled.

Shaking her head, Billie forced her mind to focus on the problem at hand and not her expanding libido.

"No, listen. You're acting like a caveman and I'm acting like a sex-starved nymph. Is any of this ringing a bell?"

Tomás came closer to her, placing his hand on the side of the wall, sealing her in. "No one touches you."

"Got your words, alpha...jerk." Billie accented the two words with a well-placed poke on the heart badge, which bore the same expression.

Instantly Tomás's eyes cleared and he stepped away, much to Billie's lustful dismay. Being near him, smelling him, feeling him, had her creaming and desperate to knock him to the ground and fuck him until he needed hip replacement surgery.

"You think that's what's going on?"

"Let's see, I went from teasing you for a kiss, to humping your leg and begging you to make love to me, and you went from cool and collected to completely irate the second another man touched me. I think it's more than a coincidence."

"Fuck." Dashing his hand through his hair in frustration, Tomás muttered under his breath as he stepped further away from her.

Billie eyed him warily, glad to see him getting himself back under control. Not as if it really mattered though, because the longer she looked at him, the hornier she became. He was pissed off. She was salivating. What a twisted pair they made.

Shaking his head in irritation, Tomás tossed his hand out towards the few people still lingering about. "Look at everyone."

Jenna's house was completely messed up now. Windows broken, chairs smashed, holes in walls, a few holes with actually heads still stuck inside of them. There were women crying and scarfing down food, people fighting, and even a few people having sex.

It was amazing and frightening all at the same time. Billie didn't know what she wanted to do more -- stay and watch, or figure where the hell Jenna and Eros...

"Wait a minute." Damn, she felt like an idiot. "His name is Eros..."

"Yeah."

"You know who that is, right?" It couldn't be, but then again, it was the only thing that made sense.

"Jenna's magician ex-husband."

"He's not a magician." Billie couldn't believe she was about to say this. "He's a god."

Okay, whatever was affecting the rest of the group had officially made Billie go mad. Speaking of mad, a groan caught his attention as the man between them finally began to crawl away. Just the sight of him filled Tomás with rage.

"Try to pay attention, Tomás." Billie snapped her finger in front of his face, bringing his attention back to her.

"To what?" he growled, angry to have the focus of his wrath creeping away. Tomás wanted to kill him for even looking at her. Moving closer to Billie, he watched the room with narrowed eyes, daring anyone else to come near her. If one more person even looked in her direction, he was going to…

"Come on, we have to talk to Jenna."

"And say what?" With a concentrated effort, Tomás zeroed in on what Billie was saying, and amazingly, his anger began to subside.

It was the weirdest thing. One moment he wanted to do as much damage as possible to a man he didn't know, just because he had touched Billie, and the next second, he felt completely calm, like his old self.

Pausing, Billie turned back to him with a peculiar look on her face. "What do you know about Greek mythology?"

Tomás snorted. "Dick."

"Then this is going to sound really strange to you."

"Billie, a guy just shot an arrow into the middle of the room and disappeared." Tomás could barely say that aloud with a straight look on his face. "We're surrounded by people doing really weird things, ourselves included. I think it's pretty safe to say whatever you're thinking can't be any odder than what's going on."

"IthinkErosisCupid." She said it so fast the words collided into one another.

Was she kidding? "Cupid...like, Cupid Cupid?"

With a firm nod of her head, Billie repeated, "Cupid Cupid."

Good Lord, she wasn't kidding. "Okay, I was wrong, that is strange."

"Tomás, you said it yourself. Eros disappeared in the midst of a crowded room. We've all morphed into the very essences of our name badges. You've become the aggressive date from hell, and I'm acting like the horniest woman on earth. I think we've entered the land of the strange."

"Horniest?" Now that was something he wanted to hear more about. "What do you mean?"

Billie lowered her voice as she stepped closer to him. "I mean I want to unzip your pants with my teeth and take your cock deep within my mouth until you come, screaming my name."

Damn. Tomás went from confused to aroused, faster than the speed of light. But Billie wasn't quite done yet.

"Right now, I feel strung tighter than a bow, and if I touch you, if I even think of you touching me, I might go insane. But then again, if we don't touch, the same thing might happen."

"And that's..." Clearing his throat, Tomás tried again, "That's not normal for you?"

"Wanting you is," Billie said with a faint smile. "But being willing to do you now, in front of a room full of strangers, isn't."

"You can't just say something like that and expect me to be able to walk upright. Or breathe, for that matter."

"I would have never figured you as one for dirty talk."

"I would have never figured you could pull my zipper down with your teeth."

"Help me get to the bottom of all this name badge voodoo and I'll show you." With a teasing grin, Billie headed back down the hall, leaving Tomás staring after her.

It took him a second to get back into focus, and when he did, his mind jumped on the one thing that made the least amount of sense. Entering the den behind Billie, Tomás felt compelled to remind her, "Mythology isn't real."

"Oh, it's real, all right."

"Shit." Turning around quickly, Tomás stared at Jenna, who was sitting in a chaise lounge in the corner.

She was curled up in the chair, sipping a martini, looking as calm as could be. Jenna's causal demeanor only furthered Tomás's irritation at the situation. There were people mutilating themselves in the other room, and she was taking time out for a cocktail. "What the hell did you do?"

"Me?" Jenna had the nerve to look offended. "I'm the victim here."

"Funny, you don't seem to be as affected as, say, your guests."

"You're a man, you wouldn't understand."

"Then make me understand." Billie's voice sounded a lot calmer than Tomás would have thought she'd be. "Who are you, and how did Cupid do that? He is Cupid, right?"

Jenna waved her hand in the air as if to dismiss what Billie was saying. "That's just one of his many names. I personally prefer 'asshole.'"

"But he is Cupid?"

"He's not Cupid. Cupid isn't real," Tomás reiterated.

"He's real, all right, and a big baby." Looking up at the ceiling, Jenna yelled, "Did you hear me? You're a big baby! By the way, I'm not sorry I sodomized your picture."

"Jenna," Billie called loudly, turning the angry blonde's eyes back to them. "That's not helping."

Helping! Was he the only person who hadn't lost his grip on sanity? "Billie, he's not Cupid."

"What do you know, mortal?" Jenna's cheeks were flushed with anger, or too much alcohol -- Tomás couldn't tell the difference.

"I know you're insane." It was the one thing he was sure of.

"You're not helping," Billie hissed, grabbing his arm. That was a big mistake. The second she touched him, her control broke and she plastered herself against him. Passion flared in her eyes as she grasped him to her, rubbing her body against him like a cat in heat. "Make love to me, Tomás."

Fuck. This *so* wasn't normal.

Billie's hand cupped his straining erection through his slacks, seconds before her warm mouth brushed against his neck. Cursing, Tomás gripped her roaming hand in his and pushed her away.

He was going to kill Eros...Cupid...whatever his name was.

"Jenna, bring him back now!"

"Don't you think I would if I could?"

"I don't know anything. Fifteen minutes ago I thought your husband was a fairy tale."

Jenna smirked knowingly. "Imagine what you'll know in another fifteen."

"Tomás..." Billie begged, trying to pull him to her.

"Billie, snap out of it."

"Good luck," Jenna toasted him with her glass. "Cupid may be annoying but his spells always work."

"I can tell they work." Firmly grasping Billie's hands in his, Tomás moved her to a chair and stepped out of her reach. The sooner they weren't touching, the better it would be for the both of them. "The question is for how long."

"Until he wants them to come to an end." Jenna shrugged her shoulders nonchalantly.

"Fuck," Billie murmured as she crossed her arms over her chest. She looked like she might break at any moment, but at least her eyes were lucid again. "What are we going to do?"

Sighing, Jenna stood up. "I'll try to get him back here, but I'm not going to make any promises."

"And in the meantime?" Tomás asked, eyeing Billie hungrily. She returned his look with one of her own, and he knew they wouldn't last another hour, let alone the whole night, without giving in to temptation.

"Give in to it, until he comes around. The harder you fight it, the worse it will be."

For some reason, Tomás had known she was going to say that.

Chapter Five

After their less than forthcoming conversation with Jenna, Billie and Tomás decided to leave the doomed party. It didn't make any sense to hang around. Who knew how long it would take Cu…Eros and Jenna to work out their little drama. Billie wasn't going to stick around and find out, that was for sure.

She also couldn't get the four little words Jenna had said to her out of her head.

Give in to it.

The words reverberated in her mind. It wasn't just the words, or the way Jenna had said them; it was the simple fact that Billie agreed. She wanted to give in to temptation, and the best part about it was she wouldn't have to hold herself accountable for her actions later.

Cowardly yes, but honest too.

She could be as lewd, as wanton, as down and dirty as she wanted, and tomorrow they could chalk it up to a love spell. The thought brought a quick smile to her face.

Unfortunately, Tomás didn't seem to be in as good as mood as she was. He was acting like he was the one walking around with the soaked underwear.

"My car is down here." Tomás gestured down the lane, speaking for the first time since they had left the party.

"I brought my own car, Tomás; you don't have to drive me home." Not that he looked like he wanted to anyway. Cupid's little spell had ruined whatever chance they had of hooking up tonight.

Fucking arrow-wielding busybody.

"The hell I don't," he growled. "Just my luck, you'll get pulled over by a cop, he'll accidentally touch you, and you'll attack him."

"I don't think it works with just anyone." There were other men at the party, including the one who had touched her, and Billie hadn't felt a fraction of lust for them. Her body knew exactly whose slave she wanted to be.

"Let's not test that theory." He had a point. Even if he was acting pissy.

Billie held back her smart retort and followed Tomás to his car. He was very careful not to touch her as they walked. Too careful. There was practically an ocean of space between them and it was driving her insane.

The reason behind their distance made sense, but Billie just couldn't get it through her thick skull that they shouldn't be touching. Especially since everything inside of her was crying out for them to do just that.

He was still silent by the time they approached his car, much to Billie's annoyance. Enough was enough, already. "Is this possessiveness thing your name badge or just your hidden personality?"

Tomás snorted in lieu of a comment as he opened the passenger door for her.

"Well." Billie wasn't going to budge until he answered her question. Alpha jerk she might be able to handle, but a flat-out possessive asshole wasn't something she was even going to try to understand.

Frowning, Tomás looked away, his checks flushed. "A combination."

"Goodie." Billie rolled her eyes as she sat down. This evening was just going to get better and better.

By the time Tomás got into the car and she had given him directions to her house, another thought slipped inside of her already overworked mind. "Do you think he'll be back tonight?"

Tomás snorted as they pulled away from the curb. "Even if he is, do you think he'll be a lot of help?"

Billie shuddered at the thought of Cupid not helping. "I hope so. He is Cupid, right? A doer of good. And this would do us a world of good."

"So anxious to be away from me." Possessive Gene Number One kicking in.

"No," she said with a sigh. "I just want to know how long it's going to last. I need to know if it's only you it will work on. I mean, if I go into the grocery store, could I touch the checkout boy without having to take him in the produce department, where they have all of those long useable fruit and vegetables?"

Tomás chuckled. Finally! "Usable vegetables?"

"I have a *very* active imagination."

When they pulled up to a red light, Tomás glanced at her with a shit-eating grin. "Really?"

Happy to have him smiling again, Billie winked suggestively. "You have no idea."

They stared at each other for several long seconds, only breaking eye contact when the car behind them honked.

Tomás shook his head as they went under the light. "This is insane."

He wasn't wrong about that, but that was neither here nor there. "You're acting as if you're still in doubt that he's Cupid."

"You're acting as if this is the most normal thing in the world." His knuckles paled under the strain of his grip on the steering wheel.

Billie shrugged her shoulders with a smile. He was right. She felt completely peaceful. "Maybe it's part of the spell, but things do make a bit of sense now."

"Sense left town a long time ago. I mean, we're talking Cupid and love spells for Christ's sake," he argued, cursing under his breath.

Tired of pussyfooting around the issue, Billie blurted out, "I think we should just take Jenna's advice and give in."

"Give in!" The surprise in his voice was downright amusing.

"Can you think of a reason not to?"

"Several. The main one being that, I don't want to make love with you when you're all roofied up."

"Then don't. Fuck me instead." At his sharp intake of breath, Billie turned in her seat until she faced him. "Tomás, is there any doubt in your mind that I want you? Think back to where we were before the whole Cupid episode started."

"If you regret this…"

"I won't."

"But…"

This was crazy; Billie had never had to beg a man to make love to her in her life. Part of her understood what he was saying, and she respected it, but another part, the horny, going out of her mind part, just wanted him to push his seat back so she could straddle him and ride him into unconsciousness. "Where did the alpha jerk go?"

Tomás glanced her way, a wry grin splitting his solemn face. "Alpha jerk doesn't mean insensitive date rapist."

"You can't rape the willing."

"Are you?"

"Why don't you find out for yourself?" Billie unbuckled her seatbelt and reached over the console, bringing his hand to her lap. The second she touched him, her desire kicked into overdrive, but she held out, wanting Tomás to know that it was her, and not Cupid's spell that made her want him.

Parting her legs, she moved his hand up her knee to her thigh and back down again, this time slipping his fingers under her skirt. Air rushed out of his lungs as his fingers grazed against the damp cloth covering her moist center.

"Cupid can make my mouth say I want you, but he can't make my body quiver. Only you can, and you've been doing it for months, long before we knew there was a Cupid. Long before tonight."

* * *

It was hard for Tomás to remember what the right thing was to do when he was a hair's breadth away from being fingers-deep inside her sweet pussy. His over-worked conscience was going toe to toe with his cock. His cock was winning.

Common sense told him to pull his hand free from her tight grip so he could drive them somewhere secluded, but Billie's moan of pleasure overruled all protests made from his brain. He had to touch her, even if it was for only a few seconds.

"Does it feel like I'm unsure about us...about this?" Her words were choppy, stunted by her quickened breath. Billie moaned as she turned more towards him, her legs spreading as wide as the console and the door would allow.

Just as her passion seemed to flare the moment he touched her, so did his controlling side. She was wet, and begging for him, just the way he liked it. Tomás wanted Billie. He had for as long as he'd known her.

"I won't let this be just a quick finger-fuck and we're through." His voice was rough with passion and need.

"I want more than your hand."

"But for now it will do, right?" The devil inside of Thomas made him ask as he turned his hand around so that he was cupping her sex.

"God...yes..." Groaning, she gripped Tomás's hand in her own, pressing it more firmly between her legs. The heat radiating from behind the slip of clothing had him biting back a groan of his own.

Fuck being noble. He had to have a taste of her now.

Tomás's fingers slipped past the dampness of her panties, into the warmth beckoning from within. His cock, hard and aching, pressed against his straining fly, begging to take the place of his fingers. "Tell me you want me to fuck you. I don't want there to be any confusion later."

"It's what I've been telling you all along."

Tomás pressed his fingers deeper into her moist opening as her juices flowed around his hand. "That's not what I told you to say."

"I want you to fuck me!"

"Much better."

"Good." Billie moaned, turning slightly towards him. "Now don't stop."

"Greedy." Her sweet, spicy scent began to fill the warm car the more he delved between her supple thighs. The warm air heated her scent until Tomás could not only smell it, but virtually taste it. His mouth watered with the desire to sample her delights firsthand, but that was something he wanted to do once they were in her home. Tomás needed room to maneuver and act out every depraved fantasy they had.

Shit, he had to be closer.

One of her feet was up against the dashboard while her opposite thigh was pressed firmly into the console. The little room they had to maneuver in was being hindered by her underwear, damp and in the way.

"Fuck this," Tomás muttered. Moving his hand from under the cotton restraint, he gripped the soft material in his hand and ripped with all of his might.

The sound of the material ripping drew both of their hungry gazes to one another, but it also drew Billie's hand down between her legs, where she teased her clit while watching him intently.

A horn blaring from behind him, forced Thomas's eyes back on the road, but he could see her pleasuring herself from his peripheral vision.

Damn it, he was going to kill them both if he didn't concentrate, but he couldn't stop glancing her way. The little vixen looked close to her release, but there was no way in hell he was going to let her get off by herself. If anyone made her come, it was going to be him.

Dropping the ripped material onto the floor, Tomás reached over to her and lightly smacked her hand out of the way. "Mine."

"Yours," she whispered back, pulling her hands away, choosing to cup her breasts instead. The twin dark beauties plumped up through the V-cut of her dress, another temptation he would have to wait to indulge in.

"That's right." Slipping his hand back up her thigh, he returned his fingers to their newfound home and caressed her feverish flesh.

His gaze was as intent on the road as her moans of pleasure could allow. It took every ounce of willpower

Tomás possessed to keep them on the road and driving in the direction of her home.

There were many side streets and dark pathways that beckoned him, urging him to pull over so they could make love. But he was so hell-bent on their first time being inside an actual house that he fought the need coursing through his body. At this point a bed wasn't even a necessity, just four walls and a ceiling.

"Yes...Tomás...yes..." she chanted, as her body quivered under his touch.

With a tight grip on the "oh, shit" handle, Billie bore down on his hand, grinding harder and faster onto him. Her breathing sped up to soft little gasps as he pressed down firmly with his palm, manipulating her clit as he pumped his fingers into her welcoming channel.

The car filled with her cries of pleasure as she found her release, her lips murmuring his name like a pagan chant. Unable to help himself any longer, Tomás brought his moist fingers up to his mouth, partaking in his first taste of Billie. Her flavor was a little shy of the most exquisite pleasure in the world. His tongue bathed his fingers, drinking in every drop of her sweet taste.

Saying a silent prayer of gratitude, Tomás pulled up onto her street and parked in front of the address she had given him. Cutting off the engine, he quickly unbuckled his seatbelt and leaned over the console, taking Billie's waiting mouth with his.

He shared the tangy flavor of her essence with her as he slipped his tongue between her lips and into her welcoming mouth. They drank from each other as they moved to get closer, prohibited only by their environment.

The windows began to fog as things between them heated up. Tomás couldn't remember the last time he had made out in a car, but he was sure it hadn't been as frustrating. Especially in the wake of her glorious orgasm.

All he wanted was to be buried balls-deep inside of her. His cock ached to fill her body, to posses her. And heavy petting in the front seat just wasn't going to cut it.

Fortunately for him, Billie seemed to feel the same way.

Billie pulled away from him, her eyes dazed with lust. "Inside, now."

Sweeter words had never been spoken. "Oh, yes."

With narrowed eyes, Billie grasped his shirt and pulled him even closer to her, "And if you try to chalk up our attraction to Cupid again…"

Tomás silenced her with a quick kiss before pulling away. There were no longer any barriers standing in his way. He knew what he wanted and he knew that she wanted him. "Cupid…Cupid who?"

Chapter Six

The passion hadn't cooled on the short walk up the sidewalk to her apartment. More than likely because of the way Billie could feel Tomás's eyes devour her as she walked ahead of him. It was obscene how his simple stare, and the deep, satisfying sounds of his tongue slipping out to caress his lips, as if savoring the last remaining drops of her dew, made her feel.

And she had plenty of dewdrops left for him to savor.

Billie couldn't remember the last time she had ever been this turned on. They weren't touching, so she knew it wasn't Cupid's spell; more than likely the spell that Tomás had bewitched her with from the moment they had met.

Taking her keys out, Billie dangled them in front of the lock. "Once this key goes in, all bets are off."

Tomás arched his brow teasingly. "Are you warning me or tempting me?"

"A little of both." Billie licked her lips, not suggestively, but more born out of anticipation. Finally she'd have him right where she wanted him, naked, hard, and hers.

As she inserted the key into the lock, she looked over her shoulder at Tomás and smiled. "Ready to play?"

Tomás moved up behind her, quickly capturing her hand under his, turning the lock at the same time she did. His show of unity proved that not only was he wanting her as desperately as she wanted him, but that they were in it together. "Do you really have to ask?"

When the door flew back, key still stuck in the lock, Billie pulled him into the house by his shirt. "One rule, Tomás."

He peered down at her with a devilish grin and eyes filled with desire. "What?"

"There are no rules." She released his shirt and stepped back, daring him to contradict her.

But he didn't. Instead, his eyes went wild momentarily as he burst into laughter. "Now those are my kind of rules."

Still chuckling, Tomás pulled the keys out of the door before slamming it shut and locking it behind him. Billie watched him all the while, like a lion watches its prey. The moment he turned back around, she pounced.

"Hey." He chuckled, falling back into the door. "Slow down."

"Oh, I don't think so." A wicked little smile spread out across her face as she took a step away from him. When she was sure she had his full attention, Billie looked him in the eye and dropped her gaze slowly until it was centered on the bulge in his pants. "In fact, I think there are a few things I need to see. Now."

The word "Billie" was barely out of Tomás's mouth, before she had dropped to her knees before him. All the while she unbuckled his pants, she kept her gaze locked on his. She wanted Tomás to see, not only feel, every second of this. "You had your taste of me. Now I want to taste you."

Leaning back against the door, Tomás pressed his hands flat against the wood. "Well, who am I to tell a pretty lady no?"

"Exactly." The word slid out the same instant his zipper parted, bringing his prized possession springing forth into her waiting hands. "Ohhh…"

"Is that a bad 'ohhh' or a good 'ohhh'?"

His penis was long, large, and thick; three qualities she admired most in a penis. Brushing her fingers against his ridged length, only a few shades lighter than her own darker skin, Billie couldn't help but study the wonder of creation. So many beautiful shades, so many beautiful colors, some similar, some not, but all beautiful.

"Definitely a good 'ohhh.'"

"I've pictured you before me, many sleepless nights." His light tone had dissipated, leaving in its place words heavy with need.

Her own excitement had risen from merely touching his cock. The smooth, thick member, coated in pre-cum, glistened and beckoned for her to come forward for a taste. Her mouth seemed dry, because the wetness had morphed down to her sensitive pussy, still tender from their dalliance in the car. But tender or not, there was no way in hell she wouldn't have him stuff her full of his thick meat.

Oral sex to Billie was like an art form. It should only be done by those who truly loved the craft. Lucky for Tomás, she did. Inhaling deeply, she brought his cock up to her mouth. She slowly lowered her tongue to the tip, to tease her senses with his flavor. The first taste of a man's jism was almost as exciting as the first stroke of him inside of her.

"Don't tease, Billie. Suck."

Looking up so she could watch him watch her, Billie slowly parted her lips and engulfed the head of his cock with the warmth of her mouth. Tomás's groan of pleasure was all it took to get her going.

With a rhythm as old as time, Billie began to pleasure his cock, taking him as deep into her mouth as she could, and pulled back with just a hint of teeth to keep him on edge. When she reached the head, she swirled her tongue around it before plunging down on him again. She couldn't get his entire length in her mouth, but she made up for it by moving her hand up and down his shaft, pumping his cock as she sucked him.

"That's right, *querida*, suck me." Tomás punctuated his words by moving his hands from the door to her hair.

The feel of Tomás wrapping his hands in her hair as she pleasured him with her mouth was almost come-worthy all on its own.

"Ahh…" He groaned deep in his throat as he powered into her mouth, carnivorous, animalistic sounds that sent off tremors in her own body. Heat and moisture began to gather once again between her thighs. Her pussy ached and her breasts swelled with desire as her nipples rose hard and rigid beneath her bra. Billie shifted restlessly between his legs, dying to feel him between hers.

As if reading her mind, Tomás pulled his stiff cock from between her lips. His breathing was ragged as he pulled her to her feet. Surprising her, Tomás took her mouth with a hard, demanding kiss. He flipped her around, until her back was against the door, and he was pressed against her.

Groaning, Billie opened her lips and eagerly welcomed the plunge of his tongue. Never would she have thought his kisses would be so intoxicating, but she shouldn't have been so surprised. Everything about him was.

Tomás seemed utterly absorbed in the taste of her, but for Billie it wasn't enough. She had to touch him. Shoving her hands under his shirt as he ate at her mouth, Billie familiarized herself with his body.

The lines and grooves of his body were so defined Billie felt like she could draw him blind. His chest was hard and felt muscular under her touch, and his nipples pearled under her wandering fingers.

With a moan, Tomás tore his mouth away from hers. His expression was hungry, filled with an intensity that made her catch her breath. Tomás's need was so raw, so exposed that it made her desire feel calm in comparison.

"You've had your fun. Now it's time for me to have mine."

* * *

Her face was flushed, her full lips parted in ecstasy. Billie looked like a women who needed a good a fuck and Tomás was just the man to give it to her. "I thought you had your fun in the car."

Tucking his erection back into his pants as carefully as he could, Tomás laughed at her naïveté. "There's fun, *querida*, and then there's *fun*."

Before Billie could utter another word, Tomás picked her up and tossed her over his shoulder. With a smack on her upturned ass, he took off down the hall. It was hard to walk with the hard on from hell, but it was a price he would pay to get into her sweet pussy. "Which way?"

Laughing, Billie raised up, hands digging into his shirt. "To where?"

"You know where, woman," Tomás growled, delivering another slap to her tempting ass. "We need a bed, and we need one now."

"I don't know. We seem to be doing pretty good without one."

"We'll do even better with one." So much for his earlier thought of just four walls and a ceiling. Now all Tomás could think of was getting Billie flat on her back and her legs spread open, with something spring-loaded to help them get their bounce on.

"Promises, promises. My bedroom is around the corner and to the left."

Quickly following her instructions, Tomás took off down the dark hallway, eyes on the prize, the open doorway just steps away.

Pausing in the threshold, his eyes lit up when they landed on the bed. Pale moonlight spilled through the open blinds, filling the room with shimmering light. He couldn't make out the color of the walls, but he could make out the position of the bed.

"Now this is what I'm talking about." His teasing tone caused Billie to erupt into laughter again.

Her laughter shook her body as he laid her back on the mattress. The lyrical tone stirred him as much as her sexy, throaty moans in the car had. Still smiling, Billie rolled to her side and turned on her bedside table lamp. With the soft glow filling the room, she got up onto her knees and went over to him.

Her eyes were filled with desire as she reached the hem of his shirt and pulled it up and over his head. When his bare chest came into view, Billie greedily latched onto his left nipple with her teeth, nipping at the puckered tip.

Billie laved the tormented peak with her tongue when Tomás growled. Pulling back, she looked up at him with a smile. "Can't handle a bit of pain?"

Her words were like arrows to his aroused groin. "You can dish it, but can you take it?"

"There's only one way to find out."

It was a dare. A challenge of sorts, and Tomás was more than man enough to take it.

"You know what I like about you?" Tomás stepped closer to her, until his legs were touching the mattress.

Billie raised a brow. "There's only one thing?"

"Oh, no, there are many." He said with a chuckled. "But one of the main things is your spirit of adventure."

"Really?"

"Oh yes. Feeling adventurous?" Capturing her hands in his, Tomás pulled her until she was pressed against his body. "Is my little sex slave, ready to obey my commands?"

Her eyes widened at his words. "Yes."

Tomás released her. "Good. Strip."

"Should I do a little dance too?" she teased, moving backwards on the bed.

That sounded good to him. "Yes."

Billie sat down on the bed, with her high-heeled shod feet flat on the quilt. Slowly, she raised one leg over the other, and dangled her left foot at him. "Care to help me out?"

Without saying a word, Tomás complied. Slipping his hand underneath her calf, he raised her leg, sliding his hand up her shapely limb, loving the feel of her smooth, chocolate skin under his touch.

The soft caramel color of his skin against the dark, deep chocolate of hers was finally coming together in the sweet resting space between her thighs. In his eyes, color meant nothing more than an erotic visual aid of what went where, a color-coded guide for their hurried need.

Billie's smile diminished into a soft moan as he caressed then massaged her feet after he removed each of her shoes. By the time he had taken off both of her heels, humor was the last vibe either one of them was sending.

Holding his hand out to her, Tomás helped her rise to her feet, and looked up at her hungrily, as she began to sway to music only she could hear. Slowly but steadily she brought her hands to the hem of her dress, and leisurely began to ease it up her lissome thighs. Her panties still lingered somewhere in the car, torn off in the heat of passion. There was nothing under her skirt, giving Tomás his first glance of her slick bare pussy. His cock jerked, pleading to be free from the constraint of his slacks. And as she lifted the dress all the way off, revealing the laciest black bra, he'd ever seen, Tomás granted his cock its wish by unbuckling and unzipping his pants.

It was quite lewd the way she looked, clothed only in the lacy confines of her bra. Her dark, plump globes spilt over into his waiting hands as Billie unhooked her brassiere from the back. When hands cupped the abundance of her breasts, Billie groaned and moved into his touch. Like the tit man he was, Tomás latched onto her nipple, hungry for his first taste of them. His fingers strummed, plucked, twisted, and teased her nipples.

With eager moans, Billie urged his mouth to her breasts, gasping aloud as soon as he took one of her tasty morsels in his mouth. Bold and aching with desire, Billie cupped her other breast and teasingly pushed them together, offering Tomás a two for one deal. He feasted on her mounds until he couldn't stand not being in her a second longer.

"Lie back, *querida.*"

His clothes disappeared as quickly as Cupid did in his rush to be inside of her, but not before Tomás pulled a condom from his wallet for their protection. All the while he was readying himself for her, Billie was returning the favor.

Sprawled on the bed, Billie spread her legs open and caressed her body as she watched him lustfully. Tomás caught himself staring at the erotic picture she was making, forgetting for an instant what was about to happen. But his hungry cock didn't let him forget for long, and neither did Billie's knowing smile.

She was such a tease. He'd show her what happened to dirty little teases.

"Hands above your head," he ordered as he climbed onto the mattress.

Billie quickly complied, her nipples hardening to rigid little peaks. For someone who had first been offended by the sex slave badge, she was surely taking to it like a pro.

"You will do what I say, when I say." Climbing above her, he settled himself between her thighs, cock in hand, strumming it against her hot pussy. The first stroke against her moist flesh had him gripping his cock harder, fighting his need to just plunge straight in.

"Yes."

"Do you want me to fuck you?"

"Yes."

That wasn't enough for him. He needed the words. "Tell me, now."

"Fuck me, Tomás. Fuck me."

She no sooner spoke the words than Tomás pressed forward, sliding deep inside her moist passage. His teeth clenched as the rush of pleasure inundated his mind.

Billie was hot, wet, and felt tighter than humanly possible. They fit each other as if they were made for one another.

Staring down into the brilliant pool of her eyes, Tomás did everything he could to hold back from the orgasm threatening to drag him drown in an undertow of pleasure.

She was a wet dream come to life. Her face flushed, her teeth sank deep into her bottom lip as she murmured incomprehensible words of pleasure. Their bodies were completely in tune with one another -- when he pressed down, she lifted up; they met one another thrust for thrust.

Billie quivered and rocked against him, urging him on with pleas and thrusts of her hips. Her inner muscles tightened around him, milking his cock as he pushed into her. Her nails dug into his hips as he powered into her body, the bed bouncing with every downward stroke.

It was too much and not enough, all at the same time. The damn alpha thing kicked in, putting the desire to be in control in his bloodstream, and the next thing Tomás knew, he had raised up until he was on his knees, and Billie's hips rested in an angle on his lap. Still powering into her, he grasped her hands, bringing them above her head. His fingers squeezed around her wrist as he used his grip on her as an anchor. "You're mine. This sweet pussy is mine. Say it."

"It's yours. I'm yours."

Their bodies melded into one, their breathing echoes of the other's passion. Tomás worked his hips into a frenzy, fucking Billie with everything inside of him.

Her legs gripped his hips tighter as she pumped up onto him. "More," she whimpered, thrusting her head back and forth on the mattress. "Harder."

Taking her at her word, Tomás pounded harder into her, squeezing her wrists tighter, marking her dark flesh with his fingers.

"Yes…Tomás…Tomás." The last word was cried out as she came, her pussy pulsing around his cock.

Tomás was mere seconds behind her. Head thrown back, back bowing, Tomás ground himself into her, crying her name as he came in a torrential flood. His body shook with wave after wave of aftershocks, and he trembled above her, lost in pleasure, before collapsing forward onto her.

It took all of his reserve strength to move off her panting body, but he did for her sake. Reaching over to her nightstand, he grabbed a tissue and removed the remains of their loving from his still fevered body. After disposing of the trash, Tomás laid down next to her, ready for slumber to take him. He felt more than saw her turn her face towards him, her warm breath escaping out onto his damp skin. The bed moved under her weight as she shifted so that she was lying on his shoulder.

Skin to skin. Billie's pounding heart beat a random rhythm against his side, as they both heaved, lungs aching for the much-needed oxygen that Tomás had heard such great things about.

There was so much he wanted to say. So much he wanted her to know about, like his feelings for her, his dreams for them, yet the only coherent thing he could get out was "Happy Valentine's Day."

Billie's hoarse laughter made him feel foolish for a second, before he himself found the humor in his words. Chuckling, he turned and faced her and brushed his lips against her nose. "I can't wait to see what you have planned for St. Patrick's."

"You know what this means though, don't you?" Billie could barely get the words out, she was laughing so hard.

Confused, Tomás stared at her. "No, what?"

"That there really *is* a little leprechaun guy running around looking for four leaf clovers."

"Oh, my God." Good lord, what a horrible thought. "Remind me later that we're staying in on that night."

"We?"

Tomás raised a brow. "You have a problem with that, sex slave?"

"Not at all."

Chapter Seven

The strong aroma of coffee eased Billie from her peaceful slumber and back into the land of reality as she reluctantly opened her eyes to the harsh light of day. Of course, after a night of bliss with her dream man as his sex slave, and the startling truth that mythological creatures weren't exactly part of man's creative imagination, the land of reality didn't seem so real.

Rolling over, she smiled when she saw the indentation in the pillow next to hers. No matter how freaked out she was about last night, one thing was for sure -- Tomás was a gifted, gifted man. From her whisker-burned breasts to her tender vagina, there was no doubt in her mind that last night wasn't a dream.

Billie stretched her hand out to caress the pillow and froze when she realized what she was doing. "Oh, my God." She laughed as she buried her face into it in shame. She was about to molest the pillow. How sick was that? To say she was sprung was so putting it lightly.

"Morning, sleepyhead."

Startled, Billie rolled over on her side to face the door with her laughter lingering in her voice. Dressed only in the pants he'd had on last night, Tomás stood in her doorway looking better than she remembered. His dark hair was slicked back and looked damp, as if fresh from the shower, and his chiseled jaw line was covered in the sexiest stubble. Damn, she hadn't even brushed her teeth yet. "You're still here."

Billie felt the heat rise in her checks at the hopeful tone in her voice. *God, she sounded so desperate. Why didn't she just throw herself at his feet and beg him to never leave? It might be less pathetic.*

With a chuckle, Tomás walked into the room carrying a breakfast tray. "Is that a bad thing?"

Get yourself together, girl. "Is that coffee for me?"

"Most definitely." Tomás tilted the tray down so that she could see it more clearly. "Along with the homemade waffles."

Waffles…the man made her waffles after making her come over a dozen times. There was absolutely no question about it. Billie was in love.

Easing up into a sitting position, Billie tucked the sheet under her arms, covering her nude body from his probing stare. "Then it's a great thing"

"That's what I like to hear. Now move over in the middle so I can put the tray down on your lap."

That wasn't going to be as easy as it seemed. Although Billie considered herself to be far from a prude, she wasn't trying to give him a show either. Not when there was hot coffee nearby. It was stupid and she knew it, but in the bright light of day, Billie was beginning to feel a bit embarrassed about her wanton behavior the night before.

Tomás waited patiently for her to ruffle the blankets and center the pillows around before he placed the tray down on her lap. "Are we shy now, *querida?*"

Billie flushed. "Me, shy? Please, don't be ridiculous."

"Ridiculous? You're the one bundled up like a virgin bride."

"You may not have noticed last night, but the boobs are huge. And if I don't get the twins situated, the only thing that's going to be covered in syrup is my nipples."

Tomás's eyes dropped down to her chest briefly before zeroing back on her face. "And that would be a bad thing, why?"

Damn it, he was cute, great in bed, and just when she thought it was perfect, he had to ruin it by being in a good mood. "You're one of those dreadful morning people, aren't you?"

"And you're not."

Billie snorted as she picked up her coffee. "What gave me away?"

"Does it have to be just one thing?"

Billie bit back a smile. Even in the face of her morning persona, Tomás was still being nice. They hadn't touched once since he had come into the room, and she was feeling like her normal, semi-reserved self. She was nothing really like the woman he had spent the night with. Maybe that was what he was waiting around for? If so, boy, was he going to be disappointed. "Wasn't this so much more fun last night?"

With a wrinkled brow, Tomás sat down on the bed next to her, picked up the syrup, and began to pour it. "I'm having fun now."

"You are?" Okay, she hadn't been expecting that.

"Of course. I wake up this morning next to this beautiful, amazing woman who snores louder than my Uncle Julio and holds onto the quilt like a lifeline, and you know what the first thing I thought was?"

"Where's the nearest exit?"

"Uhh, no." Tomás set the syrup down and began to cut into her waffle. "I hope you like powdered sugar on them. It was in the refrigerator so I took a chance."

"No, it's fine." Billie watched him warily, wondering where he was going with all of this.

"Good. I sprinkled some on in the kitchen. Would you like a bite?"

Eyeing him carefully, Billie waited for the shoe to fall. "Sure, but please get back to what you were thinking."

"Oh yes, that." Cutting off a perfectly square piece of waffle, Tomás dipped it into the syrup and brought it up to her mouth. Billie opened her mouth, slightly amused, her attention solely focused on him.

"Like I was saying, the first thing I thought was…how right this felt. Waking up with you just felt right. Something I could get used to on an everyday basis."

Swallow…you have to swallow, her brain warned her as she stared at him with her mouth wide open. *Swallow, Billie.*

Swallow now. Trying to obey her brain, Billie closed her mouth and swallowed, then promptly choked.

Damn, she forgot to chew.

Coughing, Billie tried to breathe as she stared at Tomás with watering eyes. "Every day. Just right. Are you serious?"

Leaning forward, Tomás moved to pat her on the back, but was stopped by Billie holding her hand up to ward him off. The last thing she needed right now was to go into super-slut mode.

"Completely serious, but with a few mild adjustments."

"Like?" This had to be the weirdest conversation she had ever had with him, and yet Tomás seemed to be taking it very lightly. Like it was something they would be talking about over coffee at the office.

"Well, I could have lived without the psychotic Cupid episode."

Billie nodded as she took a sip of her coffee. That made two of them. "And?"

"I think things would work out a lot better if you weren't flinching from me when I touch you."

"I'm not flinching."

Tomás raised a brow. "Really, what do you call it?"

"Waking up."

"So this is you waking up, not you regretting last night?"

In the midst of taking another drink, Billie froze. Is that what he thought? "In truth, I'm still a little weirded out about last night, and having you here in all your morning glory is taking me back a few steps, but I don't now, nor will I ever, regret making love to you."

"And that's all? You're just weirded out?"

"Cupids, spells, and being turned into a sex slave has that effect on me." Billie smiled. "But you have an effect on me that all the arrows in the world couldn't counter."

"Hmmm..." Tomás moved the tray from her lap and onto the floor. "I think I have a cure for your morning blues."

Damn, that sounded good, but the instant he moved closer, Billie pulled her head back. "I have to brush my teeth."

Tomás didn't let that deter him. "I'll take my chances."

He wanted to kiss her, morning breath and all...she could get used to this. "Do you think the spell is still in effect?"

Tomás paused, his eyes shimmering with laughter. "There's only one way to find out."

* * *

Tomás heard her quick intake of breath and saw the desire blaze in her eyes as he moved to capture her lips. But instead of kissing her as he'd implied, Tomás stopped. "Then again, maybe we shouldn't.'

Startled, Billie pulled back in surprise. "We shouldn't?"

It took the last of his willpower to move away from the bed, especially when she was looking all kinds of good. Even with sleep lingering in her pretty doe eyes, she was still tempting.

Her dark brown shoulders, framed so delicately by the mauve sheet she had wrapped around her, made her appear like a delicious, dark chocolate candy bar, just waiting to be unwrapped. Her breasts were jutting up from their silky confines, looking like ripe honeydew melons, large and juicy.

Tomás wanted to brush his skin gently against hers but he was afraid that with one touch the spell would flare to life, rearing its ugly head. He really wanted some "just them" time before all that happened.

Despite that, he couldn't help but remark, "I could make love to you all day."

Her eyes widened and she let out a shaky breath. "Don't let me stop you."

Tomás abruptly pulled away and stood up. "I think we should stop for now."

"Excuse me?"

"Let me run you a bath."

The mauve sheet that she had meticulously tucked around her came down like a flash as Billie rose to her knees. "How about you climb in bed and fuck me instead?"

Now there was the feisty woman he'd come to love. Her words were filled with the same frustration he was feeling, but with a hint of attitude.

"As tempting as it is, and trust me, *querida*, it is *very* tempting, I think we should gather our resolve and figure this thing out a bit more before we settle in to enjoy."

With a disgruntled mutter, Billed plopped back onto the bed, crossing her arms over her breasts.

Damn! He had been enjoying that view.

"I take it you have a plan."

"Not a plan, just an idea."

With a sigh, Billie rolled over, presenting her delectable ass up in the air as she picked up the breakfast tray and set it back on the bed. In the seconds it took her to do that, Tomás had completely lost all sight of what he had originally wanted to talk about.

Curvaceous, succulent ass, plump and ready, inches away from his tingling fingers. Now *that* was seriously fucked up. A nice round ass was his kryptonite.

Her rear end had been one of the first things he'd noticed about her, and last night he hadn't been blessed with the opportunity to worship it in all of its glory...but tonight...tonight that would be rectified.

With that image in his head, Tomás's erection rose hard and ready in his pants, wanting to get a piece of the work of art she had unknowingly unleashed before him.

"Tomás! Did you hear what I said?"

She'd said something? Shaking his head, Tomás tried to get back on focus. Now that Billie was seated again and covered, he might be able to keep his libido in a headlock, at least long enough for him to leave the room before he embarrassed himself.

"Could you repeat yourself, please?"

"What's the plan?"

"I think we should do some research of our own."

Billie gestured between them with her fork. "And you'd rather we do it sans touching?"

"Rather, hell no, but I do think it would be best." Tomás didn't want her to get the wrong impression. There was nothing more he wanted to do than touch her. But what he wanted and what he needed to do were two separate things."

" Best for?"

"You, mainly. Going to be kinda hard for you to search on the Internet with me pounding into you from behind."

A playful smile tugged at the corner of Billie's lips. "Sounds kinky."

"Great, I'll keep that in mind on the kinky sex list. But before we break out the whips and chains, I'll go run you a bath so you can relax."

Annoyance flashed across her brow. "You're still hell-bent on that bath. Is the intermingling odor of us really bothering you?

Is that what she was thinking? "Hell, no, I think they should seal this room up and bottle the fragrance and sell it at Sak's. Nothing is bothering me. I just want to take care of you for a bit. I saw the way you winced when you sat up. I want you to go get in the tub and relax for awhile, while I make some phone calls about last night. I want to pamper you, and make you feel good."

Billie's smile was all out now. "And you plan to do all of this all without touching me."

"Without touching you...for now. Don't get me wrong. There will be touching, and lots of it. I just want you relaxed and at peace. Let me handle the stress, you enjoy me here waiting on you, taking care of you. So by the end of the day, I'm not the only one thinking about how right this morning felt. And although I can't wait to ravish every single inch of your body, I think we need to get some answers."

"And more condoms."

Smiling, Tomás concurred. "A lot more condoms. We should probably make some phone calls to keep everyone away. Cancel any dates you might have."

"Cancel any dates *you* might have."

"The only person I've wanted to see since moving here seven months ago is you. Haven't you figured that out by now?" Unable to stop himself, Tomás perched at the head of the bed and leaned into Billie. He didn't make any attempt to touch her. He just wanted to make sure that she heard him a hundred percent clearly, so that there would be no misunderstandings. "You're it for me, Billie. Whether you are my sex slave or just my best friend hanging out, there will be no other women in my life from now on."

At her shocked expression, Tomás stood. But he couldn't stop himself from adding one more little comment. "That is, until you give me a daughter."

"A daughter!" Billie's cry of surprise had him chuckling as he headed out of the door.

Chapter Eight

Four hours later, they were no closer to answers than they had been the night before. Jenna was nowhere to be found, and every single coworker who had attended the party acted as if they didn't have a single clue what Billie was talking about. It was the strangest thing. If it hadn't been for Tomás sitting across from her, still shirtless, with her scratches still fresh on his back, Billie might have thought she'd made the whole damn thing up.

The situation would have been completely frustrating if it wasn't for present company.

Tomás was true to his word. He had pampered her, spoiled her all day, and like he promised, Billie was definitely thinking it was something she could get used to.

Yet it wasn't just the pampering. It was also the little things. Like the loving glances he sent her way when he walked into the room. The way he would crouch down close to her chair so they would be on eye level when talking. And even the way his eyes twinkled and crinkled at the corners when he smiled. It was everything big and little about him; Billie loved it all. Just like she loved him.

Love. She was in love with Tomás, and she wasn't scared. Okay, not very scared.

"What are you thinking about, sitting there so quietly by yourself?"

Tomás's words drew her from her self-imposed stupor. He had caught her staring at him like a lovesick groupie. How embarrassing was that?

Looking away, Billie couldn't help the smile that came to her lips as she wondered what he would say if she told him the truth, that she was planning to lock him up and never let him go.

"After that smile, I really want to know." Setting the phone book down, Tomás walked over to the counter and leaned back against it.

"What smile?" It was hard to look innocent when nothing but dirty thoughts were popping into her head.

"That little secretive smile of yours that tells me you're up to no good."

Billie brought her hand up to her chest as if she was surprised, "*Moi?*"

"The innocent act won't work on me."

"What does?"

"So far you're the only thing that has."

"You know..." Billie walked closer to him, her hand trailing slowly behind her on the counter. "We've been awful good for the last few hours."

"Yes, we have."

Stopping next to him, Billie peered up at him from beneath lowered lashes. "Really, really good…"

"And you're thinking…"

"Now it's time to be bad."

Billie raised her hand above his, ready to touch him.

"You know what will happen if you touch me." His voice was husky and his eyes were filled with need.

"I know what I'm hoping for." Reaching her hand out towards him, she came up short when Tomás crossed his arms across his massive chest and stared down at her.

"What?" With a raised brow, she mocked his stance.

"Are you willing to be my little sex slave again? Give into what ever demand I make of your lush body? Because this time, Billie, I won't hold back. I'll let my alpha side come roaring back and take you every single way that you can imagine, and some I'm sure you haven't. Unfortunately, for you, the alpha side of me isn't just the spell. When it comes to our loving, I want to be in control of your passions at all times. These are things that you really need to think about before you touch me again. Because the second you do, I'm going to see it as a sure sign that I have your permission to ravish you any way I please. So tread lightly, *querida*, because once we give in, there will be no going back. Ever!"

"The spell will come to an end, Tomás. Someday, possibly today."

"But that spell won't change a thing, because I'm still going to want to dominate you in the bedroom, and pamper you out of it. I don't think it's an accident that my name badge was *alpha jerk*. I think that at times it's who I am. So if you're waiting for Cupid to come down and change that about me, well, baby girl, it's not going to happen.

"Laying all of your cards on the table?"

"Yes, because I don't want there to ever be any doubt in your mind about the kind of man you're getting involved with."

"And we're getting involved?"

Tomás chuckled. "Oh no, *querida*, we're already involved. There will be no going back for me after this. And I think I can make the same assumption about you."

There were many ways Billie could have backed her way out of the situation, but plain and simple, she just didn't want to. She knew how serious she was about Tomás. Hell, she loved him. Had for a very long time. "You can assume."

"There's love here, waiting for you, if you want it."

Heart in her eyes, Billie moved to kiss him, but was stopped again by his words. "I just really need you to know that this stupid name badge is who I'm more than likely going to be for a good part of our relationship."

"I can handle that, if you can handle the fact that I'm not going to be my name badge. I want to be with you. Always have, but this sex-slave-dropping-my- panties-at-your-every-beck-and-call isn't really me."

"I want all of you. And if the sex slave thing doesn't work for you, then I want what does. I don't need a wicked wish to get you to behave naughty with me. I'm more than sure I can inspire that in you all on my own."

"You're awful cocky."

"No, I'm just a man in love."

The words were out there. Giving her the freedom she so desperately needed to say them right back. "In love with a woman who's in love with you right back. You must have done something good in your other life."

"Thank God for karma," he laughed.

"Thank God for you." Billie cornered him at the counter, narrowing his escape. "I'm going to touch you, Tomás, because I can't just stand this close to you and not touch you. Because it's been hours since I felt your warm skin against mine. And because we might find out any second what the key to our little dual-multiple-personality-existence is, but before that happens, I would really like to make love with you again. With the freeing knowledge that I'm yours to do whatever it is you want. Can you give that to me?"

Nostrils flaring, Tomás moved closer to her. "I can give you that and more."

The instant his hand touched her waist the switch flipped on, and Billie went all passive in his arms. But this time Tomás didn't feel an ounce of guilt. This was what she wanted. Hell, it was what he wanted, to be in command of her body and her soul, to have her at his sexual command. And the thing that made all of that so damn wonderful was knowing that she wanted the same thing.

"I'm going to fuck you."

"God, I hope so." Her breasts rose and fell with every desperate breath. The sexy slave light was on in her eyes, and she was as passive and open to him as she had been last night. But tonight he wasn't going to allow any backseat judgment to keep them from what they both wanted.

Picking her up, Tomás sat her on the counter. He kept eye contact with her the entire time he slid the plush pink robe down her arms, baring her from the waist up. She looked so unbelievably sexy, her wild hair tossed around her angelic face. Her smooth dark skin, like a starless night, beckoned to him to taste her. To take every inch of her body and worship it with his tongue.

But there was another part of her, a part he longed to worship for much longer. And Tomás felt like he wouldn't be able to take another breath if he wasn't able to get her sweet nether lips in his mouth now.

"I'm feeling the need to sit down and have a great meal."

"You want me to cook now?"

"Oh, no." Tomás reached back and grabbed one of the kitchen chairs and brought it over to the counter. Sitting down in front of her, he grasped her knees in his hands and spread her silky legs until each of her feet rested on the arm of the chair.

Slipping his hand up her thigh, he rested his thumb against the smooth fabric covering her mound. "When did you put this on?"

"After my bath." Her voice was husky and thick with need.

Tomás tsked, shaking his head. "That will never do. Lift up."

Billie rose, lifting up as he worked the tiny wisp of silk down her hips and off her long legs.

"Now this is more like it," he remarked, as he tossed them over his shoulder.

Tomás moved in slowly, wanting the memory of the first time he'd tasted her to linger in his mind forever. He stared as if captivated at the sight of his tanned fingers parting her dark slick folds. Billie's clit was heavy with desire, erect inside of her creamy sex, beckoning him forward for a taste.

The aroma of her passion had his mouth salivating and desperate for a taste of her sweet nectar.

"*Querida*," he whispered, before taking her bud into his mouth. Slipping his tongue around her cleft, Tomás savored the sweet taste of her on his lips. She was sweet like sugar. Her honey flowed over his tongue, past his lips.

He could feast from between her legs all day. Taking his time, Tomás roamed her heated flesh, tasting her, teasing her, enjoying the way she cried out in pleasure as he laved her clit with his tongue.

Slipping his hands between her quivering thighs, Tomás pushed his fingers inside of her tight channel, fucking her as he teased her clit with his mouth.

"Tomás…To…" Billie's hips undulated under his assault. She pushed at his shoulders at the same time her nails dug into him, gripping him closer. It was as if she didn't know whether to beg him to stay or stop, so Tomás pressed on. He alternated between fucking her with his tongue and screwing her with his fingers, until she was whimpering and moaning his name.

He slipped his tongue lower, dipping into the soft recess of her body, fucking her juicy pussy with his tongue. He worked her over and over, until he thought her buttocks would be bruised from the thrashing she was doing.

"Oh…oh…oh.." She grasped him to her, her fingers entwined in his hair as she shuddered around him. "Yes!"

Billie cried out and bucked underneath him, her cream soaking his fingers as she came. When her body started to still, Tomás pulled away, first his tongue then his fingers. His mouth was damp with her pleasure and he felt drunk on her essence. Raising up, he stood between her trembling thighs and fought his own desire to release his cock and plunge deep into her waiting body.

She was flush from her orgasm and her body was trembling as if she was trying to catch her breath. And to Tomás, Billie had never looked more beautiful.

With a groan, he fisted his hand in the tight ringlets crowning her head and pulled her tighter into his embrace. Tomás kissed her like a man possessed. Obsessed with the flavor of her, his mouth devoured hers, his tongue darting over hers like a freight train. She moaned her hungry approval, her nails biting into his shoulders as she tried to pull him closer.

"I can't get enough of you," he murmured as he tore his mouth away, his lips running over her neck.

"I don't want you to," she panted, her body quaking as he raked his teeth down the side of her neck. "Fuck me, Tomás. Please, please fuck me."

Her words tugged on his groin. His cock ached to be free, to delve into her delights, giving them both what they wanted.

Tomás drew away from her tempting nape, his own ragged breathing matching hers. They were both consumed by the fires of passion and he knew exactly what they needed to quench the flames.

Billie wrapped her legs around him as he picked her up from the counter. They kissed hungrily as he carried her to the bedroom. It was the quickest, yet at the same time the longest walk in his life. By the time they entered the bedroom, Tomás was frenzied with desire.

Setting her down quickly onto the bed, they grappled with his pants, stumbling over one another's hands in their quest to free him. Tomás would have laughed if he wasn't in so much pain.

"Lose the robe," he ordered harshly as he slipped his pants to the floor.

"Hurry up and fuck me."

"I give the orders around here, *querida*." Tomás grabbed her quickly and pulled her body against him. "Or did you forget?"

Billie leaned forward and bit him gently on his neck. "Maybe I did. You probably should remind me."

"I agree completely." Snapping his wrist, Tomás delivered a quick slap to her ass. "Lay down."

"Yes, sir." With a salute, Billie winked and dropped back down onto the bed with a laugh.

Sheathing his cock, Tomás climbed up next to her and loomed over, watching the way the light played against her skin. "You're so fucking beautiful."

Billie's face flushed as she looked away with a tiny grin. "Stop it."

Tomás reached out and touched her chin, applying pressure on it until she turned back to face him "Never."

With love shining in her eyes, Billie nodded her head. It was the affirmation Tomás had been looking for. Sitting up on his haunches, Tomás slipped her legs open and apart, resting each of her legs on one of his opposing thighs. It gave her hips a slight angle to them and it gave Tomás an eagle-eye view of what he most wanted to possess.

Slipping his hands down her thighs to her hips, Tomás lifted her up, settling her forward so that she was sitting on his lap.

He wanted them to be face to face when they made love this time. He wanted to watch her expression as she came for him, over and over. With one hand Tomás held her up as he steered his cock to her moist hole, lining up his entrance with that of her inner sheath.

"Come down on me...slowly," he ordered as he watched her.

Her teeth bit down into her bottom lip as she painstakingly lowered herself down onto his engorged cock. For every inch she took in, a sexy little cry slipped out. The noise, the lip, the beautiful women taking him inch by inch was the sexiest thing he had ever seen, and he was a man that had seen lots of porn.

It looked sexy, sounded sexy, and he was damn near close to blowing his load before she even took him completely into her depths.

When she finally took him into her hot box, Tomás almost died. "*Querida*," he groaned as she tightened her muscles around him. Heat, such blinding heat, gripped his cock, tighter than a lover ever had.

"Fuck, baby." Cupping her rear with his hands, Tomás moved her up and down his shaft, sometimes slowly, sometimes fast, but always while he was watching her expressive face. He saw every good spot, and visited it twice to make sure, and he learned from reading her face when she wanted it faster or harder, and then he delivered it in spades.

"Hmm...mmm...Tomás...right there. Right there!" she chanted, her head thrown back in ecstasy.

"You mean here, baby," he teased, pumping up into her, giving her what she wanted.

Like a sexual seesaw, they worked up and down, Tomás raising her up and then Billie slamming herself down, and when she was trembling and panting above him, he started to bump up into her body with deep, sharp thrusts, one hand gripping her ass, the other hand supporting her back.

"Come for me, *querida*."

The angle allowed for a deeper thrust and for him to graze across the sensitive spot buried deep within her. When he hit it just right, the heavens opened up and she all but sang his name. "Oohhh ohhhh Tomás...Tomás..."

The sweet wet walls of her pussy embraced him tightly as he surged deep inside of her depths, clinging like Velcro when he withdrew. His balls felt tight and heavy, ready to burst, but Tomás was having none of that. There was something more he wanted before he spilled his seed. And it was to be buried balls-deep inside of her other tempting hole. Easing her down onto his rigid length, Tomás stopped her from ascending, cupping her damp body to his. Her breathing was ragged and her body was trembling. And more than ready for another round.

"Why...why are we stopping?"

"Because I want more." Tomás inserted his index finger into his mouth, and moistened it before sliding it out and down her back to the top of her buttocks. Billie's knowing chuckle brought a smile to his lips. "That's not a no."

"You haven't asked a question yet."

Slipping his fingers between her plump checks, Tomás gently ran his finger over her puckered hole. Billie sat up, but didn't jerk away, giving him the silent go-ahead for his exploration.

"Do you like this?" Tomás's accent had thickened with his need. "Will you allow me to fuck you here, my little slave?"

"Anything you want, Tomás. Anywhere you want."

"Anything...anywhere?" Her words had his cock aching.

Wordlessly, she pulled away from him and rolled onto her stomach, easing up onto her knees so her ass was raised. Looking over her shoulder at him, she peered up with a sensual smile spread across her full lips. "I want to be filled by you in every place possible."

Chapter Nine

Nervously, Billie waited for Tomás's next move. Finger play was the closest she had ever come to anal sex, but a digit or two was nothing compared to Tomás's cock. The thought of him buried in her backside had her squirming with anticipation, but nothing prepared her for the sharp smack he delivered to her upturned cheeks.

"Hey!" Billie shot a grinning Tomás an injured look. "What was that for?"

"I couldn't resist."

"Try."

"Stop liking it and I will."

"What makes you think I..." Tomás's fingers found her slick entrance, cutting Billie off in mid-sentence. "Besides that?"

His chuckle rolled over her body, sending goose bumps up her spine. It was the sound of a confident man with a handful of wet pussy who didn't need words to know what his woman wanted.

"You're too cocky for your own good." And he was so right. Billie felt like she was on fire.

"Once again," Tomás's fingers pumped inside of her, as he leaned forward to nip at her earlobe, "as soon as you stop liking it, I will."

"Bastard."

"You love it. You love me, don't you, baby?"

Gritting her teeth, Billie pushed back on his probing fingers. "Yes."

"And you love what I do to you, don't you, baby?"

"God, yes!"

"That's what I thought." Tomás slipped his wet fingers from her dripping sex and ran them around her tight hole. "Do you have anything?"

"Like KY..." She hissed, her breath catching in her lungs as he eased a finger into her passageway.

"Yes."

"In the top drawer."

Tomás slipped his finger out. "Stay right where you are."

As if she could move. Her body was on fire, her mind ablaze. The bed dipped as Tomás moved to rifle through her drawer. If this was any other occasion, Billie would have retrieved the oil herself, but she could hardly move, which was a good thing, since Tomás ordered her not to. Like a good little slave, she stayed exactly where he wanted her, waiting impatiently for him to come back to her.

Tomás was like a drug in her system, and Billie never wanted to come down.

Her body tensed when she felt him move back in behind her. The very unladylike position she was maintaining only further fanned her flame. She felt naughty. Exposed like she had never been exposed before, and she loved it, almost as much as she loved him.

Billie jumped when his tongue swiped from her drenched opening to her puckered hole. Her squeal of surprise quickly morphed into a cry of pleasure as he teased her with his tongue, dipping into each entrance as his hands spread and kneaded her flesh. Body tense, nails digging into the bed, Billie tried to muffle her cries as she gave herself over to this new sensation.

She was beyond all comprehension, whimpering mindlessly as he tantalized her with his tongue. The pleasure sizzled through her body like an electrical storm. Her nipples were rigid peaks. Her clit ached for contact of any sort. Billie felt like she was on the verge of coming undone. One wrong -- or right move, as the case might be -- and she'd go over the proverbial edge.

"Tomás." His name was a plea on her lips. For him to stop. For him to continue. For him, period.

As if obeying her unspoken command, Tomás added his fingers to his divine torture. Slick with a mixture of the lube and her own slippery juices, he circled her rosette with his probing digit, easing his way into her body. Billie tried to hold her trembling body still as she fought to relax.

Moving slowly but steadily, Tomás penetrated her reluctant opening, taking his time to stretch her one finger width at a time. Every plunge went deeper and felt thicker than the last, until Billie could no longer tell one finger size from the next.

She was on fire. Her body was drenched with sweat; she felt too heavy to hold her own weight. The pleasure was all consuming, mind numbing, utterly indescribable.

"Relax, my love." His voice sounded strained, as if the positions were reversed and it was his remarkable ass thrust high in the air. "Push out, *querida*. Let me in."

Easier said than done, Billie wanted to retort, but the words died on her lips as the slick head of his cock teased her rear entrance. Ever so slowly, he eased the plump crown past her resisting ring, allowing Billie to gradually get used to his girth.

There was a flash of heat bordering on pain as he seated himself inside of her. But just as quickly as the stinging sensation had come, it all but dissipated in a cloud of wonderment. He was inside of her, deep inside, and it felt remarkable. Before Billie could get used to the heavy sensation, Tomás pulled back, sliding his cock almost completely out, before plunging slowly back in.

Billie didn't know how he could possible be going as painstakingly slow as he was, especially when she had to resist the urge to push back on him herself. As he pushed forward again, Billie moaned with pleasure.

"Are you okay, baby?" Tomás eased back slowly.

Okay wasn't the word. Billie wasn't sure what was, though. All she knew was if he stopped, she wouldn't be able to bear it. Never had anything so naughty felt so good. "Don't stop."

"Never." Tomás pumped inside of her as he eased his fingers over her hips and down to toy with her aching clit. His hand moved at the same rhythm his cock did, but on a different beat, keeping Billie off balance with the gentle thrusts. "You feel like hot satin, *querida*. So tight...so tight, and yet so soft."

His sexy words were as dizzying as his thrust. Billie was on pleasure overload. "Shut up and fuck me, Tomás. Fuck me."

"As...you...wish."

Taking her at her word, Tomás sped up his thrusts. He moved his hand from her hungry cunt to her hip, and pistoned in and out of her ass with a speed that took her breath away. Billie placed her fingers on her abandoned clit, rubbing her aching bud to relieve the tension coiling deep inside her.

Out of the dark, her orgasm blindsided her, catching her off-guard, throwing her into a mind-numbing tizzy. Billie cried out in ragged pants, her moans of pleasure spilling out past parched lips. Billie didn't know if Tomás was coming or going; all she knew was that she had never felt so full in her life.

Her body spasmed as Billie saturated her hand with her juices. Quivering, her muscles clenched down onto Tomás's pumping cock.

"Fuck. So good...so good." Tomás groaned as he came undone, pumping her ass as he filled her with spurt after spurt of his seed.

Gripping the sheet with all her might, Billie tried to hold herself up under the onslaught of his pounding hips, but failed when he collapsed half on her and half on the bed.

Thankfully, Tomás had the good sense to pull out before he did, or her ass would have been in a world of pain.

"Wow," was all that Billie could mutter, and even that took a few minutes. Never had three little letters said so much, yet not quite enough, all at the same time.

Tomás chuckled. "That's exactly what I was thinking."

"I don't think I'm going to be able to walk…for, like, a week."

"That's okay." Rolling over, Tomás spooned her. "I think I like the idea of you naked in bed, at my whim."

"Funny, I can't say that that surprises me at all." Their joint laughter filled the room before tapering off to a peaceful lull. Billie shifted to get more comfortable but was rewarded by a gush of fluid down her thigh. Yuck. "I'm thinking that this isn't one of the sessions where I can just doze off and worry about cleaning up tomorrow."

"Well…I think my cock is stuck to your butt, so if one of us rolls over in the middle of the night, I'm in a world of trouble."

"I'm really fond of him. We might want to shower."

"Only if I can bathe you."

Billie rolled over and faced him. "I don't know if that's such a good idea. You know the more you touch me, the more I want you."

With a deadpan expression on his handsome face, Tomás replied, "I think I'll take my chances."

If he had to die tomorrow, Tomás would go to his grave a happy man. After the marathon sex in the bedroom, he had somehow managed to raise his impressive penis for one more go in the shower. Billie wasn't going to be the only one who couldn't walk tomorrow. He felt practically bowlegged from all the extra curricular activity they had indulged in.

And as if that hadn't been heaven in a box, Billie was now astride his back, wearing nothing but a thigh-length T-shirt, giving him a massage.

Life just didn't get much better.

"Now don't you two look cute?"

With a startled scream, Billie rolled off of his back and promptly fell to the floor. Cursing, Tomás bounced up to confront the interloper, and damn near had a heart attack of his own. Bold as day, Eros and Jenna sat upon the loveseat, watching them with twin amused expressions.

As if sensing danger, Jenna quickly rose and eased behind the seat, but not Eros, who was still smiling wolfishly and eyeing Billie's fumbling frame.

Without thought to the consequences, Tomás pounced over the end table and onto a surprised Cupid, who went down over the arm of the chair rather quickly for a man his size. Eyes bulging, the deity stared up in surprise at Tomás, who was trying his best to wring his muscle-packed neck. It was a difficult task, but he managed to get a mighty good grip on the bastard before Billie and Jenna were at his side.

"Tomás, stop it," Billie yelled.

"After he stops breathing." Tightening his grip, Tomás pressed on.

"You can't kill him, if you do, we'll never find a cure."

"Technically you can't kill him at all," Jenna reasoned, sounding remarkably calm for someone whose husband was being strangled. "All you're going to do is get a cramp in your fingers."

"He can't die?"

"Nope."

Her words put a damper on his rage. No good trying to choke the life out of someone who wouldn't die. It also explained why the bastard wasn't fighting back. He was just watching Tomás with a curious glint in his eyes. The damn fool looked more intrigued than worried.

"Fuck," Tomás muttered as he released him.

"If it makes you feel better, it did kind of hurt," Eros offered apologetically as he stood up, not even winded.

Jenna rolled her eyes. "It did not."

"I said kind of." Eros shrugged his shoulders with a sympathetic grin as he offered Tomás his hand to stand.

Tomás slapped his hand away and stood on his own. "Get out of here before I ram the table leg up your ass. It might not kill you, but I promise you, you'll feel it."

That, at least, got the other man's attention. "Man, you've been awful hostile and I came all this way to say I'm sorry."

"You're sorry -- well, hell, why didn't you say so?" Billie chuckled at Tomás's sarcasm, earning an injured look from Eros.

"I do feel sorry, and to make up for it, I'm willing to reverse time and fix it so you'll never know any of it happened."

"You can do that?"

Billie's words quickly caught his attention. Was there hope in her tone? "Do you want him to?"

With a snort she slapped him on the arm. "Of course not, I was just asking."

"Don't." Tomás felt only marginally better. "Remove the spell and leave."

"It's not that simple."

"Why isn't it?" Billie and he spoke at the same time.

"It's a complicated thing. Very hard to explain."

"Try us."

Hedging, Eros tried again. "It has to do with true love and spells."

With her hand on her hip, Billie faced off with the backpedaling Greek. "You're telling me that you can erase over fifty people's memories but you can't take back a spell?"

"Oh...you know about that."

"That's it." Tomás headed towards him again, intent on rearranging Eros's insides with the table.

"Oh, Eros, stop it." Jenna sighed dramatically, stepping between them. "Just say you were wrong and fix it."

Frowning, Eros crossed his hands over his chest. "It's always a blame thing with you."

"Only because you refuse to accept any," Jenna countered.

"This is why we have so many problems, Psyche."

"And your wandering arrow doesn't help."

Tomás couldn't believe what he was hearing. They were mad! Grade A certifiably insane.

"Good Lord, will you two just stop it?" Billie's bellow silenced the dueling duo. "Eros, I would really like it if I could keep my memory but lose the craving. And Jenna..."

"Yes?"

"Lose my number."

"It really wasn't my fault." At Billie's withering look, Jenna blushed, "Not all of it, anyway."

"Look, before I do this, I just have one question to ask." Arms crossed, Tomás nodded his head in consent. "You guys are in love, right? I was right about that."

"Yes."

"See, I told you." Eros shot Jenna a cocky grin. "The arrow never lies."

Billie's jaw dropped open. "You struck us with arrows?"

"Nah, grazed would be the right word." As soon as the words left his mouth, Cupid looked ill at ease.

But not ill enough for Tomás's piece of mind. "You bastard!"

Eros grabbed Jenna's hand and pulled her in tight to him. "*Rivestimento di periodo.* Nice meeting you folks. Later."

The two disappeared as quickly as they had entered, leaving Tomás and Billie staring after them in their wake. Walking over to Tomás, Billie placed a restraining hand on his arm. "Just let it go."

"Let it go, he struck us with an arrow."

"But we didn't feel it or even know about it. And besides, look how good it turned out."

Tomás turned startled eyes to her. "You're fine with it?"

"I'm fine with it being over. I feel calm. I'm actually touching you and I don't want to jump your bones."

And that was supposed to be a good thing? Not in his book. "You don't?"

Rolling her eyes, Billie leaned her head on his arm. "You know what I mean. I'm touching you because I want to, and not because I have to. Isn't that great?"

"Yeah…great…" Tomás teased, wrapping his arm around her pulling her in close. God, he loved this woman. "Yet I haven't changed, isn't that wonderful?"

"Yeah…great…" She tossed his words back at him with a wink. Pulling out of his arms, Billie held his hand as she stepped back from him. "There is one thing I'm extremely happy about, though."

"Yeah…what's that?"

"I'm happy that the dreaded day is over. Jenna…sorry, Psyche, had it right. Fuck Cupid. Fuck Valentine's Day. Fuck it all."

"Hey, hey, hey, now…" Releasing her hand, Tomás cupped his hand over her mouth. "Not too loud. We don't want them to come back. I mean the bastard already struck us with an arrow, jinxed us with a wish, and saw some of your goodies. I think I can officially say, I'm Valentined out."

Billie pulled his hand from her mouth. "But not out of love, right?"

Tomás turned her around until he was looking down into her deep, dark eyes. "There's no such thing as being out of love, especially where you are concerned."

"I guess we're kind of stuck with each other, because I feel the exact same way."

Wouldn't it figure the little pest wasn't as stupid as he seemed? "Looks like Cupid got it right, after the misguided arrows and all. He knew real love when he saw it."

"I guess he and I have something in common, after all." With a broad smile, Billie jumped into his arms and his heart filled with joy.

Cupid's arrow or no Cupid's arrow, she was the one for him and he didn't need a hyped up deity to prove it.

It was love, plain and simple. And she was his.

Epilogue

"Are you still watching them?"

Jumping, Psyche hastily swiped her hand in mid air, erasing the hologram image of Tomás and Billie cuddling on the couch. She'd been watching them off and for the last couple of hours, secretly -- or she had thought -- but from Eros's knowing chuckle and words, Psyche guessed she wasn't fooling anyone but herself.

"I was just checking up on them."

"You were just being the dirty little voyeur that I know and love."

Psyche bit back her sardonic reply as she turned to face her husband. She would have thought that after a millennium he wouldn't be able to get to her so easily. She was wrong.

"I'm not a voyeur. I'm a romantic."

Eros smirked. "Romantic…right."

Narrowing her eyes, Psyche moved a step closer. One of these days, she was really going to leave him…maybe… "See, this is why I sodomized your picture."

"Ahh come on honey, I'm just teasing…"

"Do you really think they'll be okay?"

"Of course." Eros sounded as if he was offended that Psyche doubted him.

"And everything is cleaned up?"

Eros nodded. "With the exception of Tomás and Billie, everyone who was at the party has had their memories erased. Your reputation as the best party thrower in the world is still intact and Billie and Tomás will live happily ever after.

"You really think so?" Psyche couldn't help the soft tone that came in her voice. Whether Eros thought so or not, she was a romantic. And the thought of Tomás and Billie happy forever made her tear up. They were two of her favorite coworkers and they desperately belonged with each other.

"So do you forgive me?" Eros walked up behind her, his spirit embracing her long before his hands ever did. "I really am sorry that I ruined your party."

"Good, you should be. It was a grand party."

Eros gently lifted her hair up from her collar and rained kisses down her nape. Damn him, he knew that was her spot. Resolve firmly in place, Psyche refused to give in to him so easily, especially if she could guilt him into helping her with a new project of her own.

"You can't just kiss your way out of this."

"But I can shower you with kisses until you tell me what my punishment is.'

"It's not a punishment. It's a job."

That surprised him. "You want me to get a job."

"No I have a job for you."

"But I'm off duty."

Stepping away from him, Psyche turned and faced her handsome husband, undoing the belt on her robe all the while. "If you're too busy to help a beautiful woman who's been having a few love issues...I'd understand."

"Love issues." His mouth was moving and the right words were coming out, but that was as far as he got.

"So you'll help me find Niki Alexander's true love?"

"Of course...it's what I do." Dropping his pants, Eros quickly disrobed as he eyed his wife's perfect, nude form.

But as he stepped forward to take her in his arms, Psyche held her hand up to keep him at bay.

"But no wicked wishes this time, Eros. Niki is a by the books kind of girl. She just needs a gentle push in the right direction. Push, not shove."

"Baby." Eros pushed her hand down and pulled her into him. "Trust me, love is my job. Have I ever let you down?"

Did he really want her to answer that? She loved the big galoof, even after all these years. But despite his heart being in the right place, his big head wasn't. "I'm trusting you to get this right.

"Now come give me some of that tasty body." Gleaming blue eyes called to her in ways his wicked words never would. Right or wrong, the arrow wielding baby was hers.

Dropping a quick kiss on her frowning lips, Eros smiled charmingly and added, "I'm all over it, honey."

He was all over it, so why the hell did she feel so worried all of sudden?

Lena Matthews

Lena Matthews spends her days dreaming about handsome heroes and her nights with her own personal hero. Married to her college sweetheart, she is the proud mother of an extremely smart toddler, three evil dogs, and a mess of ants that she can't seem to get rid of.

When not writing she can be found reading, watching movies, lifting up the cushions on the couch to look for batteries for the remote control and plotting different ways to bring Buffy back on the air.

Visit Lena on the Web at www.lenamatthews.com.

* * *

TAG'S FOLLY

Eve Vaughn

Dedication

I would like to dedicate this book to my Valentine,
Andrew.

Prologue

Tag leaned against the side of his office building and took one final drag of his cigarette, relishing the smoke that filled his lungs before exhaling. He casually tossed the butt on the ground and smashed it with his heel. He should quit. It was a nasty habit, but he justified it because he only smoked in times of stress. There were months where he didn't even think about lighting up, but lately it was becoming a crutch more often than he liked to think about.

His mind drifted to his live-in lover of the past twelve months. In his thirty-eight years, no woman had ever made him feel the way Alex did. She wasn't beautiful in the conventional sense, but she was definitely striking. With just one look from her exotically slanted, light brown eyes, his cock would jump to attention.

Alex knew exactly how to use her God-given gifts to her advantage and turned heads wherever she went with her soft, medium-brown skin, full, bow-shaped lips, and an ass so round and juicy it was perfect for riding. Tag loved fucking her from behind and smacking that luscious ass of her while pulling on her glossy, shoulder-length black hair.

It was always music to his ears to hear her scream and moan his name as his cock plowed into her. Tag also loved to run his lightly tanned hands over her dark body, the color contrasts of their skin adding yet another erotic element to their lovemaking. There was nothing Alex wouldn't let him do to her in bed. Nothing. She let him take her in any hole, in any position, and anywhere. Sexually, everything was perfect.

Their home life ran smoothly as well. She cooked all their meals, cleaned, never hassled him when he wanted to hang out with his friends, and watched sports with him. He wasn't one of those misogynistic men who thought it was a woman's place to do housework, but it just wasn't his thing, either. When she'd agreed to move into his townhouse, he'd offered to hire a permanent housekeeper instead of the one who only came by once a week, but Alex had insisted that she could do it herself.

Tag supposed she did spoil him. He liked coming home and inhaling the aroma of the fruity-scented candles she favored. He enjoyed partaking of her home-cooked meals, and had become accustomed to having freshly laundered clothes, all folded neatly in his drawers. To him, things already were perfect. Tag's philosophy in life was that if it wasn't broke, and then don't fix it.

But now Alex was driving him crazy. As far as he was concerned, things were in great working order. The problem was that Alex didn't think so. On the anniversary of her moving in with him, she had brought up the "M" word. It had been only the first in a long series of heated arguments, and the last one had been particularly nasty. Why did she have to get on this wedding kick? Damn it, *why* did she want to mess up a good thing?

No one knew more than Tag that matrimony didn't guarantee a happily-ever-after. Alex had argued that he couldn't possibly know since he'd never experienced it. Well, one didn't have to put their hand in fire to know that it was hot. His parents, sister, brother, friends -- all miserable, and marriage was the reason.

He fumbled with his lighter. When Tag looked up, he saw an old woman crossing the street just as a Mack truck was bearing down on her.

Holy shit!

He was a renowned plastic surgeon but knew that even he wouldn't be able to put that lady back together again if she got hit by that huge chunk of moving metal. He dropped his cigarettes and dashed into the street, grabbing the woman's arm and pulling her out of the truck's way even as its horns blared on the way past them. In the nick of time, thank God!

Their momentum sent the two of them flying to the ground. Tag immediately jumped back to his feet, holding out his hand to the elderly woman and helping her up. "Are you okay, ma'am?"

"Oh, my goodness, me! You saved my life." She was panting and seemed really shaken up, which was understandable, considering how close she'd come to death.

"It was nothing. Do you think you'll be okay? Maybe you should come up to my office and have a seat until you've had a chance to rest."

"You're such a nice young man." The woman looked up at him with a weather-beaten, wrinkled face, but her hazel eyes were surprisingly clear and youthful. They didn't seem to fit her old, old face. "Oh, no. I couldn't. I have to meet someone. I'll be fine." Her voice sounded young, too.

"Are you sure?" he asked, concerned. She appeared really feeble.

"Of course, but I must repay you for your kindness. My name is Psy-- I mean, Sally." She held out her frail-looking hand, which he immediately shook.

"You don't have to repay me, and I'd rather you didn't."

"But I must. My husband would be furious if he knew I was here like this."

"Really, ma'am, I don't need any kind of payment. Just knowing you're okay is rewarding enough."

Sally grabbed his wrist in a surprisingly tight grip. "I'm not what I appear to be. One wish. Anything you want will be yours. You just speak the words and I'll make it happen."

Chapter One

Alex stiffened when she heard Tag enter the bedroom. Usually, on the nights when he did pro bono work, she was asleep long before he arrived home, but tonight she was restless. It was hard to sleep when the man you loved and wanted to spend the rest of your life with thought you were good enough to fuck, but not good enough to marry.

He'd never come right out and said it, but what else could it be? Wasn't she the perfect partner? She cooked, cleaned, supported him, and hardly ever nagged. She was already performing the duties of a wife, so why the hell wouldn't he make things official? She knew he'd had reservations about their age difference, and though he never mentioned it, Alex often wondered how much race played a factor in his decision, too. Tag claimed that had nothing to do with anything, but it didn't stop her from thinking otherwise.

She'd come from a truly racially blended family with a full-blooded Sioux grandfather, a couple of white aunts, a

Latino uncle, and a handful of bi-racial cousins. Her family ranged from high yellow to coal black. There probably wasn't a more liberal family unit where race was concerned. Alex had dated black, white, Middle Eastern, and Asian men, but she'd never wanted to commit to any of them. Until Tag had come into her life.

Even now, just thinking about him made her pulse race. Her mind flicked back to the time they'd first met. When her then five-year-old niece, Tiffany, had been bitten in the face by the neighbor's rottweiler, the child's appearance had been dramatically altered. Alex's sister, Olivia, was just going through a divorce and money had been tight. Tiffany's medical expenses should have fallen under her father's insurance, but Bill had removed both her and Olivia from his policy.

Through a friend, they'd heard about a plastic surgeon who often did pro bono work and who could possibly help Tiffany. Alex had gone to the appointment with her sister and niece for moral support. And met Dr. Taggert Webster. She'd wanted him. Badly. When he'd smiled at them, revealing perfect white teeth, Alex had fallen head over heels. A quick scan of his left hand had thankfully revealed no rings or a telltale tan line.

He wasn't drop-dead gorgeous. He wasn't even particularly handsome, but something about him had attracted her and made him appear sexy as hell. Though he didn't possess the beauty of Brad Pitt or Colin Farrell, he had the type of rugged appeal that would make women give him a second look.

As far as Alex had been concerned, he was a powerful, rawboned work of art, just an inch shy of reaching six feet in height. A crop of short, blue-black hair had fallen carelessly over his forehead, as though he couldn't be bothered with a comb. On most men, it would have looked unkempt; on him, it worked. The harsh lines of his face and intensely black eyes gave him a menacing, but compelling appearance, and his sharp blade of a nose rested over a pair of full, wide lips. Separately, his features were forceful, but together they made a devastating combination.

His body was lean, with the look of time well spent in a gym. And his air of cocky self-assurance was somehow appealing, and likely garnered more than one glance from the opposite sex wherever he went. All in all, Tag Webster was the kind of man who could walk into the room and command all eyes on him without saying a word.

That first meeting had impressed Alex a lot. That a reputable plastic surgeon with a successful practice would do charity work for underprivileged patients spoke of his great character. And she'd really liked the way he had handled Tiffany. It seemed that he had quite a winning way with children.

At the time, she could tell by the way he'd looked at her that he wanted her, too, but Alex instinctively knew she'd have to be one to make the first move. She'd taken his business card and called him the very next day. They'd had an instant rapport and had started initially with talking nightly on the phone. Then the calls had turned into lunches, which had transformed into real dates. Pretty soon, their relationship had progressed to sex, which hadn't been what she'd expected at all.

It had been even better.

No one else made her body sing, stroked her to a frenzy, or made her pussy so damn wet she soaked the sheets. After four months of dating him, Alex knew for certain that her feelings were based on more than the physical and was sure that Tag's were as well. When he'd asked her to move in with him, she'd jumped at the chance, giving up her cozy apartment over the beauty salon where she worked as a hair dresser.

She'd thought, of course, that by moving in with him he'd really wanted marriage, but a year later, she was nothing more than a glorified mistress and housekeeper. It galled her to think of all that she did for him while still holding down her job at the shop. Though Tag had told her that she didn't have to work if she didn't want to, quitting her job would really have made her feel like a kept woman.

It was humiliating to go to family functions and be asked when they were going to tie the knot. It had been even worse when Tag had responded by stating in no uncertain terms in front of her entire family that he wasn't interested in the institution of matrimony.

Maybe if she'd known before moving in how he felt about getting married she wouldn't have done so, but now Alex was in too deep. She loved Tag so much it hurt. Other than their difference of opinion on wedlock, he was a wonderful man, a considerate lover, a great listener, and the best cuddler ever. He always had a way of making her feel like she was the most beautiful woman in the world. In his field, he saw gorgeous women who were obsessed with their looks on a daily basis, but he always came home to her.

Really, he was perfect in almost every way. It was his outlook on marriage that soured everything. Something else that bothered her a lot was that she'd never met his family. Was he ashamed of her? Every time Alex brought up the topic of meeting his relatives, he'd blown her off.

She sighed as she listened to him move around before he came to their room. The pretense of happiness was getting harder to maintain.

The minute he slid into bed, she knew he wanted to make love. He always did, but if he thought he was getting some black tail tonight, he had another think coming, especially after he'd told her earlier today to get off his back and stop nagging him about forming a permanent union.

Tag moved closer to her, a hand landing on her shoulder.

Alex forced herself not to respond. She wouldn't let him do this to her. He'd have to learn that he couldn't always have his way.

"Alex, I know you're awake, so stop pretending you're asleep. You're not even breathing like someone sleeping," he whispered, brushing his lips against her ear. She held herself tightly to keep from shivering.

"I'm not in the mood, Tag," Alex hissed through clenched teeth. She knew without looking that he was already naked. He never wore anything to bed.

"Oh, I can change that." She heard the amusement in his voice and wanted to punch him. He captured her earlobe between strong teeth, the slight sting of his bite making her gasp in surprise and pleasure. Damn him. Tag knew how nibbling on her ear drove her wild with desire.

"Tag. Please don't. I told you I'm not in the mood." She groaned, and her pussy starting to tingle. He continued to nip at her sensitive flesh like he hadn't heard her. "Tag," she moaned, knowing that she was on the verge of giving in.

"Yeah, babe?" He turned Alex onto her back. She looked up into his twinkling black eyes.

"Why do you always do this to me?"

"Because you like it. What's up with the nightgown?"

"I told you --"

"And I told you that if you ever wore a nightgown to bed, I'd rip it off." The feral gleam in his eyes told her that he wasn't kidding. Before she could protest, Tag ripped the covers away, gripped the front of her nightgown in his hands, and tore it down the front.

"Tag, stop it!"

"Never. You knew the consequences. I bet you even wanted me to do this -- you knew it would be like waving a red flag in front of a bull. Well, you've messed with the bull and it's time for the horns." When Tag went into Alpha-mode, Alex knew there wasn't a damn thing she could do to change his mind. Besides, he was right. Hadn't she secretly wanted to him to do this?

He continued his task of stripping her with urgent movements before sliding on top of her and burying his face against her neck. He pressed hot kisses into her heated skin, such that there was only one thing she could do.

Surrender.

Her fingers dug into his thick, black hair, holding his head against her. The warmth of his breath sent pulses of ecstasy down her spine. Tag's kisses were making it hard for her to think, but at this point, Alex didn't care. The angry words of this morning's argument no longer mattered. The only thing worth thinking about at this moment was the pure, unadulterated lust coursing from her head to her toes.

"Oh, Tag." His tongue grazed the hollow of her throat.

"That's more like it," he growled.

Tag nudged her thighs apart with his knee, rubbing the length of his cock against her moist slit. The rock-hard shaft pulsed and rubbed, teasing her. She wished he'd hurry up and move it into her, but she knew he'd only give in when she could no longer articulate her desires. That was one thing that made him an excellent lover. He always took her body to the heights of passion, making her so hot she could barely breathe before he screwed her senseless.

He shifted to the side of her and trailed a finger down the center of her body.

"Tag," she moaned helplessly, the way she did every time he touched her. His finger didn't stop until they reached her throbbing cunt. "Touch me, please," she begged, arching her hot sex against his palm.

"You want it bad, don't you?" A knowing grin lit his face.

"You know I do, dammit. Don't tease me!" Alex grabbed the hand cupping her and mashed it against her pussy. She felt certain she'd die if release didn't come soon.

"Eager, aren't you, babe?" he taunted, and if she weren't so damn horny, she'd knee him in the nuts for torturing her like this. "I thought you weren't in the mood."

"Shut up, and fuck me!"

"No dice, babe. I want to play with you a little first." His middle finger slid between her folds, grazing the sensitive button nestled at the top.

She gasped from the delicious delight of his touch. "Oh, God, Tag."

"That's it, baby. Moan for me." His lips brushed against her cheek. Her body was hot, scorched by the heat generated from Tag's flesh rubbing against hers. Only he could push her to this burning need for fulfillment. Another finger joined the first and Tag squeezed her clit, eliciting a soft moan from her throat. Her hips ground against his hand. Highly aroused and wanting more, she said, "Tag, you're a bastard. Do you know that?"

He chuckled, seemingly unconcerned with that statement. "Maybe so, sweetheart, but you want this bastard, don't you?"

She didn't want to say the words, but knew Tag wouldn't let up until he had his way. "I do, dammit."

"Not good enough." His fingers clamped down tighter on her sensitive bud, sending shockwaves of pleasure soaring through her body. A thin line of sweat ran down the side of her face. Lord, she was burning up.

"I want it bad, Tag. Really, really bad."

White teeth appeared. "Very good," he said before lowering his head to take one taut nipple between his lips. His mouth was hungry, hot, and savage like a wild man as he suckled and nibbled.

"Ouch!" Alex yelped when his teeth clamped on the tight bud. She'd cried out more from surprise than anything else because the pleasure far outweighed the pain. She loved it when he got a little rough with her. Nice, sweet lovemaking was great, but sometimes a little bit of low-down, dirty fucking was the only thing that would do. Alex didn't want to be made love to right now. She wanted to fuck.

"Give it to me, Tag! I need it!"

"You don't get it until I say you do. This is your punishment for trying to deny me and yourself when we both know you want this." He transferred his attention to her other rigid nipple, then released her clit. Fingers plunged into her slick channel, probing, digging, seeking.

Her nails dug into his shoulders, breaking skin.

He lifted his head, black eyes locking with hers. "You little wildcat," he groaned passionately. His lips returned to her breast in a warm caress. She shivered. Desire pulsed within her body, matching the rhythm of her heart. She wanted to grab him by the cock and demand that he fuck her, but Tag had an almost superhuman amount of restraint.

He was the master of her body and secret desires, firing up her blood more than any man she'd ever been with. She was his slave, helpless against the passion he unleashed inside her.

Alex arched her back against his touch as Tag finger-fucked her with quick, steady thrusts. Moisture dripped down the inside of her thighs.

Lifting his head to look at her, he appeared slightly dangerous. "Moan for me again, Alex. You know how I love to hear you."

"Tag!"

"Who do you belong to?"

"You. Only you."

His hot tongue stroked the valley of her breasts. "Whose body is this?"

She trembled. "Yours!"

"And don't you forget it!"

How could she, when he handled her body so deliciously?

"You're so beautiful." He groaned again, covering her mouth in a fervent kiss. Her mouth opened eagerly under the savage assault of his. Tongues pushed forward, tasting and exploring the recesses of each other's mouths.

He sucked her tongue, dominating the kiss. When Tag finally lifted his head, they both panted for breath, although the intensity of his stare threatened to steal hers away. He straddled her once again, his arms holding him braced above her. She lifted her hips to meet his cock, but he shook his head.

"Uh uh, babe. I want you on all fours. I love fucking you from behind. That big beautiful ass of yours is just waiting to be spanked. You want that, too, don't you?" A cocksure grin lit up his face.

She did. She wanted it more than anything. Alex answered without hesitation. "Oh, God, yes." Before she could utter another word, Tag scrambled to his knees and flipped her over. She positioned herself on hands and knees, shaking with anticipation, and her pussy was so wet that she dripped.

Thankfully, Tag didn't torture her further. She sighed with relief when the tip of his cock slid between her folds. Alex pushed her hips back as he moved forward, savoring the delicious length of him. He was so deep within her. They were one and she loved it.

Tag wasn't the largest lover she'd ever been with, but his seven and a half inches, combined with an impressive girth, was enough to make her cream with each powerful thrust. He gripped her hips, digging his fingers into her skin. She wiggled impatiently when he paused.

"Hurry, Tag!"

"You took your pill this morning, didn't you?"

"Of course I did. Why --"

His cock slammed into her before she could finish. What the fuck?! This was the third time he'd asked that question during sex, and now it finally dawned on her why. How dare he?! About to voice her displeasure with his words, Alex decided to forget everything just as his cock hit the right spot. Forget temporarily. She'd confront him over his words later.

His thrusts were hard and deep. She tilted her head back, fully expecting him to grasp a handful of her hair. She knew he loved to tug and play with its length. Alex had been thinking of cutting it for a while, but had kept it long for him. Besides, she kind of liked him yanking her hair during all the action.

She wasn't disappointed; he grabbed a hold of her ponytail, pulling it roughly. She didn't mind one single bit. That, combined with his pounding cock, drove her insane with lust.

"That's it, Tag!" she cried. "Fuck me hard!"

Smack.

His hand cracked down on her ass. "God damn, you're tight, baby. You have the tightest pussy I've ever fucked, and it's mine. All mine. I'm not going to let anyone else fuck this pussy."

Smack.

His hand came down on her tender rump again, this time on the other cheek. The pain was minimal, but the pleasure was immense.

"Yes! This pussy is yours and only yours. Harder! Faster!" she screamed, wanting it dirtier and rougher.

Tag surged forward, increasing the pace of their motions, his cock slamming into her sopping cunt. Alex knew she'd be a little sore in the morning, but this was well worth it. Only Tag could make her want it like this. She felt like a wanton, always craving more of his cock. She could sense a build-up in her body that slowly spread from the tips of her toes up her legs, then traveled along her spine. When the sensation reached her head, Alex thought she'd lose consciousness.

He carried her to an intense, frenzied peak. She yelled when she achieved her mind-shattering release. "Tag! I love you!"

His grip tightened on her hips for several more strokes until he came. "Oh, fuck, yeah!" He continued to grind into her, his balls emptying into her thirsty pussy.

When her arms would no longer hold her steady, Alex collapsed, with Tag following. He rolled onto his back and gathered her in his arms. She turned around until she faced him, resting her head against his broad chest.

They remained silent for several minutes. Alex wondered what was going on in his mind. As usual, he hadn't said he loved her. Was this what their relationship was destined to be? Would he never utter the words she wanted to hear? Alex realized she should leave him, but the prospect of never seeing him again scared her.

Chapter Two

The smell of turkey bacon filled the air and his stomach responded with a low growl. Still, Tag knew something was wrong the moment he entered the kitchen. Alex was already up, cooking breakfast like she usually did, but her back was stiff, and without seeing her face, he knew she was upset. Great. The last thing he needed was another argument this early in the damn morning.

He had a day full of consultations and a breast augmentation surgery later. Going into the office with angry words on his mind wasn't how Tag had planned to begin his day. He decided to play things cool.

"Morning, babe." He walked over to her and planted a chaste kiss on her warm, brown cheek.

"Hmm," was all he got for his effort. No "good morning," and Alex was already dressed, which was odd, because she usually didn't go to her shop until ten. Tag decided to follow the example of the military by not asking. He didn't want whatever was on her mind to turn into another argument.

He put on a fresh pot of coffee and poured her a cup before sitting down at the table. His newspaper rested on his place mat as usual, but a niggling feeling told him not to pick it up as he usually did. Tag just couldn't shake the feeling that something was up and, as much as he wanted to ignore it, doing so was tough.

He knew he'd regret it, but found himself asking anyway. "Alex, is anything the matter?"

She slowly turned around and gave him a tight smile. "Why do you ask, Tag? Everything is just peachy. What could possibly be wrong?"

He knew that tone well. She was spoiling for a fight. Well, if Alex was going to play games and not tell him what was on her mind, then he wouldn't give her the satisfaction of probing.

"Okay, in that case..." He shrugged and raised the paper. Without looking up he could tell she was glaring. He could feel her stare burning him like he was an ant under a magnifying glass on a sunny day.

When he didn't face her, she finally turned away from him, banging pots and pans noisily around the oven range. What the hell? Tag tried very hard to attempt an air of nonchalance while he flipped through the pages of news. However, once Alex practically threw the food onto his plate, Tag realized she wouldn't let him have any peace until he found out what the issue was.

"What?" he asked in defeat, tossing the paper aside.

"For a man with a medical degree, you aren't very bright, are you?"

His hackles were instantly raised. Though Alex couldn't possibly know this because he never spoke of his childhood, nothing angered him more than when someone questioned his intelligence. Having been raised in a home where he was constantly called stupid meant he had a very low threshold on the topic.

"What the hell is that supposed to mean?"

"Last night, you asked me if I'm on the pill."

Was that what the fuss was all about? "Huh?"

"Huh, nothing. It wasn't the first time you've asked it, either, and I won't let you disrespect me like that again. How dare you ask me that? How...dare...you!" By the time she finished, she was practically screaming.

"How dare I? What are you getting so upset about? It's a simple question. We agreed you'd take the pill at the beginning of this relationship."

"Exactly, because you don't want children."

"So what? I've made it no secret. What are you getting so mad about?"

Arms crossed over her chest, her nostrils flaring, she glared at him. "Do you think I want children out of wedlock? I wasn't raised like that, but the fact that you'd ask me that, and during sex of all times, was hurtful." Her light brown eyes flashed with righteous indignation. With arms unfolding and hands flying to her hips, Alex looked pissed.

Tag stood up, his appetite lost. "What the hell's the big deal? So I asked you if you're on the pill. It wasn't the fucking Spanish Inquisition." He didn't mean to curse at her, but his temper had reared its ugly head.

"You may not think it was a big thing, but it was to me. It wasn't even the question itself, but the reason you asked me last night and the same reason you asked me before. But I know why you did it."

"Oh, do you, Miss Know-It-All? Why, then?"

"Don't play dumb with me, Tag. You asked because you wanted to make sure I wasn't trying to trap you. You think if I got pregnant, you'd have to marry me, and that's the last thing you want, right?"

He couldn't deny it. Children and marriage had never entered into the equation for him. He liked kids a lot but didn't want any of his own because he believed they should be born within the union of marriage, and as he had no intention of ever getting hitched, there was no point in having them.

He'd grown up dirt poor and living off the state's system with four brothers and two sisters, all of them by a different father, and an abusive mother who was also a functioning alcoholic. It had been a nightmare. His mother had been married three times before she took off with another woman's husband, leaving Tag and his siblings to their own devices. He'd been only fourteen.

After spending a year and a half in the foster care system, his mother had returned. The state of Virginia, in their infinite wisdom -- not -- had returned him and his siblings to her care, this time with husband number four in tow, a low-life biker named Scott. When Scott wasn't beating the hell out of his mother and the kids, he was spending their welfare checks on booze and drugs.

One day, Tag had snapped. He and Scott had gotten into it, and he'd ended up breaking his stepfather's jaw. The man had taken off the next day, but was his mother grateful to be free of the tyranny? Hell, no. Melissa Webster had taken to the bottle even harder and became more verbally abusive than ever.

Unable to handle it anymore, Tag had left home shortly before his seventeenth birthday. He'd gotten his GED and, with the equivalent of a high school diploma in hand, he had begun taking classes at the local community college. He'd then applied to, and, being white, had received a minority scholarship for Howard University. Not only had he discovered his love for medicine there, but he'd also realized his love for black women. Tag enjoyed women of all races, but he had a soft spot for black women. Their skin coloring spanned different shades, and they had shapely asses and an air of confidence they always carried with them.

After graduating summa cum laude from Howard, he'd won a partial grant to medical school at Georgetown University. Those years were difficult. He worked hard, struggled, and made many sacrifices, but he'd never forgotten his family. He had tried to help them as best as he could, but you couldn't help people who wouldn't help themselves.

Two of his brothers were in jail, and one was in a mental institution from years of abuse. His two sisters had followed the example of their mother and became teenage mothers. One was married and already divorced; the other was on her second baby with a different man. His youngest brother, who'd Tag had always thought had the greatest chance of success, had married young and was miserable, working a crummy nine-to-five job and supporting a woman who refused to work and help out with bills.

The life he'd led, coupled with his family's dysfunctional outcomes, had proven to Tag beyond a shadow of doubt that marriage and children were not a direction he wanted to ever go. He adored Alex, but he'd been honest from the beginning, had told her up front that he had no desire to marry. He wouldn't apologize for his feelings now.

"Yes, that's exactly why I asked. I wanted to make sure we were still on the same page."

The next thing he knew, an open palm flew toward his face. Thankfully his years of Tae Kwan Do training had taught him to react quickly.

"Don't you ever raise your hand to me again, Alex! I would never ever lay hands on you, so don't even think of doing it to me."

Her nostrils flared. She looked unrepentant. "Why? You deserve it. How could you think I would try to trap you? Hasn't this past year meant anything to you? Do you really think so little of me that you think I'd pull a stunt like that?"

"You're the one who keeps bringing up marriage after, I might add, I've repeatedly said I'm not interested."

"You didn't answer my question. Do you think me capable of trying to trap you?" The sheen in her light brown eyes looked suspiciously like tears.

He sighed. Tag hadn't meant to question her integrity, but this was an issue he wouldn't budge on. "Alex, you're young. You'll soon learn that marriage isn't the be all and end all of everything." He patted her on the shoulder, which only seemed to enrage her.

"Don't you dare patronize me, Taggert Webster."

She never used his full name unless she was really angry. He'd have to tread lightly. "I'm not trying to patronize you. I'm just trying to say that marriage isn't for me -- something you've always known."

"Why?"

"The way I see it, marriage is just a lousy piece of paper that represents nothing but lies and broken promises."

"How can you say that? My parents have been married for over thirty years, and happily, I'll have you know."

He lifted a brow. "Are they?"

"Yes! And you have a lot of nerve to imply otherwise."

"What about your sister? Her marriage didn't end so happily ever after."

"So she married a jerk. That doesn't mean all marriages don't work."

"Fifty percent of marriages in this country end in divorce, and the other half may not be living as happily as they appear to be."

Her eyelids fell and the fight suddenly seemed to leave her. "Is that what you really believe, Tag?"

"You've always known how I felt. I've said it on numerous occasions."

"Yes, I know, but I thought..."

"Thought you could change my mind? Sorry, my dear, but that's not going to happen. Look, we have a good thing going here. Why rock the boat?"

"Although we basically live as husband and wife already, I don't get the benefits of a legalized union. What if you were seriously injured? I wouldn't have the right to decide what to do with you as your next of kin, and vice versa. You'd have no recourse if something were to happen to me."

"Now you're being ridiculous. You're thinking about things that may or may not happen. There are people who are paid to do that -- they're called insurance agents. Look, you knew the deal. Let's just sit down and have breakfast. In fact, tell you what, why don't you cancel all your appointments at the salon and have a day at the spa. My treat. You can use the Titanium Visa."

"Is that your solution to everything? Give me your credit card so I'll shut up? That's not going to work this time, Tag."

He raked his fingers through his hair. "What do you want, then?"

Alex shrugged. "Besides marriage? Your love and respect would be nice."

"I do respect you, Alex. As far as love is concerned, I don't believe it really exists."

"How can you say that? I love you, Tag."

"You don't really love me. I know you don't, and one day you'll realize that, too."

"Then what do we have?"

"Mutual respect, understanding, companionship, and mind-blowing sex. Now, come on, Alex, let's have breakfast and, tonight, I'll take you out. We can go down to the Wharf and go to the new seafood restaurant you wanted to try." He hoped his offer would mollify her.

She shook her head, a desperate look in her eyes. "Maybe I won't be here when you get back."

His eyes narrowed. She'd threatened to leave him on several occasions these past couple of months, but she never had. He was getting damn tired of her threats.

"Oh, you'll be here all right, dammit, and this is why!" He grabbed her, his arms wrapping around her body. The minute his mouth clamped on to Alex's, the same turbulent feelings rushed through his body the way they always did. She always had this effect on him. He couldn't get enough of her taste, scent, and the way she felt in his arms. His cock became rigid, and his tongue pried her lips apart, demanding entrance. Alex struggled against his hold, but Tag wouldn't release her until he'd gotten what he wanted.

God, she was sweet; the petal-soft lips beneath his were nearly more than he could take. Every time he kissed her was like the first time, each touch making him feel like his body would burst into flames from the heat they ignited together.

He ground his pelvis against her crotch. Only when she relaxed and returned his hungry kiss did he loosen his grip. Tag lifted his hands to cup the sides of her face, probing deeper into her mouth. He wanted to taste all of her. The soft moans she released filled him with masculine pride. It was he who had brought her to this state of arousal.

If he didn't have to be at his office in an hour, he'd take her to their bedroom and make love to her until the thought of leaving never crossed her mind again. Tag lifted his head, looking down into her slightly dazed eyes.

"Let's not argue about this again, okay?" he coaxed.

Alex gasped, pulling away from him. "You've got a lot of damn nerve! Did you think a mere kiss would get me off the topic? I'm very serious, Tag."

That was it. He refused to continue this conversation. "Grow up, Alex. I wish you'd leave me alone and forget about this marriage crap. If you absolutely have to have marriage, then you can forget about me, too!" He knew he was laying it on a bit thick, but he wasn't about to give into emotional blackmail.

Just then the house shook and the lights began to flicker on and off. What the hell? "Are you okay, Alex?"

She nodded, a strange look in her eyes. She was probably shocked.

"Who would have thought an earthquake would occur in Maryland? Maybe we'll hear something about it on the news later," he said lightly.

Again, she only nodded. Tag sighed, not wanting to leave for work with the way things were. "Alex, say something."

She looked at him, but didn't speak. It was almost like she was looking past him. His lips tightened. If this was another one of her games, he wasn't playing. "I'll grab breakfast on the way to the office and see you when I get home."

She stood still. Tag turned away in frustration and gathered his car keys. She'd get out her funk soon enough.

Alex would just have to learn that sometimes you couldn't always get what you wanted.

* * *

"Psyche!" A screech rang through Eros's Temple of Love.

"Oh, boy," Psyche muttered. Aphrodite was in a rage again and, as usual, the anger was directed toward her. One would think that the woman would have mellowed out after a couple of millennia. At least she learned not to take the goddess's outbursts personally. Aphrodite would have hated anyone who married her precious son, Eros. Besides, with the God of Love as your husband, an evil mother-in-law was a small price to pay.

She turned around to face the blonde goddess. Aphrodite was so beautiful at times it was difficult for mere mortals to look directly at her. What a shame it was that her main flaw was being a jealous shrew.

Psyche pasted a smile on her face. "Yes, Mother, dear?"

Aphrodite's eyes narrowed. "How many times have I told you not to call me that? I'm not your mother, nor will I ever be."

Ignoring the goddess's rant, Psyche's smile remained. "What can I do for you today?"

"You know damn well what I'm here for. I've told you many times not to get mixed up with humans. You may be the wife of a god, but that doesn't give you the right to interfere with our jobs."

Blinking innocently in the face of her enraged mother-in-law, she asked, "What are you talking about?"

"Don't be an even bigger idiot than you already are. I'm talking about Taggert Webster. I have personally taken an interest in his case."

Psyche gulped. Had she screwed with something she shouldn't have? It wouldn't be the first time, but usually her husband smoothed things over. As it was getting closer to Valentine's Day, Eros was on his yearly sojourn, shooting arrows at unsuspecting lovers, and wouldn't be back until the holiday ended.

When she'd visited Earth, Psyche sometimes granted wishes to humans, but knew to be careful not to bother any humans who were under the gods' or goddess' protection. "But...he, uh, he said... Well, why would you be interested in someone who doesn't believe in love?"

"That's exactly why I'm interested in him, you dumb, dumb..." Her mother-in-law sputtered, apparently unable to find a suitable insult, and poked her finger into Psyche's chest with every word. "He's a challenge. You had better fix this or else!"

She was in big trouble. "Oh, dear."

"'Oh, dear,' is right! You're going to be kicked out of Olympus for this."

"But how can I fix it when he's been granted a love wish, blessed by this temple? They're hard to reverse."

"Humph. Maybe you should have thought about that before you did this idiotic thing!" Aphrodite was screeching, not looking very beautiful at that moment.

Psyche's patience was wearing thin. "Instead of hurling insults at me, tell me what I can do to make things right."

Her mother-in-law tossed a golden lock over her shoulder. "I don't know what my son sees in you."

"Would you get over yourself for once? This wicked witch act is getting really old. You could never stand the fact that you're no longer the most important woman in Eros's life and, besides, you've always been jealous of me."

Ice-blue eyes glared at her. "One day, my son will come to his senses and when he does, I'll be dancing for joy."

"If it hasn't happened yet, it ain't gonna. Are you going to help me or are you going to stand there bitching?"

The goddess shook her golden head. "You'd better watch carefully what you say to me. Of course, you know I will have to go to Zeus about this, and you do know what will happen, don't you?"

Psyche smiled, knowing she had one last card to play. "Oh, I don't think so, and this is why..."

Chapter Three

Gone. Son of a bitch, she was really gone. Tag lit his third cigarette in ten minutes. If Alex had been here, she'd have had a fit seeing him smoking in the house. But she wasn't here and hadn't been for nearly a month.

How could she have walked out on him without so much as a goodbye? The morning after their big argument, as ticked as he'd been, he'd never really expected her to leave him as she'd threatened to do so many times before. When he'd come home that night, however, flowers and candy in hand, she had been nowhere in sight. Not only that, but all traces of her had disappeared, too, as if she'd never lived there at all.

His house had looked the same as it did before she'd moved in with him. The pictures she'd hung, her knick-knacks, even the hole in the wall she'd created when trying to hammer in a nail was gone. The fresh scent of a clean house was absent, the hint of her sweet perfume no longer lingered in the air, and her clothes were missing.

How could she have removed all traces of herself in so short a time period? With her disappearance from his home, other things flew out the window, too. Almost immediately, he'd taken up smoking as much as he had before she'd met him. His nurse at the office never asked about Alex as she usually did, and everything that had been remotely connected to her was gone. It was incredibly stressful, not to mention eerie.

In the beginning, Tag thought Alex was trying to force his hand, but as time passed without contact from her, he'd come to the realization that she might be serious, after all. He'd tried to brush it off, told himself he didn't need her. He wasn't the marrying kind and she knew it. Fine. There were plenty more women out there who'd kill to be in the position she'd been in.

When a week went by, then turned into another and yet another, he'd begun to miss her like hell. He knew then that he'd made a huge mistake. It wasn't just the things she'd done for him around the house that he missed, but it was her smile, intelligent conversations, and the way her eyes would light up when he'd walk into a room. And Tag hadn't known how hard it would be to live without her. His cock stayed in a constant state of arousal at the mere thought of her. Masturbation was no longer enough, and waking up in the middle of the night without her warmth or soft body curled next to his was torture. It made it difficult for him to fall back asleep.

He missed her. All of her.

Dammit! Why did it take her leaving for him to finally realize that love truly did exist?

He loved her. And if this wasn't love, what could it be? Why else would he think of nothing but her morning, noon, and night? Why else was he now up to two packs of cigarettes a day and unable to rest at night? Hell, earlier today, he'd almost left a tube inside a patient during surgery because he was thinking of her! For one of the most sought-after plastic surgeons in the D.C. area to nearly make a critical error like that during a simple liposuction procedure not only could have resulted in a nasty malpractice suit but also possibly damaged his reputation and practice. Alex's departure had him more twisted than he ever thought it possibly could, all right.

He stubbed out his half-smoked cigarette. He'd call her. Yes. That's what he'd do. Feeling better than he had in the last few weeks, he grabbed the cordless phone beside the couch. It was not quite five o'clock so the beauty shop she worked at should still be open, as Tuesdays were their late nights.

Tag punched the number impatiently into his phone, then waited for someone to pick up.

"Blessings Beauty Salon," a gum-snapping receptionist answered.

"May I please speak to Alex?"

There was a pause on the other end of the line followed by the sound of muffled conversation before the receptionist came back on the line. "Alex is with a client right now, may I take a message? Or if you want to make an appointment with her, I could do that for you." Her gum popped with every word, smacking loudly in his ear.

"Could you tell her it's Tag?" She'd always told him that she'd drop whatever she was doing if he phoned her at work.

He'd only done it a couple time in the course of their relationship but, true to her word, she'd always answered.

Again, muffled conversation. "Can I get a number for her to get back to you?"

"No. I actually need to speak with her."

"And I said she was with a client. If this is a solicitation, we don't want it." The receptionist sounded slightly belligerent. Was Alex screening her calls?

"I'm not soliciting anything. This is personal business."

"I told her your name, but she's busy."

"But I'm her boyfriend. I know she may not want to speak to me because we argued, but it's important that I talk to her."

"You don't say? Funny, Alex never mentioned she has a boyfriend. Hold on a second." The phone clacked loudly on the other end, practically blasting his ear. He waited for what seemed like forever before someone came on the line.

"Who the hell is this?" It was Alex.

"Didn't the receptionist tell you?" He knew he'd have to humble himself, so getting annoyed wasn't an option.

"Yes, Trish said some guy was on the line saying that he's my boyfriend. I don't have a boyfriend."

"Alex, please. I know I was wrong, but if we could just talk about it, maybe you'll see your way to forgiving me."

There was silence on the other end of the line.

"Alex? Say something. Please."

"Why are you calling me? I don't know you, and I'd appreciate it if you don't call here again. There are laws against prank calls and stalkers."

About to respond, Tag was cut off by a loud click. He knew she had every right to be upset with him, but to pretend that she didn't know him was somewhat extreme. He immediately stabbed at the redial key.

"Blessings Beauty Salon." This time, Trish's high pitched voice was thankfully without the accompanying snapping of gum.

"Could you please put Alex back on the line?"

"Is this the weirdo that just called? Don't call here again, you creep!"

Click.

This was not going to fly. If this was what Alex wanted, then he'd have to play it, on her terms. He'd crawl on his hands and knees if that was what was required.

He just had to get her back.

* * *

Alex swept the hair from her station into the dust pan. It had been a long, agonizing day, and her head felt like it would split wide open.

She glanced at her watch. Nearly closing time. Her sister, Olivia, was supposed to come by to borrow a couple DVDs in a few minutes. It was nice that Alex didn't have a long way to travel to get home so time wasn't an issue for her. Living over the shop was a convenient arrangement. The rent was cheap, and since there was no need for transportation to and from work, there were no commuting expenses to worry about. She was able to save a fair amount of money...money that would help her realize the dream of opening a shop of her own.

Today had been especially tough because her first client had been a crying child; then there was the woman who had insisted on a style that was too young for her. That wouldn't have been so bad if the client with extremely damaged hair -- split ends nearly to the roots -- threatened to beat her up when she felt Alex had cut off too much of it.

Ha. Alex had only cut two inches when she actually should have shaved the woman bald in order to get a healthy head of hair. At the client's insistence, however, she'd refrained from cutting a lot. In the end, she let the woman go without paying. It wasn't worth the fight especially when there were other people waiting to get their hair done.

To top things off, some nut had called claiming to be her boyfriend. He had sounded sexy on the phone, with a deep voice that had momentarily made her forget he was a lunatic, but a lunatic he was, nonetheless. Why else would he call her shop making such an outrageous claim?

She'd wondered how he had gotten her name and work number, but then realized he had probably found one of her business cards somewhere. She'd handed out quite a few out to potential clients.

Why the nut claimed to be her man, she wasn't sure. It would have been nice to have a boyfriend, but she thought it was more important to find the right guy. She wouldn't settle for just anyone. Her parents were a shining example of what marriage should be. After nearly thirty-five years of wedlock, they still carried on like a couple of teenagers.

They had taught her that happily-ever-after did indeed exist. On the flipside, however, her sister, who'd ended up marrying the man who'd taken her virginity, had taught Alex not that she'd rather be alone than be unhappy, but that sometimes finding Mr. Right requires some patience. None of the family had ever really warmed to Bill, a superficial, jealous man, but Olivia had stuck by him through the carousing, the drinking, and even the verbal abuse.

It was only when he'd raised a hand against their daughter that Olivia had gained the strength to leave that jerk. It was so unfair that her gorgeous, sweet sister had ended up with someone so unworthy of her.

The jingling of bells signaled that someone had entered the shop. She looked up to see Olivia, followed by Tiffany, who came running through the shop, pigtails flying behind her.

The child screeched, hurtling into her with a big hug. "Auntie Alex!"

"Hey, Babycakes. How's my favorite niece?"

Tiffany giggled. "I'm your only niece."

Alex smiled at the child's wit. "But you're still my favorite."

The six-year-old smiled slyly. "My birthday is coming up."

Alex laughed, glad she only had one niece; otherwise, she'd be broke. As much as she spent on this child, it was almost like Tiffany was *her* daughter. Not that she minded. Tiffany was a sweet little girl who'd suffered so much. It tore at Alex's heart to look at her niece's face and see the extensive damage from that dog savaging her.

Fortunately, the rottweiler that had attacked her hadn't bitten hard enough to cause any nerve injury, but it had been enough to leave extensive damage on the side of the child's face. The doctors had done the best they could for her, but there were still noticeable scars. It had broken Alex's heart when Olivia had told her that the kids at school called her a monster and wouldn't play with Tiffany. And it angered her that her ex-brother-in-law, Bill, refused to lift a finger to help. A good plastic surgeon could have fixed the worst of the scars, but without the funds, there weren't many options for the child.

Still, Tiffany had managed to stay positive and upbeat. How this child persisted in waking up every morning and keeping a smile on her face amazed Alex. Though her niece was just a little girl, she was Alex's hero.

"So what do you want for your birthday?"

"I want the Amazing Amanda doll, but the brown one, not the white one."

"Well, I'll definitely see what I can do about it."

Tiffany clapped her hands together and jumped up and down, excitement blazing in her dark eyes. "Oh, goodie!"

"I have some cookies in the back room. Why don't you go get a couple?"

"What kind of cookies?"

"What's my name, little lady?"

"Auntie Alex!"

"Darn tootin', and what's Auntie's favorite cookie?"

"Chocolate chip!" Tiffany shouted with a fist raised in the air.

"That's right, you little monkey. Now, why don't you go get some so I can talk to your mom?"

"Okay." The little girl turned to her mother. "Will you be okay without me for a few minutes, Mommy?" As a result of her parents' breakup, Tiffany had become very protective of her mother.

Olivia smiled. "Of course I will, baby. Go ahead."

Apparently satisfied, Tiffany raced to the backroom without a backward glance. Olivia stepped forward, her smile falling. She sighed.

"I don't know where she gets that energy from."

"She's six. Remember when you were six?" Alex grinned.

"That was twenty-two years ago, although I feel like I'm forty-eight right now." Olivia brushed the bangs from her forehead.

"Is everything okay? Any more drama with Bill?"

"The same as usual, of course. His support check bounced this month so now my account's overdrawn because I had checks written against it."

"Did you call him?"

"Of course, I did. And as usual, he gave me some lame-ass excuse. This time he said there must be some kind of mistake. That sorry bastard. I get paid tomorrow at work, but the overdraft fees are going to eat a big chunk of what's deposited."

"I can give you the money to cover those. How much do you need?"

"No. I absolutely will not let you dip into your savings again to solve my problems. You've helped me out too many times. At this rate, you'll never get a shop of your own opened. I'm your big sister. I should be the one coming to your rescue, not the other way around." Olivia looked on the verge of tears, and it served to infuriate Alex even further because it made her want to thrash her good-for-nothing ex-brother-in-law.

As a kid, Alex had always looked up to her sweet, older sister, the beauty in the family. Although they were both roughly around the same height at five feet six, and had the same curvy build, Olivia was stunning with smooth, dark-brown skin, large, dark, slightly up-tilted eyes, a straight, proud nose resting over lush lips, and a head full of naturally curly hair. Men often followed her around like puppy dogs, but the amazing thing was that it never went to her head. The downside of being such an attractive woman was that Olivia sometimes drew the type of men who were solely interested in her looks rather than her as a person. Bill was a prime case in point.

"O, that's what family is for. If you can't come to us when there's a problem, who can you turn to?"

"I'm tired of turning to Mom, Dad, and you when I have a problem. You all warned me not to marry Bill, but I thought he loved me and that I loved him. For him, I threw away the opportunity to finish college and I can't afford to go back to school. I refuse to ask Mom and Dad for the money because I'm no longer their responsibility." A tear ran down Olivia's cheek. She quickly wiped it away. "Now I don't know what I'm going to do with myself. I don't have any major talents and I'm in two dead-end jobs going nowhere fast. Look at you -- you do hair like a dream. That's a gift. To top everything off, I'm a lousy mother."

Alex's hands flew to her hips. "Don't you ever say that again. You're an excellent mother. Anyone who sees you with Tiffany can tell how much you guys love each other."

She couldn't believe her sister was getting down on herself again. Not only was she drop-dead gorgeous, Olivia was loyal, dependable, compassionate, and loving. Not a lot of people possessed so many fine qualities. And, sometimes, she had such a serene quality about her that she was almost angelic, practically too good to be true. Still, every now and then Olivia would start feeling sorry for herself and Alex would indulge her woe-is-me party. But only for a few minutes before the tough love kicked in.

"Of course I'm a bad mother. Just look at Tiffany's face. That's my fault. I'm the one who left her with our neighbor so I could go out with friends. I knew the woman had dog, but I didn't think twice about placing Tiffany in her hands. Because of my negligence, my baby will probably look like that for the rest of her life!" She burst into noisy tears.

Alex pulled her sister into a tight embrace. "Shh. It's okay. These things happen for a reason."

"What possible reason could there be for what happened to my baby?"

"I don't know. Only God knows for sure. Look, I'm going to lock up, we'll go upstairs and I'll fix you some tea. I'll write you a check for those overdraft fees and if you argue with me, I'm going to slap the silly out of you." Alex pulled away from a now-contrite Olivia.

The older woman gave her a weak smile, dark eyes shiny with tears. "You're too good to me."

"You're my sister, girl. I know if I were in your position, you'd do the same for me." She walked over to her station and grabbed a couple of tissues. "Here. Wipe your face. You don't want Tiffany to see you like this, do you?"

Olivia took the tissue and dabbed her eyes. "Thanks, sis."

Alex nodded and walked to the front of the shop to lock the door. Everyone was gone for the day, and since she lived over the shop, the owner trusted her to lock up the salon.

Just as she reached the front door, it opened. A tall, dark man with intense black eyes entered the shop. He didn't look like the type to frequent a beauty salon like this one. In fact, judging from his designer khakis, black Polo shirt, and Kenneth Cole shoes, he was more the kind of man who frequented only the most exclusive salons for his haircuts.

He wasn't good-looking but had a certain something about him that made it hard for her to drag her gaze away. Even more intriguing was that Alex had the strangest feeling they'd met, but she couldn't remember where or when. She was attracted to him. Very attracted. Regardless, she had Olivia and Tiffany to deal with right now.

She smiled at him. "I'm sorry, sir, but we're closed, but if you'd like to make an appointment for another time I'll be happy to take your information." That strange familiarity was not going away.

"Alex, what are you playing at? I know we parted on bad terms, but don't pretend you don't recognize me. Don't cheapen what we had. And what the hell did you do with your hair?"

Alex's hand flew to her head, self-consciously smoothing her chin-length hair into place. Who the hell was this? Was he nuts? Suddenly, a light went off in her head. If she didn't recognize his face, she certainly recognized his voice. It was the weirdo who'd called earlier. She felt a stab of disappointment that she could be that drawn to someone who obviously had some kind of mental imbalance.

"You're going to have to leave."

He moved forward. She retreated. "Don't come any closer." She ran to the closest workstation and snatched up the first thing she could get her hands on.

"If you take one step closer, I'm going to spray you."

He laughed. Tall, dark, and crazy. But he had a great laugh. Why did the weirdos have to be so hot?

"You're going to assault me with hair spray? That's hardly threatening. Alex, c'mon, be reasonable. Put that down and let's talk about this like two adults." He approached her, and she pressed the button on top of the aerosol can. He lifted his arm to shield his face, and with the other arm he grabbed the container from her hand.

"Now you're just being ridiculous, Alex. How can we work things out if you don't give me a chance?"

"Work what out? I don't know you."

Olivia shouted from the back of the shop. "I'm calling the police!"

The stranger lifted his head and looked toward her sister's direction. "Olivia, talk some sense into your sister."

Alex gasped. How did this man know who they were? This was getting way too creepy. She looked over her shoulder. "O, grab Tiffany and get out of here. Go out the backdoor."

"I'm not leaving you here with that psycho." Olivia charged at him with the broom Alex had been using earlier.

Whack! The handle connected with the man's shoulder.

"Ow! Cut that out! Are you women nuts? Alex, I'm not leaving until we talk this out," he said with obvious determination, leaving no doubt in her mind he meant every word. What was his problem? When Olivia raised the flimsy broom to strike him again, he caught it, grabbed it, then snapped it in two over his knee.

Alex was truly frightened now. Were they about to die?

"Now, will you listen?" he asked impatiently.

Before she could open her mouth, Tiffany came running from the back room, mouth covered in cookie crumbs. "Mommy, I brought you some cookies." The child stopped short and smiled up at the nutcase. "Hi, are you here to get your hair done? My auntie is the best hairdresser in town."

Alex and Olivia both broke out of their stupor at the same time, each taking one of Tiffany's little shoulders and pushing her behind them. Alex's eyes darted to the stranger who had paled significantly. He looked as if he'd just seen a ghost. In fact, he almost looked like he'd faint.

"Oh, my God! Her…her face."

Chapter Four

Alex crossed her arms. "Get out of this shop right now and never come back! What kind of insensitive jerk are you?"

"But-but her face...it shouldn't be like that. I-I...fixed it," Tag muttered, stunned by Tiffany's appearance. Although he hadn't been able to restore her face to exactly the way it used to be, the scarring had been so minimal that when she grew up, it'd barely be visible. But now, the little girl's face looked exactly as it had, if not worse, before he'd operated on her.

What the hell was going on, and why was Alex acting as if she'd never laid eyes on him before? And why didn't it appear to *be* an act? Something weird was happening.

The shop door opened and a little elderly woman walked through the door. She looked at him and her eyes brightened. She looked oddly familiar. "Oh, there you are. I've been looking all over for you." She smiled at him.

"You have?" he asked dumbly.

"Of course, I have, silly. You forgot to take your medication again, dearie." She turned to the two perplexed women and the child peeking from behind her mother.

"I'm sorry my son has bothered you. He...he's not exactly well. It's been so hard for me to keep up with him since his father died, but I do my best. I'll take him off your hands, dearies."

Tag's jaw dropped. Oh, yeah, things were definitely amiss, but a niggling feeling told him that this woman somehow held the key to what was going on. He took one last look at Alex, who wore a baffled expression on her face, before he allowed himself to be led out of the salon.

The minute they stepped outside the doors and got a couple yards away from the shop, Tag turned on the old lady. "Will you tell me what the hell is going on? Why are you claiming to be my mother?"

The woman laughed. "Well, I had to think of some explanation to get you out of your predicament; otherwise, those ladies would have called the police. Look, Taggert, you were floundering and needed my help. Besides, Alexandra doesn't have a clue who you are."

"Whoa! Whoa! Whoa! First off, what are you talking about? And why wouldn't Alex know who I am? We've been lovers for the past year."

"Yes, you were, until your wish changed things."

This was going from ridiculous to farcical. He hated being in any situation he didn't understand. "Has the world gone nuts? What are you talking about?"

"Don't you recognize me from a few weeks ago, Taggert?" the woman asked.

He finally took a good look at her. "Holy shit. You're the crazy wish lady."

"Sort of, but haven't you ever been taught to look beyond the surface?" The most phenomenal thing happened next. Before his very eyes, she morphed into a whole new woman -- an extraordinarily beautiful woman, with curly brown hair that nearly touched the ground, a youthful face, and sparkling green eyes.

He couldn't possibly have seen what he thought he did. Or could he? "How did you do that?"

"Oh, I usually take on different forms when I leave Olympus. My real name is Psyche, by the way, but you're probably more familiar with my husband, Eros, and perhaps my monster-in-law -- I mean, my mother-in-law -- Aphrodite."

Greek mythology had been one of his interests in college, but he'd put it aside because his passion for medicine had been stronger. Either this woman was shooting up or he was in the middle of a dream because there was absolutely no way he could be standing here talking to Psyche -- the God of Love's wife.

"Tell me I'll wake from this wacky dream or that I'm on *Candid Camera* or something, because you're not supposed to be real."

She sighed. "Yes, I get that a lot. Eros doesn't really like it when I interact with humans, but I used to be human and sometimes I like to visit Earth. Anyway, I'm very much real and very much in a world of shit."

"What?" Tag thought his head would fall off if things didn't start to make sense soon.

"The wish you made had repercussions for me and you both. Me, because the monster-in-law may finally have some ammunition to get me tossed out of Olympus, and you, because now everything that had to do with you and Alex in the past year never happened."

"I don't understand."

"Well, you're the dummy who wished Alex would leave you alone and forget you. You know, when you have a love wish at your disposal, you really ought to be careful with your wording."

It finally occurred to him exactly what she was talking about. No. It couldn't be.

"So what you're saying is that because of something I said in the course of an argument, it has now wiped out the past twelve months of my life?"

"It hasn't exactly wiped out everything, just the stuff between you and Alex. That friend of hers never made the suggestion for Olivia to take Tiffany to see you. No Tiffany and Olivia, so no Alex tagging along. It's really a shame because you'd done such a good thing for that little girl."

"I didn't do it for the thanks."

"I know you didn't, and that's what makes you a good person. A man of your status doesn't need to give his services away for free. A lot of people in your position never give back to the community. That's one of the reasons I granted you that wish. I saw in you a trait that's been lacking in mankind recently -- compassion."

Tag raked his fingers through his hair, not believing he was actually having a conversation with a woman who was claiming to be someone from a Greek myth. "So how do we fix it? Can't you just undo the wish?"

"It's not that simple. Love wishes are difficult to reverse."

"Then I'm to pay for the rest of my life for something said in anger? I never asked for the damn wish in the first place."

"Well, you did a good deed, and I only wanted to reward you."

"In that case, the next time I see a truck about to hit an old lady, I'll just let it happen."

Psyche bit her bottom lip, a look of contrition on her face. Maybe he was being a little hard on her. She couldn't have known that he'd make such a jackass wish.

"I'm sorry. I didn't mean to be so nasty, but I've recently discovered that I love her. If only it hadn't taken her leaving for me to find out."

"I said the wish would be difficult to reverse. I didn't say it was impossible."

Tag gripped Psyche by the shoulders, practically shaking her. If there was something he could do to win Alex back, he would do it. He didn't care if he had to assassinate someone; he'd do it if only for a chance to tell her of his love. "What do I need to do? Tell me, I'm desperate."

She laughed. "I'll tell you if you stop shaking me."

He let her go and waited to hear what she had to say.

"First, I think you need to calm down."

"Lady, I'm as calm as I'm going to get, considering the situation."

She shrugged. "Fair enough. Nothing jars the memory better than lust. You can forget events or people, but you never forget how you felt in the throes of passion. You're going to have to make her remember what you two shared."

"So I basically have to get her to have sex with me? How in Heaven's name will I go about convincing her to do that when she thinks I'm certifiable?"

"I'll think of a way. And you have to do it by Valentine's Day or else the results of your wish will be permanent."

"That's next week! Are you kidding me?!"

Psyche sighed, twirling a lock of luxuriant brown hair with her finger. "I told you it would be difficult, but I'll help you, of course. I'll just have to come up with a plan. We both have a lot at stake here."

"And what is yours?" Tag almost wished he'd never seen her crossing the street that day, but didn't. It was wishing that had caused his current problems in the first place.

Psyche stopped twirling her hair, a dark brow lifting, green eyes almost appearing to emit fire. "This isn't all about you, buddy, and if you think about it, my giving you that wish didn't cause your problems. Your stubbornness did. Had you just admitted your feelings for Alex were based on more than just sex, had you told her why you don't believe in marriage, you wouldn't be in this predicament."

"How --"

"How do I know? I live on Olympus. There's not a lot I don't see, and let me tell you something, buster, there aren't a lot of women out there who would put up with you the way she did. And all she asked in return from you was a deeper commitment. The two of you already lived together, so what would have been the big deal if you did marry her? I know you'll argue the opposite side and say that since you lived together, what did a piece of paper matter. Well, that piece of paper mattered to Alexandra, and if it didn't to you, what would have been the harm in giving her what she wanted?" She shook a finger at him. "You really ought to be ashamed of yourself, Taggert Webster. You treated her abysmally, but she loved you, anyway. You *knew* she loved you and did things for you out of that love, which you took for granted. Now you have the audacity to rail against me when most of this is your own damn fault. If I didn't have my own interests to consider, or the other people your selfish wish affected, I'd say to Hades with you!"

Tag felt like an asshole. Everything Psyche said was absolutely correct. His selfishness had gotten him into this mess. He'd used his childhood as an excuse and, as a result, he'd ended up losing the very best thing that had ever happened to him.

He'd never been as close to tears as he was now. "I'm sorry, Psyche," he said, and meant it.

"You've gone pale as a sheet. Come on, I see a Starbucks down the block. They make great coffee." She took his hand. "You know, they're in negotiations to open one on Olympus."

He allowed her to lead him to the coffee shop. "Why don't you get a table for us, and I'll get us both a cup of the evil brew. How do you take yours?"

"Black, just a little sugar," he said automatically. Alex used to make the best cup of coffee, knowing exactly how he liked it. Why was he now remembering all the little things? Sex had been a big factor in what he'd been missing lately, but nothing compared with the other things she'd done for him.

When Tag found an empty booth, he sat down and stared absently out the window, wondering how he could get himself out of this mess. His heart twisted when he remembered Tiffany's face. No child deserved to suffer what she had. The one thing he most remembered about dealing with the little girl was her sunny disposition. A lot of his pro bono stuff involved children, but by far Tiffany had been one of those special kids you couldn't help but like because she had a light about her that one could almost see.

And to think, because of his wish, that precious darling was probably ostracized by her peers. No one knew as well as he how cruel children could be. Hadn't he been teased mercilessly in school because of his thrift-store clothing and no-brand-name shoes?

He shuddered to think what children had to say about Tiffany. He wondered who else had been affected adversely by his ill wish. So much had happened in the year he'd been with Alex.

"Here you go. I got you a cup of the Kenyan. The coffee there is excellent." Psyche handed him his drink, then took a seat.

Tag smiled gratefully, not really wanting it, but thought it impolite to refuse.

"Now, let's think of a way to get you back with Alexandra."

"You said that you had a lot at stake in this. Care to elaborate?"

Psyche grimaced before taking a sip of her coffee. "Aphrodite has wanted to get rid of me from the very beginning. Even before I married Eros she tried to destroy me because of my appearance. I can't help the way I look, and it's certainly not my fault that people traveled from all over to pay me tribute -- tribute that she felt was rightfully hers. I never disputed that and what happened between Eros and me...well, she would have made any woman who joined with her precious son miserable, but she hates me tenfold." She sighed. "Anyway, because she tried to finish me when it was discovered that Eros and I had married, my husband went to Zeus and asked for intervention. Although we'll never be friends, Aphrodite and I have had somewhat of a truce as long as neither one of us interferes with the other. By granting you that wish, I've broken the spirit of the truce. Because of this, I could get kicked out of Olympus. This time, Eros can't help me."

Tag's brows furrowed. He frowned, trying to make sense of what she'd just told him. "I'm not quite following you. How did granting my wish interfere with Aphrodite?"

"You were her pet project, or at least one of them. She's the Goddess of Love and you didn't believe in love. She was working on a way to change your mind, when I inadvertently stepped on her toes by getting involved. She could go to Zeus and get me expelled from the only home I've known for the past several centuries. She's such a horrid woman sometimes, but I've been given until Valentine's Day to fix everything between you and Alex."

"If she wants you out that badly, why is she willing to wait until Valentine's Day?"

A mischievous smile crossed the brunette beauty's face. "It's February."

"And?"

"And Valentine's Day falls in it. Anyone seeking a favor from her can ask her in the month of February and not be denied. As much as she hates me, she couldn't say no to my request."

"So why didn't you ask for more time?"

"Well, that's the thing; I didn't specify how much extra time I needed. I know I should have, but I wasn't thinking clearly. The woman gets me so flustered sometimes. Valentine's Day was her stipulation."

"Damn," he muttered.

"'Damn' is right." She sighed again and placed her elbows on the table, resting her chin in the center of her cupped palms.

"I hate to ask, because God knows I don't think I can take any more bad news, but what else has been affected by the wish besides what's been stated...and Tiffany?"

Psyche shook her head, a sympathetic gleam in her green eyes. "Well, because you never met Alex or her family, Olivia used up all of her savings to take Tiffany to a doctor she could afford, but he turned out to be a hack. He messed up her daughter's face worse than before. Since there was no insurance, the subsequent hospital visits put her in serious debt. She took on another job to make ends meet. Alex's savings are slowly dwindling away because she's constantly bailing her sister out. Unless she wins the lottery, she'll never realize her dream of owning her own shop." Psyche scrunched up her face, obviously trying to remember more. "Hmm, let me think. Oh, yeah, there's also --"

Tag held up his hand, sure that he didn't want to hear another word. The last thing he needed was a laundry list of the consequences of his stupidity. "I get the picture. So what's our next move? How do you propose I get Alex alone and convince her that we're sexually compatible?"

"You leave the getting together part to me, but first tell me her likes and dislikes."

"I thought you were all-knowing," Tag taunted.

"Watch it, smart ass. My name is Psyche, not Zeus. Now, how about giving me that list so we can get your woman back?"

Chapter Five

Alex felt excited for the first time in a while. What luck it had been to receive a packet in the mail for a Valentine's weekend getaway at the downtown Washington Ritz Carlton. It was funny to have won because she didn't remember entering this particular contest, but everything had turned out to be legit. She planned on enjoying herself, and since she didn't have a significant other to share her prize with, she invited Olivia.

Her sister really needed this weekend of relaxation more than anyone, courtesy of her thankless jobs and wretch of an ex-husband. Their parents had agreed to watch Tiffany, so everything was set. Not only were she and her sister going to have the weekend getaway, but they'd also received tickets to the Annual Valentine's Day Ball, which was also at the Ritz. Some of her favorite musical acts would be performing, and all kinds of celebrities would be there. These tickets were the hottest items in town, and they'd been included in her prize pack.

She turned to her sister and held up a spaghetti-strapped, red mini dress and an even smaller strapless white dress. "So what do you think, O? Which one should I wear? I don't know why, but I just get the feeling something wonderful is going to happen to me tonight."

Olivia eyed each dress critically. "Uh, yeah. Something is definitely going to happen to you if you wear either one of those dresses."

"Oh, come on, sis, why don't you get into the spirit of things? Maybe you'll meet your Mr. Right tonight."

The other woman snorted, a derisive look on her face. "Hardly. I made a mistake once. I'm not going down that road again."

Alex placed the dresses on the king-sized bed and walked over to her sister. "Sweetie, I wish you wouldn't talk like that. Don't let that jackass, Bill, affect you this way."

"Its really hard not to. I...I thought he was my knight in shining armor, but instead, he was only a big loser. He turned my life upside down and left me in debt without a qualm. How do you think I'm supposed to feel? I hadn't even been lucky in love before him."

"I absolutely hate that he's done this to you."

"I hate what he's done to me, too, but I especially hate what he's doing to our daughter. He hasn't so much as attempted to visit her since..."

"I know."

Olivia sighed. "I guess I always knew what a superficial bastard he was. When I was carrying Tiffany, I'd gained some weight, of course, and he wouldn't touch me. He called me a disgusting pig. Even when I lost the weight, the name stayed because he knew how much it hurt me. I realize she's better off without him in her life, but that's hard for a six-year-old to understand."

"Then why can't you see that he's the one with the problem and not you? He's an asshole, always was, and always will be. There are lots of good men out there."

"You sound so sure, Alex."

"I am. Look at Mom and Dad. They knew each other for only a day before they eloped. Don't stories like that make you believe in the power of love?"

"Too blindly in your case, I'd say. You wait until it happens to you, Alex. It might not be the sweet, perfect bliss you think it will be. That kind of attitude will have you shacked up with a man as his glorified mistress."

A shiver rippled down Alex's spin. A strong feeling of *déjà vu* struck her and she wasn't sure why. What did this mean? Why did that comment bother her so much? A face suddenly flashed through her mind. The man from the salon. She took a seat on the bed, careful not to sit on the dresses, her legs no longer able to support her.

"Alex, are you okay? You lost a little color there for a minute. Can I get you something to drink?"

"No, I'm fine."

"Are you sure?"

"Yes. I...something you said made me feel strange."

"What?"

"The part about being a glorified mistress. That statement...I've heard it somewhere recently."

A pensive look crossed Olivia's dark face. "That's odd. Look, I'm not sure if I'm up to going to this party. Maybe I'll just read a book or something."

"Oh, no, you don't. You're coming to the party. You promised. Besides, that beautiful peach gown we brought would go to waste. That dress is way too fierce to just sit in a closet."

Olivia rolled her eyes. "Whatever. It's not like I can really enjoy myself. This is the first time I've had a weekend off in ages and I should be spending it with my daughter."

"You spend plenty of time with her. Having a weekend getaway doesn't make you a bad parent."

"But didn't you see her sad little face when I left?"

"You're imagining things. She's probably having a great time with Mom and Dad. She always does. You know as well as I do that they love having her over and they'll spoil her like crazy."

"I guess, but --"

"No buts. So are you going to tell me what dress I should wear or not?"

"Well, isn't this a formal function? Didn't you bring something that would cover more flesh?"

Alex giggled. "Oh, come on. These are classy dresses. Look." She held the red one up. "It has sequins around the bottom."

Olivia lifted a brow. "And the white one?"

"It's satin. Nothing is more formal than satin."

"Hmm, I'm not really sure I'd wear either one, but you certainly have the body to carry them off."

"So do you."

"Maybe so, but I don't have your flair. You could get away with wearing something like that because you have the right attitude."

"You could, too, O. I just know something fabulous will happen tonight."

"How do you know?"

"It's weird, but when I won that prize packet, I felt there was something special about it, like it was touched with magic or something. I know that sounds crazy, but I really think something good will happen, and since this is a Valentine's party, what else could it be but meeting my true love?"

"Hmm, love schmov."

"Oh, stop it. You're the Valentines' Day equivalent of Scrooge."

"And you're naïve."

"I wouldn't be surprised if you meet a terrific man tonight."

Olivia shook her head. "I doubt it. I'm going to find the bar and I'm not moving from it until the party is over."

"We'll see." Alex laughed, unable to quell the excitement coursing through her body.

* * *

"Are you sure she's going to be here tonight?" Tag asked Psyche for the third time as he tugged on his bow tie. God, he hated wearing these damn things. They felt like a noose around his neck.

Psych pushed a long, curly length of hair over her shoulder. Tonight she wore a gold ball gown. Eyes looked her way the minute she'd stepped into the ballroom on Tag's arm, but she didn't appear to notice. She was one of those women who possessed a beauty so rare that when people stared, it never fazed her because she was used to it. Tag didn't know if it was wise to have so much attention in their direction, but he was only following her lead.

"Of course she'll be here tonight, Tag. She has to be."

"But you sent her two tickets. What if she brings a date?"

"You're such a worrier. You need to calm down or you'll give yourself an ulcer. Everything has been taken care of. I do have a few connections of my own, you know."

"What's that supposed to mean?"

"Ever heard of subliminal advertising?"

"Yes. What's that got to do with the price of tea in China?"

"It means I had some friends make subtle suggestions to her. Actually, they were invisible and she couldn't physically hear them, but her subconscious did. If everything goes according to plan, she's brought her sister along."

Tag relaxed. "That's okay, then."

Psyche looked annoyed. "That's it? No 'thank you' for my efforts? I thought it was rather clever of me."

He shook his head with a chuckle. Women and their egos. "Thank you, Psyche. You've done a great job."

"I should think so, considering we're getting down to the wire. Aphrodite isn't supposed to interfere, but she's tricky. I know she had something to do with that long errand I was sent on a couple of days ago. The thing is I can't prove it. Fortunately, she and Eros are now working as this is their holiday, which means I can concentrate on getting you back together with your woman."

"My woman. I like the sound of that." He smiled his first genuine smile in weeks because he felt hopeful. Maybe things would truly work out, after all.

A waiter walked by and offered them a glass of pink champagne. Psyche took one, but Tag declined, his gaze drifting to the entrance of the ballroom. Any minute now Alex would walk through the door.

"This party started nearly an hour ago. Where could she be?" He shifted his weight from foot to foot with impatience. The waiting was killing him. It was bad enough that he was here in this monkey suit at a function he normally wouldn't be caught dead at, but the uncertainty of whether Alex would even show up was nearly more than he could handle.

"I know you're anxious to see her, but you really need to relax. You know, for a doctor you're very high-strung." Psyche popped a bacon-wrapped scallop she'd gotten off a tray into her mouth.

"Relax? After midnight tonight I could lose the woman I love, and you tell me to relax? I thought you'd be a little more concerned for yourself, too. After all, you have just as much to lose as I do."

"More, actually." She grabbed a cheese puff from another tray as a waiter walked by. "Mmm, these appetizers are to die for. Not as excellent as ambrosia, mind you, but pretty darn close. Yummy."

"Are you just going to stand there and stuff your face?" Tag wanted to shake her. How could she be so calm?

"This is a party and I'm trying to enjoy myself. Anyway, if you weren't so busy fussing at me you'd have noticed that Alex and her sister just walked in. I must say that they both look lovely tonight." Psyche pointed toward the women and Tag's mouth went dry.

He did a double take when he saw Alex. She looked so beautiful and so...naked. What the hell was she thinking to wear that little red getup to a formal ball? She was practically falling out of the red mini-dress. Her curves had always been generous, but in that dress, she looked like a black Betty Boop. If her dress dipped any lower, he'd see nipples. Despite her scantily clad body, she somehow managed to look elegant with an expertly made up face, her hair pulled back in a style reminiscent of Audrey Hepburn in *Sabrina*, and a look that said she was aware of her sexuality.

His cock stirred. Damn, he wanted her. His hand immediately flew to the front of his pants to cover up the result of his raging hormones. Jealousy reared its ugly head when he noticed several pairs of male eyes ogling her. Tag wanted to stalk over to her, toss her bodily over his shoulder, carry her up to his room, and fuck her until she realized that she belonged to him and only him.

"Should I go over there? How do you think she'll react when she sees me?" He turned to Psyche, who was now holding up one poor waitress as she brought shrimp to her lips.

"There's only one way to find out, and that's going over there to talk to her," she answered with a full mouth, not bothering to turn away from the tray. The god's wife seemed more interested in stuffing her face than helping him. Tag rolled his eyes heavenward. How in the world did Eros put up with this bubblehead for two millennia?

"Aren't you supposed to be advising me?"

"I am advising you."

"From where I'm standing, looks like you're chowing down."

Green eyes narrowed. "If you would try these hors d'oeuvres, you'd understand. I'm going to have to put some of these bad boys into my purse to take back to Olympus. Hey, what do you think these little green squares are?" She pointed to an edible something on her napkin. The waitress, seeing the talking garbage disposal's temporary distraction, got the hell out of there.

That was it. Psyche wasn't going to be any help. He'd have to do whatever he needed to do on his own. Now if only he could figure out what that what was.

* * *

"Oh, look who's playing now! The Flow Brothers are one of my favorite groups. I can't believe they're here!" Alex squealed with excitement. The ballroom looked fantastic, a prism of lights dancing across the ceiling.

"I can't believe we're here, either," Olivia muttered, not sounding excited in the least.

"O, snap out of it. You promised me you'd at least try to have a good time."

"I'd have a good time if I were home with my daughter."

Alex bit her lip to stop herself from saying something hurtful. She wasn't going to let her sister's negative energy kill her mood. Instead, she said, "If you want to hang out at the bar, go ahead. I'll just mingle and maybe I'll meet someone who actually wants to be here."

Olivia turned to her, dark brown eyes shining with a look of regret. "I'm sorry to be such a killjoy. I just feel so ridiculous in this dress, and why you insisted on a tiara is beyond me."

"Because it goes great with your gown and your 'do. You are the most gorgeous woman here."

And it was true. Olivia's looks had been a source of envy for Alex when they were younger, but her sister didn't have a conceited bone in her body. It was hard to stay jealous of someone who seemed so unaware of their power at times.

"Excuse me, but may I have this dance?" An extremely tall gentleman with dark hair and the greenest eyes she'd ever seen had approached them. Alex knew right away that he wasn't talking to her, but to Olivia. His eyes were riveted to her sister's face.

He was fine as hell. This man by far blew any Hollywood hunk out of the water in the looks department. He had a hard-looking face, appearing as though it had been sculpted from granite, which saved him from looking like a pretty boy, and thickly lashed eyes and sensual red lips that made one want to kiss them. If his gaze wasn't glued to Olivia, Alex would definitely take him up on his offer.

"I...I don't dance," her sister answered.

"Then perhaps you'll have a drink with me?" The stranger's voice was deep and melodic, with an almost hypnotic quality about it. There was something compelling about it that made it difficult to look away from him and, oddly enough, it wasn't his looks. He almost had some kind of strange magnetic pull.

Olivia looked slightly uncomfortable, not meeting the man's eyes. "No, thank you."

Alex's jaw dropped. Her sister was nuts. Maybe she was willing to rebuff the hottie of the century, but Alex wasn't going to let her. "Of course, you'd like a drink. Before we got here you were talking about hanging at the bar." She faced the hunk.

"My sister would love to have a drink with you. She's just shy. Go on," Alex encouraged, practically pushing the reluctant woman toward the man.

Olivia glared at her before looking up at the smooth and refined man standing in front of them. "No, please. I...I don't want to. I don't mean to be rude, but I don't know you."

The stranger smiled, revealing teeth almost too white to be real. "My name is Maxwell Sterling, and you are Olivia, am I correct?"

Olivia's forehead wrinkled. "How do you know my name?"

"I must apologize for eavesdropping, but I noticed the two of you earlier today in the hotel lobby, and I couldn't help but overhear a bit of your conversation. I'm glad you're here tonight."

A light bulb went off in Alex's head. Was this *the* Maxwell Sterling, one of the richest men in the world and related to royalty as well? "Maxwell Sterling of Sterling International?"

He turned green eyes on her. "You've heard of it, of me?"

Alex snorted. "Who hasn't?"

"Then you also know that I didn't get where I was today by taking no for an answer," he said. Although the words were directed to her, his gaze remained on Olivia, who looked like she wanted to bolt. Why was her sister acting like this?

Before either woman could say another word, Maxwell took Olivia by the elbow.

"Please, I don't want..." Olivia began, but something in Maxwell's eyes halted her.

Alex didn't know what it was, but she had a feeling that something had just happened. Maxwell nodded her way before leading Olivia off. Her sister looked slightly dazed. What in the world? She sensed that whatever occurred after this ball, it wouldn't be the last time that either of them saw him.

She chuckled, thinking that he might be the person who could give her sister the jumpstart she needed to live life again, even if it was temporary. Everyone knew Maxwell Sterling was a notorious bachelor.

Barely over her mirth, Alex turned to see a figure striding purposely toward her. At first she couldn't make out who it was, but when she could, all traces of humor and her earlier excitement fled. With a look of pure determination flashing in his black eyes, the psycho from the salon was closing in on her.

She did the only thing she could think to do. She ran. Rushing out of the ballroom, Alex headed for the elevators, not daring to look back. If she could just make it to the lobby on the first floor, she could notify security. Frantically pushing the down button, Alex stole a look over her shoulder. Thankfully, he was nowhere in sight. She breathed a sigh of relief when the elevator door opened.

Home free. She walked in and leaned against the back wall, but her respite was short-lived when a body came barreling through the doors just before they closed.

She screamed. "No!"

Chapter Six

Just as the shriek tore from Alex's throat, the elevator began to rumble and the lights flickered. Tag had only experienced this one other time and that was the morning of his wish. Were things back to normal already?

Alex reached out for the button pad, stabbing the "door open" button impatient fingers. Nothing. No movement. No sound. She pushed at more buttons without much effect. "No, please tell me I'm not stuck in this elevator with this nut," she muttered, sounding frantic.

Tag knew without a doubt that other forces were at work. So, Psyche had come through, after all. He crossed his arms, triumph swelling his chest. Tag grinned, leaning against the wall. "I don't think pushing those buttons is going to do you any good. I believe we're stuck."

She ignored him and started pummeling the doors. "Help! Somebody help me! I'm stuck in the elevator with a madman!"

"If you keep screaming like that, Alex, you're going to lose your voice."

She turned on him, a snarl on her lips. "Who the hell asked you? Why did you follow me, anyway?"

"Because I had to find a way to talk to you."

"What could you possibly say to me that I'd want to hear? Why are you bothering me again? Did you take your medication this morning?"

"Could you at least hear me out before you hurt yourself banging on the doors?" he asked impatiently.

"No." She opened the panel over the buttons and pulled out the emergency phone. "Oh, no, it's dead," she cried in dismay.

Tag smiled. Now there was no escaping him, and that was exactly how he wanted it. "Alex, could you please listen to me for five minutes?"

"No, just leave me alone. Pretend I'm not here."

"I can't do that. You're the reason why I'm at this ball in the first place."

"Why me? Why did you have to use your psycho vibes to zero in on me?"

Tag grabbed her by the shoulders and pushed her gently against the wall. "First of all, you need to take it easy."

"Take it easy? I'm stuck in an elevator with a lunatic and you tell me to take it easy? If its money you want, I don't have my purse with me, but you can have my earrings. They're real rubies, just don't hurt me."

He sighed, momentarily closing his eyes. What could he say that might get through to her? There had to be something. "I would never hurt you."

"How would I know that? I don't know you from Adam."

"Yes, you do. You just don't remember me. Look, why don't you have a seat because it looks like we'll be here for a while."

"I'll stand, thank you."

"Suit yourself." He shrugged out of his jacket and laid it on the floor, sitting down on it and loosening his bowtie. "What does it matter, anyway? My life doesn't really seem worth living right now."

This statement seemed to get her attention. "What are you talking about?"

"If I told you the truth, you'll probably call me psycho again."

"I think that's already been established, so you might as well tell me since it looks like we'll be stuck here." She folded her arms across her full breasts and leaned against the wall, her skirt riding up succulent thighs.

Tag's mouth watered. He wanted to bury his head between those chocolate thighs and taste her honeyed sweetness. He missed eating her pussy and hearing the little sounds she made in the back of her throat when he did it. He ran his tongue over suddenly dry lips.

"Alex, what I have to tell you may sound crazy, but I don't know how else you're going to believe me."

"I seriously doubt I'll believe you no matter what you say, but since we're trapped I have no choice but to listen."

He took a deep breath and crossed his fingers. Here went nothing. "You and I met over a year ago, but that's not where the story really begins. It starts with an angry, bitter young boy who lived in hell for the first seventeen years of his life. He was the oldest of seven children and watched his mother go through various men, and four marriages, all of which were dysfunctional relationships. There was a time, a little over a year and a half, in which this boy was also in foster care. In the first home he was placed, his foster parents seemed nice. They appeared to be the kind of couple everyone liked and tried to emulate, but..." he broke off, still angry over the experience.

"But behind closed doors, the man was a sadistic bastard and his wife did nothing. Not for herself and certainly not for the boy. Her husband flaunted his affairs in her face, and sometimes even brought his girlfriends home in the guise that the women were only good friends. The boy once asked his foster mother why she simply accepted the man's behavior. She told him that she'd made a commitment to stay with her husband for better or worse -- an answer that served to solidify the boy's highly unfavorable impression of marriage, which had already been indelibly etched in his mind from his own family's experiences." It was painful reliving all these old memories, but Alex needed to know where he came from and why he was so adamant about not marrying. This was what he'd never shared with her, never wanted to discuss. Until it had been too late.

Tag looked at Alex, and saw that she waited for him to finish.

"Then what happened to the boy?"

"He soon went to another foster home because he dared to question his foster mother's reasons for staying in a dysfunctional marriage. This time, he was with his new family for nearly a year. It was the first time in a long while since he'd allowed himself to let his guard down. The couple treated him like he was their own son. There was finally someone the boy could look up to, and the foster mother...well, she was everything the boy had ever wanted in his real mother. The man and woman seemed to have the perfect marriage. After a time, the boy began to believe the hype about love was true. Until one day his foster mother got careless. She'd obviously forgotten that the boy had a half day at school -- he came home and found her sprawled out on the couch, naked, with her husband's best friend. Their eyes met before the boy walked out of the room without saying a word. Later that night, when her husband was asleep, she begged the boy not to say anything, even going as far as to offer herself to him to ensure his silence. It sickened him. Disgusted him. Since then, he has believed that anyone would have to be insane to enter into matrimony, especially when it seems like the only thing married people do is lie and hurt each other."

Alex slid down to the floor, tugging her dress over her thighs as far as it would go. "That's awful, but I don't believe all marriages are like that. You were that boy, weren't you."

It wasn't really a question but he answered anyway. "Yes," he said quietly. He'd broken out into a cold sweat just thinking about his painful childhood.

"As sad as your story sounds, I still fail to see why you're telling me all this."

"You'll see. There's more to the story." Tag could tell she was softening toward him, which meant his plan to get her back by opening up to her was starting to work. "So, after I caught my foster mother cheating on her husband, and after she propositioned me, things were never quite the same. I hated them both. I hated her for doing something so despicable to someone who obviously worshiped the ground she walked on, and I hated him for not seeing through her pack of lies."

"What happened after you left their home? You said you were only in foster care for about a year or so."

"My mother came back with husband number four, vowing to be a better mother. Not unexpectedly, that turned out to be a bunch of bull. The bastard beat the shit out of her, but she took it because she's the type of woman who can't be without a man. She cried more about that worthless piece of shit than over her own children. We didn't have any food in the house because he blew the welfare check on drinking and drugging. After he and I got into a huge fight, he took off. You'd think things would be better with him gone, but they went from bad to worse. According to my mother, I'd ruined her life, so I left. I've worked very hard to get to where I am today without anyone's help, and those years taught me a very valuable lesson. If I were to ever settle down into a relationship, it would be on my terms, and marriage and children wouldn't be part of it. I didn't want end up in a situation that made me feel trapped."

"And you think marriage would make you feel that way?"

"Definitely. I don't have any good examples to go by."

"My parents have been married for thirty-five years. They're happy. I'm not saying they never had problems. I mean, I think there was one time when they were going through a really bad patch, so bad, in fact, that I thought they'd break up, but they didn't."

He snorted. "They stayed together for the sake of you and your sister, I suppose? There's nothing worse than two people trying to stay together for the sake of children. The only thing that that accomplishes is that no one is happy and the children end up in therapy when they're older."

"I agree, but no, that wasn't the reason they stayed together."

"Then what kept them together when so many other marriages fail?"

"Their genuine love and mutual respect for each other. I think many marriages end in divorce because the couples didn't love each other in the first place. They probably saw getting married as something to do, rather than a real commitment, when what they should really have done was cut their losses before walking down the aisle together."

"And can you explain love?"

She shrugged. "In my opinion, I don't think love is wanting to be with someone because of who they are; it's wanting to be with someone *despite* who they are."

Tag had never looked at it from that angle before, but it made sense. He'd always been under the impression that Alex was one of those women who'd dreamed of marriage just for the sake of a wedding, and likely had planned it down to last detail from the age of five. He'd underestimated her, hadn't realized that she had such a mature view about love or the institution of marriage. More and more now, it appeared that *he* had been the childish one.

"I think that's a good philosophy, Alex."

"Thanks. I think it's the right one."

There was a brief pause before either of them spoke again.

"I no longer believe you're a psychotic maniac, but I do believe you owe me an explanation as to how you know so much about me and why you insist we were lovers."

"Do you believe in magic, Alex?"

"Like David Copperfield?"

"No. The real kind. You're going to have to suspend your disbelief while I tell you the rest of this story."

"I…I don't know. You're not a Satanist, are you?"

He grimaced. "No. I'm just a normal guy who is living through some extraordinary events."

"Please don't say anything that will make me question your mental welfare again. I want to believe that you're normal, but this talk of magic isn't helping."

"I *am* normal, I just happened to land in a not-so-normal mess." He ran his hand through his hair. "You see, the reason I reacted the way I did when I saw your niece's face was because I operated on her over a year ago."

Her brow furrowed; it was obvious she was confused. "I don't understand."

"She was bitten by a rottweiler, right? Olivia's friend suggested that she bring Tiffany to see me because I'm a plastic surgeon. I do some pro bono work, mostly facial reconstruction and breast augmentation for cancer survivors, as well as help people who were badly scarred by other plastic surgeons or doctors. You accompanied them for their first consultation with me."

"Now you're going all batty on me again."

"Bear with me, it's the truth. I operated on Tiffany, and she was almost as good as new when I finished. You and I began dating after that, and eventually you moved into my home. We lived together for a year, but then you began pressing for marriage. Because of my past, I wouldn't discuss it. I believed that I could keep you on my own terms, and you'd stay with me. I guess I wanted to have my cake and eat it, too."

He paused to see how she was handling these new disclosures. She just stared at him with folded arms, not speaking, so he took it as an encouraging sign. At least she wasn't calling him a liar or a freak.

Tag continued. "About a month ago, I met a woman whose life I had just saved. In her gratitude, she said she'd grant me a wish. At the time, I thought she was simply a fruitcake so I dismissed her words. The next morning, you and I had another of our arguments, so I said I wished you'd leave me alone and forget about the whole getting-married thing. I guess I didn't choose my words very wisely, and I'd certainly forgotten about the crazy woman and what she'd said about a wish. It was only after you were gone from my life, all traces wiped out, did I realize how much I love you. It also turns out that the woman did have the power to grant me the wish -- she's Psyche -- Cupid's wife."

"Now I know you're making that up," she said, eyes wide, head shaking in patent disbelief.

"I hardly believe it myself, but the proof is right here. You don't remember me at all, and I only have until midnight to get you to recall what we had together."

Alex stumbled to her feet. "No. This can't be possible. You're lying."

Tag stood, too, moving so that he was mere inches away from her. He had to convince her! "Then how do I know so much about you? How do I know your name is Alexandra Renee Harrison, age twenty-four? You have one sister, Olivia Robinson, formerly married to William Robinson. Your parents, Jacqué and Frank, live in Northeast D.C. You have a niece, Tiffany, age six."

"Anyone can look up stuff like that on the Internet or through some kind of vital statistics registry."

"Then how do I know that Tiffany wants to be a ballerina when she grows up? Or that your dream is to one day open your own beauty salon? You realized you wanted to be a hairdresser because you used to style all your Barbie dolls' hair with celebrity do's you saw in magazines. You have a heart-shaped mole just below your right breast." He lifted a brow. "Should I go on?"

"This can't be. No. You...I...how..."

"You broke your arm when you were sixteen after you tried to sneak out of your house to meet a boy your parents forbade you to meet. You had a dog named Lucky who got hit by a car on three different occasions, but the last time he didn't live up to his namesake. More?"

Alex looked stunned. "Stop. Just stop. This...this can't be happening. I mean, in the back of my mind, you seem familiar to me, but I still don't...can't...believe it."

"Believe it, Alex, because it's true. Believe in my love for you -- our love for each other."

"But I don't know you. I can't know you," she sputtered, looking as pale as any black woman with her complexion could.

"You do know me, and I *can* make you remember me," he said, growing bolder in his desperation, moving closer until his body crowded hers against the elevator wall.

Her eyes widened even more. There was a hint of fear in their depths, but there was also desire. That was the emotion he was most interested in, what he needed to fan to a blaze.

"How will you get me to remember?"

"Like this." He lowered his head and captured her lips. She placed her hands against his chest, probably to push him away but, at the last minute, she didn't. Instead, Alex clutched a fistful of his shirt, holding him tightly against her. God, he'd missed the feel of her warm lips beneath his -- missed their sweetness.

It was heaven, pure and simple. *This* was his true purpose in life, to be with this woman, here and now. He placed palms against the wall on either side of her head, his tongue coaxing satiny lips apart. She opened to him, and his tongue swept in to sample the honeyed recesses of her mouth.

Dear Lord, she was intoxicating. His cock grew impossibly hard, aching for action, burning to get what it had been denied these past few weeks. Long, painful weeks. Tag lifted his head slightly to look at her, to make sure she was real and that he wasn't going to wake up from some lovely dream. "You're so beautiful, Alex."

"Just...just kiss me. No more words are needed." She raised her hand to cup the back of his head, bringing it down to hers. This time, her tongue snaked out to meet his, swirling it around and twining with his tongue. Tag pulled his head back, intending to nibble her bottom lip, knowing that it drove her crazy with lust. His teeth gently gnawed at its fullness.

"Oh, God, yes," she sighed. Fingers plowed deeper into his hair. She pressed her body against his. An overwhelming heat seared through his body. Tag sucked her lip roughly into his mouth. If they were going to do it like this, fuck here, it had to be raw and dirty.

Tag gripped her forearms, digging his fingers into her tender flesh, before thrusting his tongue back into her mouth. He sought every corner and crevice, tasting and savoring. Delicious. Absolutely delicious.

When he nipped her tongue with his teeth, she released a shocked gasp, but he immediately tugged it into his mouth. Not bothering to lift his head, Tag twirled her around to the adjoining wall, pinning her body against it. His tongue traced the seam of her lips.

Alex threw her head back, offering her neck to him like a virgin sacrifice to a blood-thirsty vampire.

"You're so damn hot, Alex. You have no idea. I've missed this so much, missed *you* so much." No woman had ever driven him to such animalistic passion. The more she gave in to his sexual demands, the more he wanted to take. He trailed his lips down the side of her throat, using tongue and teeth, wanting to make her very much aware that there would never be another man for her. He wanted to brand her, possess her, make her his woman all over again.

"Tag! That feels so good," she moaned, yanking on his hair. He knew the effect he was having on her by her maddening little sighs and impassioned moans, but he wanted her to know the effect she had on him, too.

It suddenly dawned on him that she'd said his name, almost instinctively. This could only mean one thing -- she was on her way to remembering him. He couldn't let up now, not when he was so close to making her his once again.

"Feel what you do to me, babe." He took one of her hands, dragging it down the length of his body until it reached his cock. He ground himself against her hand. Tag wanted the sensation of that hand on his bare skin.

"You're so hard," she said in wonder.

"That's right. It's what you do to me, babe. Take me out of my pants. I want you to touch it."

Alex looked at him with uncertainly in her eyes, hesitating for only a moment, before tentative fingers undid his pants and pulled out his cock, circling it.

"That's it, babe, stroke me. Please."

Her grip tightened around his shaft, her fist sliding up and down his length. "Your cock is so thick." Alex's pink tongue snaked out to wet her kiss-ravaged lips. "And hard."

"You're responsible for that. You've always had this effect on me."

Her head shot up, their eyes locking. Did he see a hint of recognition, or was it just wishful thinking on his part?

"I want to taste," she whispered, squeezing her fingers around his swollen length.

"There'll be plenty of time for that. I'm going to fuck you first."

Chapter Seven

How had this happened? How had she ended up in an elevator with a man she'd thought was crazy?

Alex couldn't remember a time when she'd enjoyed someone handling her so roughly or even talking to her like this, but she found that she liked it. Maybe it was the hidden freak in her. Whatever the reason, he was hot and she was horny.

Or maybe she was the crazy one. After all, random sex -- with a stranger, no less -- wasn't something she normally did. But this man drew her to him somehow. Logically, she realized she shouldn't believe his sob story or that some crazy wish had changed the course of their lives over the past year, but there was a surprising ring of truth to it that she couldn't easily dismiss. Besides, *how* did he know so much about her?

The feral gleam in his black eyes made her shiver. And his touch…it felt right, familiar, perfect. She wanted him very badly.

Tag's hand slowly inched up her thigh, pushing her skirt to her waist. Alex cried out when his fingers dipped between her legs, rubbing the silky material of her thong against her clit. She grew damp with her need for him. "Oh, God," she moaned.

"You like this?"

"Need you ask?"

"I like hearing you say the words."

Somehow she knew that. But how did she know that?"

"I love it, Tag. More," she begged. In one deft move, he gripped the thong on both sides and ripped it off her hips and tossed it aside. "You won't be needing this for the rest of the night," he growled.

His take-charge attitude turned her on like no other man had. Fingers delved between the folds of her hot, slick pussy.

Alex leaned her head against the wall with a groan. "Yes, Oh, God, yes."

"You're so wet, Alex. How does this feel?" He thrust his fingers harder and deeper into her.

She moved her hips, grinding herself over his hand. "It feels wonderful."

"I bet it tastes wonderful, too." He brushed his lips over hers, then slid down the length of her body until he was kneeling before her, his head inches away from her throbbing cunt.

Tag pushed her leg further apart. Alex gripped his shoulders, her knees suddenly feeling weak. When his tongue touched her clit, she thought she'd burst into flames. "That's it, just like that!" If this wasn't decadent, she didn't know what was. The Aerosmith song, *Love in an Elevator*, popped into her mind. She had enjoyed that song when it had been popular, but now that she was actually experiencing it herself, she knew that if she ever heard it again, she'd relive this moment in excruciatingly fabulous detail.

Possibly getting caught added yet another thrill to what was happening between them. Who knew when this elevator would start to function again? It could be hours or a matter of seconds. Anyone seeing them would instantly know what they were up to with just a look, but that thought didn't bother her in the least. Besides, she could barely think about anything except that his mouth was ravaging her pussy.

He slid his middle finger into her while sucking on her throbbing button. She mashed her pussy against his face. Hot. She felt so hot. The delicious things he was doing to her were like nothing she'd ever experienced.

"Don't stop," she pleaded. Was she making those noises? That hoarse, impassioned groan?

When teeth nipped her clit, she let out a little yelp.

Tag lifted his head. "Too rough?"

"Never!"

He chuckled and ran his tongue over her slick labia. "Somehow I knew you'd like it. You've always liked it when I do this." An electric jolt shot up her body. "And you always like this, too." Tag nibbled gently at her sensitive bud, his fingers still embedded deeply within her damp sheath. Alex couldn't keep still, wiggling under his mouth's ministrations. "And you absolutely loved *this*," he said before he drew her clit into his mouth again, suckling it. Hard.

"Fuck me, Tag! I don't think I can take anymore of this torture. I want your cock inside me. Now!" He couldn't drive her mad like this and not expect her to burn to ashes.

Tag took his time releasing her clit, giving it one final kiss before getting to his feet. He forced his body against hers, jamming her back into the wall. Alex wrapped her arms around his neck as his head descended toward hers.

Their kiss was hungry, urgent, and needy, their tongues dueling for supremacy in a timeless dance of lust and passion. She could taste herself on his tongue, and it was intoxicating. So close; she was nearing a torrid peak. Tag's hard cock was suddenly there, pressing against her slit, demanding entrance.

She tore her mouth away from his. "Give it to me!"

"You're going to get it, babe."

Alex had always cringed whenever a man called her "baby" or "babe," but coming from Tag, it somehow sounded just right.

He grabbed her thigh, lifting it just enough to let his cock slide into her. "Jesus, you're wet. You're so hot and tight, as if your pussy was made especially for my cock."

"Mmm." She moaned, unable to think clearly, much less articulate anything intelligible. All she could do was revel in the deliciousness of his thick cock inside her. It felt almost like she'd done this with him before.

"Hold on tight, babe. I want you to wrap your legs around my waist. I need to get as deep as I can into your juicy pussy."

There was no way she could deny him. She gripped his shoulders in a vise as Tag cupped her ass, raising her so that her legs could circle him. He bucked, his hips driving his cock in to the hilt. The exquisite sensation of his cock stretching her so wonderfully made her squeal with delight. "Fuck me! Fuck me hard!"

She needed to feel more of his naked skin against her. Letting go of his shoulders, she ripped open his shirt, revealing a very masculine chest; her eyes feasted on a light dusting of black curls over his well-toned pectoral muscles. As she ran her hand over the hard planes of his body, his flesh seemed to throb beneath her touch.

Alex buried her face in his throat, kissing and nibbling his heated skin.

He groaned. "God, Alex, you have no idea what you're doing to me."

She sucked on the side of his neck, wanting to leave her mark on this sexy man. She did know exactly what she was doing to him, and it made her feel extremely empowered. Her legs tightened around him as his cock ground forcefully into her.

Tag's fingers dug into the tender flesh of her ass, squeezing and kneading. She bit into skin, breaking through the delicate tissue. She hadn't meant to hurt him, but Alex was so caught up in the heat of the moment that she couldn't help herself.

Tag growled. "You little vixen. So you like to bite? Well, I do, too." He captured her lower lip between his strong white teeth and gently bit into the already sensitive flesh.

She was sure her lips would be as swollen and large as Angelina Jolie's by the time this was over, but Alex was so highly aroused, pain didn't enter into the equation. He released her lip before turning his attention to her face, raining kisses over it.

"God, I can't get enough of you, woman. You'll never know how much I've missed this sweet pussy of yours."

Alex clenched her vaginal muscles around his cock, milking it. "Do you like that?"

"Oh, yeah," he responded breathlessly, before mashing his lips against hers. "So sweet," Tag muttered against her mouth.

She writhed against him, her body on an upward spiral of intense sensation.

Tag's cock pounded savagely into her pussy. His nails scraped her ass checks when he tightened his grip on her. He lifted his head. She looked into his dark, molten gaze just as a powerful climax surged through her body. She screamed and kept on screaming until he covered her mouth with his. Her orgasm was so strong that she shook, unable to stop herself.

"Oh, hell, yes!" he shouted, tearing his lips from hers, signaling his own release. A stream of come shot up her channel.

She held on to him, her head falling weakly on one broad shoulder. "Oh, Tag, I love you."

Tag sagged weakly against her, then his head popped up. Did he hear her correctly? Had she just said that she loved him? "Alex?!"

She lifted her head, beautiful light-brown eyes locked with his. "Yes, Tag?"

"Did you just say what I think you did?"

"That I love you?"

"Yes. Did you really say it or am I dreaming?" he asked anxiously. He pulled her away from the wall, allowing her to unwind her legs from his middle. She nearly collapsed when her feet touched the floor, but he quickly grabbed her waist, keeping her steady. "Are you okay?"

She giggled. "I am now. You can hardly expect my legs to support me after a performance like that."

Tag gripped her tighter, desperately wanting the answer to his question. "Alex, did you mean what you said?"

A slow smile tilted her swollen lips. "Yes. I remember, Tag. I remember everything. I remember you and the year we spent together."

He felt like crying in relief. Cupping her face in his hand, he stared deeply into her eyes, trying to gauge her emotions. "Tell me this isn't a dream, my beautiful lover, my friend," he said, lips brushing lightly against hers.

"It's not a dream, Tag. I do remember, although everything is a little jumbled in my head right now."

There was so much he wanted to tell her but, first and foremost, he had one thing he *had* to say. "Alex, I love you so much. My life wouldn't have much meaning if you weren't in it, as I learned painfully this past month."

Alex's eyes welled with unshed tears. "Do you mean it?"

"More than anything. I didn't realize what a precious jewel I had in you until I lost you. From now on, it's going to be whatever you want. We'll get married, a big fancy wedding, if you'd like. I want whatever you want."

Alex laughed. "Whoa, cowboy! How about we settle for a fifty-fifty relationship? Besides, I never asked for a big fancy wedding. All I really wanted was your love and commitment. If you're really adverse to the marriage thing, then I can live with that now that I know you love me, too."

"You have it and more, babe, but I must insist on getting married. I'm not going to let you walk out on me so easily again."

"Technically, I never did. How strange is this? I can remember events from my year with you and the one without you."

"Side effect from the magic, maybe? Who knows? Perhaps the memories that weren't supposed to happen will eventually fade. I hope they will."

"Could be, but when I compare the two, I know my life was much better with you in it. It wasn't the material things that you provided, either. It was always you. Just you." She gave him a quick kiss.

"I know what you mean. I went through hell this past month. I'm sorry for the arrogant way I brushed your feelings aside, as though they were inconsequential. I hope that I can become the man you deserve."

A tear escaped from the corner of her eye. "Oh, Tag. You don't know how good it feels to actually hear you say that. For the longest time I thought that you were somehow ashamed of me because you wouldn't introduce me to your family or even talk about them."

"I could never be ashamed of you, my love. I never told you about my family because I didn't want you to think less of me. I came from poor white trash. Don't get me wrong. I care for them as much as I'm able to, but I've always faced the fact that my mother is an alcoholic and sometimes drug user who refuses to get help. She was never much of a mother, and we only see each other every other year, if that. The last time I heard from her, she was shacked up with yet another biker."

He took a deep breath. Sharing his past was obviously painful for him. Alex waited patiently for him to continue, giving him as much time as he needed. Tag grimaced before continuing. "My two sisters are both living off the system with about seven kids between the two of them. Two brothers are in prison, one is in a mental institution, and the remaining one says he wants a better life but doesn't do anything to achieve it. I can only help them so much. When they come to me for money, I give it to them but, frankly, I don't think you'll be surprised to know that I'm not particularly close to any of them."

"That's really sad."

Tag shrugged. "I've grown used to it. Do you understand now why I didn't want to expose you to them? Maybe deep down I always knew that I loved you, but was too afraid to admit it." He wiped away the trail her tears had made.

"Tag, that's what love is all about -- sharing in each other's lives, the good and bad."

"I know that now. With you by my side, I can face anything." He kissed her again, heart swelling so overwhelmingly with love it almost hurt.

Her soft lips beneath his were enough to make his cock stiffen once again. Alex must have felt it pressing against her, because she tossed her head back with a laugh. "Are you ready again so soon?"

"Will that be a problem?" he asked, placing a gentle kiss against her jawbone.

"Definitely not," she murmured. "There is one thing, though."

"What's that?" He lifted his head to look into her eyes.

"This time, I want us to make love."

Tag smiled. "I believe that can be arranged." He drew back, taking Alex's hand and guiding her down until they were both kneeling on his tuxedo jacket on the floor, facing each other.

Tag wrapped his arms around her in a tight embrace, reveling in the scent of her tangy perfume while dropping kisses on top of her head. He never wanted to let her go. Her small hand glided up and down his back, rubbing and kneading his muscles. He released his grip on her waist only so he could push the straps of the red dress down her shoulders. Then he yanked the bodice down, revealing two perfect brown globes capped with large, dark, puckered nipples. His mouth watered at just the thought of tasting them, and his shaking hands cupped the generous mounds. "You have such a beautiful body. I was so damn jealous earlier, watching all of those men ogling you, wanting you."

"But there was obviously no one for me but you," she said teasingly.

"Damn right, just like you're the only one for me." He dipped his head and took one succulent peak into his mouth.

Alex groaned. "That feels wonderful, Tag."

He laved and circled the taut tip with his tongue until her body visibly trembled. He wanted this to be slow and easy, but his cock ached so badly for some more of her sweet pussy that he didn't know if he'd be able to last very long without sinking between her chocolate thighs again.

He loved the sound of her sighs and moans, aware that she was as turned on as he was. Tag transferred his attention to her other nipple, flicking it first, then taking it into his mouth. He squeezed and shaped the breast he'd just suckled with his free palm.

Alex groaned. "Tag, I need you inside of me, right now!"

He took his time lifting his head before meeting her eyes. "So soon? I thought you wanted to make slow, sweet love."

"Maybe sweet, but right now, I can't handle slow. I want your cock in this pussy. Now, now, now!"

He chuckled. "So eager and demanding. I think I like this new, bossy you." Tag pushed Alex onto her back, then positioned himself over her, his arms supporting the bulk of his weight. His straining cock pressed against her moist folds. "Take me inside of you, Alex," he commanded softly.

Tentative fingers reached between their bodies and encircled his cock. It took every ounce of his willpower to remain still. Alex lifted her hips and guided his shaft to her dripping wet cunt. She parted her labia with her fingers and gently pulled his cock forward until it rested at her entrance.

Unable to hold back any longer, Tag slid into her damp heat. He hissed with pleasure. She felt so good. It was like the first time for him all over again. Every time he made love to her it felt like the first time.

He buried himself inside of her until his balls rested against her rear end. The delicious fulfillment he felt from joining as one with the woman he loved was like no other experience. He looked down at her. So beautiful. Tag felt like the luckiest man in the world to find this priceless gem among women. The woman he'd risk life and limb for. The woman who had taught him the true meaning of love.

Tag lay on top of her and clutched her hands, their fingers interlocking as he moved within her. "I love you." He didn't think he could ever say it enough.

"I love you, too." Her pussy clenched around his cock like a vacuum, sucking him deeper inside of her. His love for Alex further intensified the desire he felt for her. Tag lunged forward. She moaned, whispering words of adoration and lust, her head rolling back and forth. He couldn't get enough of the sight or scent of her.

"Yes!" she screamed. "I'm coming!"

"Oh, God!" he cried as his seed exploded into her. When he finished pumping the last drop, Tag wrapped his arms around her pliant body. "I love you, Alexandra Harrison," he said again, kissing her sweat-slickened forehead.

"And I love you. More than anyone or anything else, Taggert Webster."

Just then, the elevator doors flew open, and standing outside was a handful of people, one of whom was wearing a gold ball gown, a satisfied smile on her face and flashing the thumbs up sign. A few of the shocked onlookers gawked at them with fascination.

Tag shielded Alex's body with his own, more embarrassed for her than for himself. However, when he heard her giggle, he knew that everything would be okay. They could face any adventure as long as they were together.

Now he had to figure out who the hell had just snapped a picture.

Epilogue

"Can I be a bridesmaid, Auntie Alex?" Tiffany asked, turning her pretty little face toward her aunt.

Tag sat back in his chair, belly full from a huge dinner Alex's mother, Jacqué, had cooked in celebration of their engagement. He couldn't remember a time when he'd been happier. The Harrison family had welcomed the news with a round of hugs and kisses.

"It's about time, boy," her father, Frank Harrison, had said.

Things had certainly changed since the night at the hotel a couple of weeks ago. Alex's shining black hair hung past her shoulders once again, for one. For another, Psyche had fixed things to the point where Alex didn't remember the argument they'd had when he'd uttered those fateful words or the alternate year without him. The month they'd been apart never happened, and she hadn't even remembered the things he'd told her about Psyche and the wish. As far as

Alex knew, they'd gone to the Valentine's Day ball together with her sister, and the only other things Alex had recalled were everything they'd discussed in the hotel elevator, plus the two of them getting caught in it after an incredibly mind-blowing sexual interlude.

Tag looked studied Tiffany's face. The side he had operated on looked just as it was supposed to. Olivia seemed to be thriving as well. Something must have happened to her at the ball, too, although she refused to talk about it. Alex had mentioned a man, Maxwell Sterling, that her sister had met, but she couldn't get any more information from her sister, either.

He turned to the woman he adored, who looked more beautiful with each passing day. He loved her more than could be put into words. Ever since he'd opened his heart to her, he didn't know how he'd survived before she had come into his life. She was his everything -- the first thing he thought about when he woke and the last thing he thought about before he went to sleep. The one thing he regretted and felt ashamed of most was how long it had taken him to realize how much she meant to him and what he had had to go through to finally acknowledge his feelings.

Because of her, he'd even reached out to his family again. She'd showed him that throwing money at them in the hopes that they'd go away would never solve their problems in the long run. So he tried to make a more conscious effort to be in their lives. Maybe his siblings would never change, but he could at least be a positive influence on his various nieces and nephews.

Tag grabbed her hand under the table, giving it a light squeeze. Alex turned to him with a smile, mouthing the words, *I love you.*

"Auntie Alex, are you listening to me? I want to be a bridesmaid in your wedding." Tiffany huffed, sounding slightly exasperated.

"Of course, I am, darling, but wouldn't you rather be a flower girl? I could have a dress made for you that looks just like my wedding dress, and we could give you a little tiara or put flowers in your hair. You'd look really pretty."

Tiffany shook her head, pigtails flying as usual. "I don't want to be a flower girl because that's for babies. I'm a big girl now. I'm going to be seven next week."

Tag threw his head back and laughed. "Spoken like a woman who knows her mind. I think the final decision is up to your aunt, but how about a junior bridesmaid?"

The child's face lit up. "Oh, Uncle Tag. I think that sounds like a super idea. What you do you think, Auntie?"

Alex smiled. "I think that's a super idea, too." She leaned over and gave her niece a kiss on the tip of her nose. "Of course, O, you're going to have to be my maid of honor."

Olivia smiled. "I think I can handle that as long as you don't do anything crazy like throwing the bouquet my way."

"Why not?" Alex asked.

She shrugged. "Once was enough, thank you, and I haven't met anyone who could make me change my mind yet."

Tag studied his soon-to-be sister-in-law and got the distinct impression that she wasn't exactly telling the truth, and that a certain Maxwell Sterling might have a lot to do with it. No matter, it was none of his business. Olivia was a woman with a good head on her shoulders. He suspected that whatever problem she had would be worked out soon enough.

"Do you know what your colors are going to be?" Jacqué asked, standing up to clear the dishes.

Her husband groaned and got up abruptly. "This sounds like women's talk. I'm going to take out the trash. Tag, I'd make my escape if I were you. Good luck, son." With that, the older man left the kitchen as if the devil himself were on his heels.

Tag laughed. He had no intention of leaving. Indeed, most men would not involve themselves with their own wedding plans, but he knew how much his input meant to Alex. He listened to the women at the table talking excitedly, full of various ideas, and nodded at appropriate intervals, letting them chatter away. He couldn't wait for the big day to come, when the law would cement their strong bond.

He knew that in his and Alex's hearts, they were already married, but Tag wanted to bind her to him in all ways. Who would have thought that a simple wish would change this many things in his life and make it so wonderful? Sure, he had had to go through hell to win back Alex, but if he hadn't made that wish, he would never have opened up to her and discovered all the sweet mysteries of love.

Tag put his arm around Alex's shoulder and smiled as he listened to her plans for them. If marriage was a prison, he hoped his jailer would lock him up and throw away the key.

* * *

Psyche looked down on Taggert Webster and Alexandra Harrison-soon-to-be-Webster with a sense of triumph racing through her. Despite all her mother-in-law had done to thwart her efforts, these two were together and happy. The love she observed between the two of them warmed her heart. It was the kind of passion she felt for her own husband.

She didn't have the ability to see in the future like some of the gods and goddesses could, but from her observations of this couple, she knew their love would last.

Eve Vaughn

Eve Vaughn enjoys writing above all else. She began writing short stories to amuse herself since she could form letters. Mischievous as a child, she lost her television privileges quite a bit and found writing to be her outlet. Besides writing, Eve likes reading, baking, volunteering, traveling, and spending time with her family. She currently resides in the Philadelphia area with her husband and turtle.

Eve loves hearing from her fans so feel free to contact her at EveVaughn10@aol.com or join her yahoo group at evevaughnsbooks@yahoo.com.

LaVergne, TN USA
11 December 2009
166712LV00003B/36/A